A World With You

M. ROCA

CRANTHORPE MILLNER
PUBLISHERS

First published by Cranthorpe Millner Publishers (2023)

ISBN 978-1-80378-134-1 (Paperback)

www.cranthorpemillner.com

Cranthorpe Millner Publishers

CHAPTER ONE

Gemma Higgins was the sort of person who took hours to decide what to order at a restaurant, only to greet the arrival of her dish with muted enthusiasm because her dinner date's food looked better.

'But you said you didn't want chips?' said Paulo, grimacing as Gemma claimed a fistful. 'And you promised you wouldn't do this again, babe.'

He proceeded to rant for a bit about chips, babes and promises. Sucking the salt from her lips, Gemma waited patiently for Paulo to finish, before setting out her defence.

'I didn't know they'd be thin ones. If I'd known that—'

Her excuse smoked out in the steakhouse air. *If I'd known that.* She sighed. That innocent phrase wasn't just applicable to this French fries fracas. It was, in fact, a common thread that ran throughout her life; a life which, as far as Gemma was concerned after a bad day at work and a bottle of white, could be summed up as a series of dubious choices broken up by the odd bout of food envy. Hoping to gaze away the malaise, she studied her man. His eyes were – how had she described them to Diya? – "like kaleidoscopic ripples in an azure pond". Diya had laughed at her. If only her best friend were here now, bearing witness to Paulo's irises. They'd gone into overdrive on the rippling front.

Gemma grabbed another chip, and a split second later, Paulo grabbed his hair. She smiled because the synchronicity of them was almost perfect, and his hair *was* lovely. Volatility in the market had not prevented the man she loved swanning from the office like a *Wolf of Wall Street* film star. Jesus, if *she* were responsible for everybody's pensions, and they'd just nosedived in value by fifty percentage points, she'd be trembling in a ditch somewhere, with bad hair. She was lucky to have this investment banker. Very lucky indeed.

'Why are you staring at me like a bunny boiler?'

'I'm not. I'm appreciating what a dreamboat you are.'

'Well can you stop please, babe? You're freaking me out.'

'Okay.' She helped herself to some more of the good stuff.

Paulo eyed his rapidly diminishing plate, and the alarm on his face was palpable. 'I'll get you some of your own.' He raised his arm to garner a waiter's attention. When the waiter didn't come, Paulo waved more desperately, like a man with a flare, stranded at sea.

Gemma sunk his hand down with a playful tap. 'No, no. I only wanted to borrow a few.'

'Borrow? How can you borrow my dinner? Are you going to regurgitate it into my mouth like a fucking albatross to her chick?'

'You've been binge-watching David Attenborough documentaries again, haven't you?'

As ever, she spoke to her alpha-male Attenborough lover with affection. She never scolded, nagged or shouted. Restrained and dignified conduct – that was the key to keeping this perfect thing in her otherwise imperfect world. Well, that and the fact she never said no to sex.

'I feel bad for nicking so many of your chips. Would you like some of my salad?'

Even with that vein throbbing in his neck, he still seemed so *together*. This investment banker, he was not like her. Not like her at all.

'And do you want all your rump, by the way?'

Paulo threw down his napkin, because he'd been pushed too far. Injustice blazed in his azure eyes. 'Fuck this for a laugh!'

'What?' Gemma was too stunned to do much about it as she watched him storm off towards the exit, then swivel, and storm back towards her again. She breathed a sigh of relief. He'd changed his mind! He did love her! He'd just suffered a temporary lapse in sanity – no doubt due to the stress of a volatile stock market. Investment bankers – it took an other half to really understand them. Gemma smiled her most understanding of smiles.

'Let me finish my food before I go. What you've left of it.'

'Oh.' Smile torpedoed, Gemma stared at her ex dejectedly as he tucked into his excellent choice of dinner. Noting he didn't offer her so much as an onion ring, she remembered what Diya had once said: "investment bankers are greedy, grim-reaping bastards of society, and no one in their right minds should ever fall in love with one".

*

'Nice evening?' called Diya, over what sounded like enthusiastic lovemaking. Diya was a devout Catholic, and fan of X-rated TV dramas.

'Give me a sec!' replied Gemma. In a very composed sort of order, she placed down her bag, removed her coat, let herself into the bathroom and puked in the toilet.

'Oh, huuuuun!'

Gemma loved Diya dearly, but if there was one thing she'd change about her, it'd be the way she expressed sympathy. Which was ironic, because as Gemma's best friend and flatmate, expressing sympathy was pretty much Diya's *raison d'être*. Although, if you asked Diya herself what her purpose on Earth was, she'd tell you it was to end global injustice and to fight for the human rights of citizens everywhere. The woman was a wonderful human being who worked for Amnesty International.

Sadly, everyone has their foibles. Diya had an infuriating habit of dragging out a "huuuuun" or a "looooove" or a "poooor thiiiiing" because in her eyes, plumping words out like cushions softened any blow.

As if pillowed talk wasn't bad enough, Diya's idea of cheering someone up was to offer them some irrelevant alternate reality, like: "Your mum posted embarrassing photos of you on Facebook, and your privacy setting wasn't as strong as you'd wagered, and all your students have seen what you looked like in the 90s? Ah well, at least you're not the victim of revenge porn." Or: "You were so scared of accidentally driving onto a motorway, you pulled into a landfill site and got locked in and had to spend the night there? Ah well, at least you weren't crushed to death by a rubbish digger." Or: "Your boyfriend is a con man? Ah well, at least you found out before he stole all your money… He stole all your money? Oh. Shit."

Diya shouted outside the door. 'Can I get you anything? Tea? Chocolate?'

'No thanks. I'll be out in a sec.' Washing her face in the sink, Gemma stared at her reflection. Like many an antihero before her, she tended to self-analyse after a shit-show. She was inclined to agree with the scriptwriters – nothing quite beats a mirror in the toilet as a place to face up to the fact you've screwed up bad and feel terribly guilty because you've shot someone. Or else, feel you have no choice *but* to shoot someone. *Ah well*, thought Gemma, *at least I haven't shot someone.*

Seeking answers from what was staring her in the face, she found nothing. A voice staggered from one side of her brain to the other, like a street drunkard crying: *I'm not good enough. Why do I always make the wrong choice? I want wine.* The drunkard crashed into the wall of her skull, and it hurt. Gemma rubbed her head and swallowed some water.

Perhaps she should change tack, save the post-mortem for another time? A time when she was more sober; a time following some glorious triumph. Gemma snorted. To be fair, in the past, there had been such a thing as a good hair day; when her brunette locks had shone, her olive skin had glowed, her nut-brown eyes had sparkled, and she'd made the right call at a restaurant.

There was a knock. 'Huuuun? Are you okay?'

Gemma emerged from the bathroom. 'Not really, no.' Diya went to hug her but was batted off. 'Thanks, but I wouldn't wish my breath on anyone.'

'Right.' Diya tilted her head, expectantly.

As usual, Diya was wearing lots of zany-patterned cloth, smelling of incense, and cupping a mug of something hot in her hands. She said something reassuring, but Gemma was too distracted by sex sounds to hear it. Each moan was an actor saying, "Fuck you, we're still gonna have fun."

'Mind if you turn that off, Dee?'

'Of course. Sorry.'

Gemma followed her flatmate through to the living room, which could have come from a home makeover show — before the makeover. The trouble was, clothes stores, as well as Ikea, existed in this world, and the women knew what they'd rather spend their money on.

Every piece of furniture was hand-me-down, mismatched, upcycled. The process of reclaiming an old object and fashioning it into something new is laudable – if you are good with your hands. Gemma and Diya were not good with their hands. The wooden crate they'd rescued from a skip looked less like the chic coffee table of the YouTube video and more like a Woodland Trust termite sanctuary.

'Another woodlouse,' said Diya, shaking her head as she scooped it up and let it out onto the balcony. On the couch, she crossed her legs the backwards yoga way, before rewinding what she'd missed, and a bit more besides, leaving the Georgians on pause, repressed once more. 'So, what happened?'

'Paulo dumped me.'

'Oh, huuuuun. I know we didn't get on but…' She lassoed Gemma into a hug. 'I am sorry. Did he say why?'

'I don't know. It's all a bit of a blur. I think it's because I ate his chips.'

'What did I tell you? Selfish, capitalist bastard.'

'He isn't. He's amazing. Too amazing for me.'

'Shut up. One day in your life making a difference is worth a thousand days making squillions.'

'Paulo did that heptathlon, remember? He raised loads for charity.'

'Let's not pretend he was motivated by a sense of social responsibility. He just wanted to prove he could do a heptathlon.' Diya's voice dipped into something even more bitter. 'Still can't believe he asked if I wanted a proper job.'

'You were saying you had no money, and there was an opening for a secretary at his work. He was trying to help.'

'He was trying to be an arsehole.'

'No, he wasn't.'

'Blinkered is what you are. Completely blinkered. You never stopped to see *who* you were bending over backwards for. You were too busy bending over backwards.'

'Remind me never to discuss my sex life with you again.'

'You guys don't even have anything in common.'

'Yes we do.'

'Like what?'

'We both have… great sexual chemistry.'

'Apart from that.'

'He's amazing with kids. And we both want a big family.'

'That's what Angelina said about Brad. Didn't work out so well for them, did it?'

'We… we love going to restaurants!'

'That's not a thing. When was the last time he went with you on one of your walks?'

'So what if he's bored by the Broads? Gives me a chance to listen to my music, and I like my own company. Which is a good thing really, seeing as how I'm now single.'

Diya sighed and squeezed Gemma's hand. 'At least you're finally free to meet someone who deserves you.'

'Look, Dee, I appreciate what you're trying to do, but I'm not at the "hate stage" yet – not by a long shot. Please don't say anything negative about him – not until I give the signal.'

'Okay. What's the signal?'

'I dunno. Whenever you hear me call him a capitalist bastard?'

It looked more like she was relieving a crick in the neck than nodding, but Gemma took Diya's action as assent.

'Oh, Dee! We would have had such beautiful babies!'

The full-scale waterworks started up again, and Diya was true to her word. 'I suppose he did have nice eyes.'

*

Rose didn't want them to be one of those families who never saw each other. Unfortunately, by insisting they met up monthly, Rose was turning them into a family who wished they could see each other less often. The truth was, everyone indulged the matriarch because she was a top-notch cook. Most people would put up with family in exchange for a nice roast dinner. Or, in Georgia's case, a nice piece of Quorn. After the main, came the tea and biscuits.

'Don't you think you've eaten enough?' said Georgia, flicking Gemma's hand away from the tin. It wasn't that she thought her daughter too chubby. It was that, as someone who lived a totally clean, fat-free, sugar-free, organic, vegan life, she didn't see why others couldn't suffer too.

'Leave my niece alone,' said Rose. Picking up the discarded digestive, she started feeding it to Gemma. Rose believed she could cure anyone of heartbreak through the sheer power of spoon-feeding. Gemma, naturally, found it a bizarre and very uncomfortable experience. 'There, there,' said her aunt, 'you eat your biscuit, there's a good girl.'

'Mum, she's not one of your grandkids,' said Ruth, chasing after the twin with a felt tip whilst carrying his screaming brother underarm like a rugby ball. 'A little help here? Someone?'

Gemma tried to get up, but her aunt dragged her back down and started tipping tea into her mouth.

'Just a bit at a time, love.'

Still with an eye on the football scores, Tony made a half-hearted beeline for the twin with a felt tip. 'Don't get anything on my lucky shirt, now.'

'Honestly, Uncle, if that thing got scribbled on, it would

be an improvement,' said Amber, Gemma's least favourite cousin.

She had a point. Tony was donning something from his Norwich City collection – a green and yellow monstrosity affectionately known as the club's "bird poo" shirt. In polls, it had consistently been voted the worst football shirt of all time.

Tony's face twitched as it struggled to contain its affront. 'How dare you insult the classic '92 kit! From the one time in history we reached the pinnacle.'

Amber gave her usual riposte. 'You finished third that year.'

'Technically, yes. But we led the table for most of the season, so by the law of averages, we won the league.'

'Whatever.'

Tony checked his phone and appeared to have a minor heart attack. 'Bloody hell, we've scored! What did I tell you! Lucky shirt!' Kissing his badge, he began jumping up and down like a loon, which of course thrilled the twins, who made a bolt for him. Tony opened his arms wide, before realising his error. His face turned to horror at the sight of the looming felt tip. 'No!' he cried, before running from his nephews. 'Sorry boys! Can't get anything on my shirt. Bad luck.' The door slammed, and from somewhere he yelled, 'I'll be back when the pen is gone!'

'That man,' said Amber, 'would make a really shit terminator.'

'Language,' said Ruth through her teeth, for once grateful her boys were being too boisterous to hear anything – obscene or otherwise.

Rose took a break from drip-feeding Gemma tea. 'Amber, I didn't bring you up to be so rude.'

'No. You brought me up to be a strong woman who isn't afraid to voice her opinion.'

One of the boys had turned his mother into a horse. With a child on her back, tugging on her hair like reins, Ruth pleaded, 'Help me, Amber.'

'Sorry, Roo. As a feminist, it's vital I don't help with anything considered *woman's work*, like childcare.'

'Screw you.'

'Isn't it telling that you turned to a woman for help, rather than asking one of the men?'

'I asked you to help because you're my sister and you're lying on the couch doing nothing. I didn't ask you because you're a woman.'

'I'm sorry,' said Amber, with a pained martyr's face, 'but I must lie down, to stand up for what I believe in.'

'She's gotten worse,' said Ruth, shaking her head at her mother. 'Ever since that Barbie movie…'

'Yes, but it was a great movie.'

Amber stuck out her tongue. 'Where's Uncle Joe?'

'In the toilet still,' said Georgia. 'I told him what would happen if he ate that pre-prepared sandwich from the petrol station, but would he listen?' She began to tremor violently, like she was suffering from hypothermia. The tremor was brought on by her next two words: 'White bread.'

'He *ate* before coming here?' asked Rose, deeply offended.

'Apparently the kale and cucumber smoothie I made him for breakfast left him starving.'

'Maybe he should have got his own breakfast,' mumbled Amber, darkly.

'I don't need another biscuit, thank you, Aunty.'

'But I want you to have it,' said Rose, tenderly wiping a crumb from her niece's mouth. 'You were so cute when you were a baby. I don't know why anyone would dump you.'

The horse and her rider had cantered to within reach.

'Come here, you,' said Gemma, evading her captor before untangling chubby fingers from Ruth's mane.

'No! Horsey!'

'Thanks,' said Ruth, staggering to her feet. 'You're a life saver.'

Gemma tried to tickle the twin, but he escaped – largely because she'd been re-captured by her aunt.

Ruth's delight at being human again was short-lived, because her other son was artistically expressing himself. 'No, Dwayne! Please don't decorate Grandma's walls! Amber! He's right next to you!'

Tony came back from wherever he'd gone, and horizontal Amber seized her chance to stay horizontal. 'Ask Uncle Tony.'

'So the pen is still here,' sighed Tony, sounding like every man who'd ever hoped a problem would go away of its own accord: disappointed. 'Well, it's half-time, so I suppose I could... Give it here, Dwayne,' he said, in a way that suggested he didn't want it here.

'What are you feeding them, Ruth?' asked Georgia, unhelpfully glued to her perch as Dwayne defaced the wall in front, and his brother threw tennis balls at the one behind. 'If it's rubbish with E numbers in it, you can't really blame them for going mental.'

'They won't eat anything but beige, Aunty,' said Ruth, confiscating the balls.

'They ate my roast chicken,' said Rose, proudly.

'Was it free-range and corn-fed, though?'

'Um...'

'Dwayne! Stop scribbling on the walls!' shouted Ruth,

whilst wrestling with her other son who, since the loss of his balls, had been trying to pull down her trousers.

'Children will be children, dear,' said Rose, braiding Gemma's hair. 'If I can't scrub it off, I'll get new wallpaper. I wanted an excuse to freshen things up, anyway. Tony, will you re-decorate the living room for me?'

'How many times? Just because I'm gay, doesn't mean I have a good sense of style.'

'You can say that again,' said Amber, eyeballing her uncle's Norwich shirt.

That small comment changed his mind. 'On second thoughts, sis, I'd love to help! How about a green and yellow canary theme?'

'Give Uncle the pen, Dwayne!' said Amber, like an encouraging mistress to her dog.

The armed child smiled angelically and did as he was told.

'No!' came Tony's anguished cry. 'My lucky shirt!'

'I'm sure it'll rub off,' said Rose, in a very unsure way.

'It better! Because if it doesn't…' Tony snatched the offending object from his great-nephew, who started to cry.

'What've I missed?' said Joe cheerfully, doing up his fly as he entered.

'Ew, Dad, put it away!' said Gemma.

Whilst her aunt was busy blushing, she escaped the woman's clutches and stuck on a children's channel. It was like a spell had been cast on the boys, who instantly sat before the TV, enraptured.

Tony turned white as he examined the pen. 'It's not felt-tip; it's permanent marker.'

'I'm so sorry, Uncle,' said Ruth, trying to clean his shirt with a baby wipe, making the stain worse. 'Mum? Next time we're over, do us a favour and lock away the permanent markers.' She screamed for her husband.

A man ambled into the living room. Gemma had never seen Marvin look anything other than oblivious.

'Yes, love?'

'Where've you been? It's been pandemonium in here.'

Marvin blinked at his sons, who were calmly watching a talking cat. 'Has it? Sorry, I was doing the washing up.'

His wife took a deep breath and a spare spot on the sofa, where she spent the next five minutes glaring at bric-a-bracs. A few more relatives (after checking the twins had been sedated) braved their way in. Fold-out chairs were fetched, but still there weren't enough seats.

'Amber, would you mind…?'

'Fine.' She swapped her supine position for something more upright. 'But don't think I'm doing this for you because I'm subservient.'

'Wouldn't dream of it.'

Even after Amber's sacrifice, there were family members on the floor.

'Take my place,' said Gemma to one of her cousins, desperate not to sit next to her mollycoddling aunt anymore.

'It's okay,' said the cousin, patting her on the knee sympathetically. 'You need the couch more than we do.'

'United have scored,' said Tony, not looking up from his phone, and sounding very depressed. 'See what happens when my lucky shirt is tampered with?'

'Does anyone want more tea?' asked Rose.

Everyone politely declined, apart from Tony, who was too depressed to speak.

'Are you sure you don't want tea, Gem?' said Rose. 'I can get you brandy, if you prefer?'

'For Pete's sake!' said Georgia. 'She hasn't lost a limb!

Only another boyfriend. She'll be all right, won't you, Gem?'

'Yes, Mum.'

'Are you taking the multivitamins I gave you?'

'Yes, Mum.'

'United have scored again.' This time, Tony gave evils to the three-year-olds staring innocently at the TV.

'I don't know how you keep messing things up,' said a different relation. 'I've been with my partner for six months, and we've not had so much as an argument.'

'That's because he's scared of you,' quipped someone else.

'Shut up.'

'3–1.'

'I wish you'd let me set you up with this lovely doctor son of my friend,' said Rose.

'Thanks, Aunty, but the last time you set me up with someone, he stole all my financial details.'

'I can't believe you were thick enough to fall for that scam,' said an uncle who wasn't as nice as Uncle Tony.

Technically, the man wasn't Gemma's uncle, she was just obliged to call him that. In truth, Gemma wasn't sure what the man's tie to her family was. She had asked her mum and Uncle Tony to spill, but they had acted all mysterious and refused to give her a straight answer, and when she had asked Aunt Rose, she had replied simply "he's an estate agent", as if that explained everything. Ruth had a theory that the "uncle" was privy to some terrible family secret, and her mum's steady supply of roast dinners was essentially hush money.

'I reckon you're too picky,' said Ruth, moving on from giving knick-knacks evils. 'I said that to you the other day, didn't I Marvin?' Her husband blanked her. 'Marvin?'

He turned his bewildered head towards her. 'What?'

Tony interrupted with an update. '4-1. This is getting embarrassing now.'

One of the room's relatively new arrivals turned the spotlight back on Gemma. 'You probably sleep with men too soon. Everyone can't wait to take their knickers off these days.' Grandma waved her hands at the screen's talking pussy. 'It's all over the TV, twenty-four-seven. How can you expect a man to respect a hussy?'

'Less S. E. X. talk around the children, please,' said Ruth, spelling out what she didn't want spoken.

'She's got as much right as a man to sleep around, haven't you, Gemma?' Amber's smile was less sister-in-arms, more bitchy grin.

Not for the first time, Gemma wanted to punch her cousin in the face.

'Maybe you're better off without him,' said Grandma. 'Everyone knows investment bankers sleep with prostitutes.'

'He wasn't like that.'

Tony sighed and shook his head at Gemma. 'What you need is a Norwich City fan. We're used to disappointments.'

'Thanks.'

'That's not what I meant. What I meant was, we'll stick by your side, through thick and thin. Oh bloody hell – United have scored again! That's it! I can't take this anymore!' Like a very upset stripper, Tony removed his shirt, threw it to the floor, and exited the room dramatically.

Joe took a swig of his beer. 'Gem's love life is no one else's business. Is it, sweetheart?'

'Thanks, Dad.' Gemma threw him an appreciative smile, which was turned down when everyone else started saying:

'Well, I think…'

The next hour was an excruciating mix of talking TV cats,

hair braiding and musings on her life. Not only did her family know what she should have done, but what she should do. Further opinions ranged from, "What do you expect if you eat deep-fried potato?" to "You should buy this new two-bed flat just come on the market". Tony even made a brief reappearance to tell his niece she should never, ever get involved with a Norwich City fan, unless she wanted her heart broken into a million pieces and to never be happy again.

Gemma tried to dress herself in a metaphorical wetsuit so she could let her family's words wash over her, rather than soak her skin, but she couldn't blank out the noise. Their snapping voices were like the snip, snip of scissors, cutting away at her sanity. What she wanted more than anything was for her family to close its mouth and quit trying to control her life.

She put her hands over her ears. 'La, la, la.'

They all stopped and looked at her like she was mad.

No. This isn't what she wanted. What she wanted, more than anything, was for Paulo to take her back.

CHAPTER TWO

'It's a beautiful day,' said Diya, opening the curtains.

Rejecting the light, the sleeper crawled further under the covers. 'Go away.'

'It's been weeks since Paulo. You can't keep wasting weekends. Come, pray to God.'

'Paulo's left me. There is no God.'

'Don't be so melodramatic. Come on, Mass will lighten your soul.'

"Mass will lighten your soul" was Diya's go-to hook, but in fifteen years of break-up angst, she had yet to catch her best friend with that one. God/no God – the lady in bed could not make up her mind either way and did not wish to commit herself to the wrong side. (Although, presently, Gemma was swinging towards the negative).

'You promised last night.'

'I did?'

'You said, if I never made you sit through a sci-fi film again, you'd come with me to church. Remember?'

Much as she didn't want to be, she was awake now and fully conscious of the deal. Being coerced into church was the price she paid for being best mates with a practicing Catholic. Gemma dragged her admittedly heavy soul up and got dressed, whacking on any old thing without a second thought. In the past, she had fussed over what to wear, but that was before Paulo had dumped her. Lately, she just didn't care. Anyway, she doubted, even if He did exist, that He would mind if her coat didn't match her shoes. Jesus had cured lepers, irrespective of their fashion sense. Indeed, Jesus had famously worn rags that had done nothing for his figure.

In double-quick time they were out. Diya tackled the cold with a brisk stride and a fabulous multi-coloured poncho, whilst Gemma was in a black widow ensemble, bowing submissively to the butt-kicking wind.

'Some beautiful day.'

'Isn't it? The sun is so bright, and the sky is so blue.'

'I'm cold.'

'Should've worn something warmer then. At least it's not—'

'Don't say it.'

'Raining.'

'Now you've done it.' Gemma looked skywards and, to shield herself from baited heavens, arched her arms over her head.

'There's The Conductor,' said Diya, tugging Gemma's ludicrous umbrella down.

The man they called The Conductor lived in a nearby home that offered supported living. Every morning at nine a.m., he would leave his flat to direct traffic at the crossroad. Pacing the same pavement backwards and forwards, he'd shout noises that weren't words. These non-words mimicked "your turn!", "right only", "keep coming", "stop there!" instructions, and were accompanied with semaphore hands, and a leporine expression. This look was due to his belief that cars depended on his direction. He didn't understand the traffic would flow fine without him; that computerised traffic lights had everything under control. As far as The Conductor was concerned, without his input, there would be some terrible accident or, at the very least, several cases of road rage. The Conductor would labour for hours at a time, braving all weathers. He was a local landmark. Some passers-by were too afraid to say hello, others weren't. The Conductor didn't have time for any of them. His job was too important and required his full concentration. If friendly commuters beeped him or waved, he would wave them on. Long ago, when Gemma had introduced herself and asked his name in return, he had ignored her, turned to a van and told it, through intonation and make-believe language, to keep coming, keep coming. It was Diya who'd christened him The Conductor.

'Morning,' sang Diya, and mumbled Gemma.

The Conductor was too preoccupied to pay lip service to the women. They nodded their appreciation his way when the light turned green, and they could cross safely. The Conductor allowed a flicker of pleasure to pass his face, before shooing the expression away, turning stern, and refocusing on the next torrent of traffic.

The church came into view. On a good day, Gemma saw the building as a quaint piece of architecture in the comforting Ye Olde stone England style. On a bad day, the spire looked like a middle finger telling everyone what they could do with themselves. Today was one of those days.

'I don't think He wants me here,' said Gemma as they shuffled their way in. 'I'm not really feeling it, you know?'

'Nonsense,' said Diya, in between greeting/air-kissing half the congregation. 'Jesus is the champion of the downtrodden.'

After taking her seat, the downtrodden one scanned the vicinity for pupils. There were none she could see. If Diya had dragged her to pray in a kebab shop, it'd be a different story.

Not for the first time, Gemma beheld her poncho-wearing friend in a sea of dowdy jumpers, and wondered how it could be she cared so little, standing out like a sore thumb. Or a middle finger. She had her faith, Diya, and she knew what was right, and what was good, and what to believe, and nothing else mattered to her. Especially not what other people thought. Gemma envied that about her. A couple of nights ago, Diya had arrived home, laughing to herself. Gemma had asked what was so funny, in the snappy way miserable people do.

'What's so funny?'

'You know it's Diwali?'

Fireworks exploded outside. 'Yeah. And?'

'Well, the new guy at work asked me how I was going to celebrate. I told him I was going to Mass this evening. The look on his face!' Diya laughed again. 'Honestly, I've lost count of how many times in my life people have assumed I worship multiple gods, many-armed gods, gods with faces I don't know. And I tell them, no. It's The One I believe in, and He died for all of us. Not just you white people.'

Gemma believed in The One too. She blew her nose as she recalled Paulo's azure eyes. A chink of light broke through the stained-glass window and fell onto her lap. Its warmth was like a cuddly bunny that had curled itself upon her, and it seemed as good a sign as any that she might, after all, be okay. But then the sky snatched her comfort away, and the disciples weren't gift-givers anymore, they were back to being glass and, before she knew it, unease took hold. What secondary school teacher spies adolescents in high-necked robes brandishing burning flames, and doesn't wonder what secret evil they're planning?

The saintly-slash-sinister figures placed their lights beside a magnificent, gold leaf Bible.

'Do you think those altar servers look shifty?' asked Gemma.

'Stop talking.'

'Sorry.'

Diya was on the brink of a hot-man-alert faint: Father Tom had entered. The congregation knelt and rose at the priest's every command, unquestioning. Then came his lecture, which was so dull, Gemma practically went into a coma.

*

'Hullo, Gemma.'

It was tea and biscuit time, Diya had gone AWOL, and a woman whose name she should know, but didn't, had come over for a chat.

'Hello… you!'

'Saw you sleeping during service. Late night?'

'Not exactly. I'm struggling with insomnia.'

'Oh no. Boyfriend trouble, again?'

'Er, yes.'

'Never mind, dear. He's not worth it. I'll pray for you to meet a nice young man.'

Gemma wanted to say "the last time you did that, I met the guy who stole my financial details", but she didn't. She said, 'Thank you.'

'Hello, Miss Higgins,' said yet another woman whose name escaped her. 'Fancy seeing you here.'

'I only drop by occasionally.'

'Hmm,' said unknown number two. 'Just started coming to St Peter's. Fell out with the other lot. But I go to one church or another every day. Every day without fail, I tell you!

Even when I had my kidney stone removed, I still made evening Mass.'

Now she was wagging her finger, Gemma remembered where they'd met before: the school council. Yeah, that was right. Hadn't this woman thrown a pencil at the headmistress because she'd disagreed with the budget?

'I must admit,' said the original lady, 'I don't come as often as I should, either. But we've come. That's all that matters. Ah – is this your friend, Gemma?'

To Gemma's horror, Diya was heading over with an inquisitive smile. 'All right there, Gem? Who are your friends?'

Neither of the women were volunteering anything. They stood expectantly as if on a champion's podium, waiting to be presented to the president.

Gemma gestured towards the first one. 'This is, um…'

'Betty,' said Betty, coming to the rescue after enough time had passed to make it apparent her name was forgotten. Her don't-worry-about-it look made its recipient burn with shame.

'And this is, um…'

Whoever it was had a wicked grin on her face. Diya and Betty laughed awkwardly.

'What's the joke?' asked Father Tom, winking at Diya, who blushed.

'Sorry, Father. Didn't see you come.'

He smiled at her, then held his hand up to Gemma. 'High five!'

In spite of her innate misery, she giggled like a schoolgirl. There was no denying it: Father Tom was almost handsome. He could have cut the "almost", but the trouble was, both ends of his body were too sharp. His head seemed to gather and stick up in the middle, and he wore tight-fitting trousers that emphasized the way his long legs thinned incrementally to the ankle. *Like a runner bean, he could do with a nice top and tail and, if he did,* thought Gemma, despite her dilapidated libido, *he might be rather tasty.* Diya was looking at the priest like she wouldn't change a single thing about him. Except, perhaps, the fact that he was a priest.

'Miss Higgins doesn't know us,' sniggered the still nameless woman who, rather than doing anything to clear the situation up, took another sip of her tea.

'Ah,' said Father Tom. Being a philosophical man, he'd misunderstood the answer. 'Still agnostic, are you, Gemma?'

'Maybe.'

'I hope, over time, we can change your mind. I take it you came to pray for a boyfriend again?'

'That'd *really* be a miracle,' said the woman whom Gemma would henceforth refer to as terrible tea lady who attacks people with pencils.

Diya barged in. 'She doesn't *only* come after a break-up. Every Christmas, and Easter, and when she has kids, she'll start coming every day, won't you, Gem? To get them into the local school…'

Father Tom gave Gemma a look that made her think Diya wasn't helping.

'Coming sometimes is better than never. Isn't that right, Father?' said Betty.

'It is,' said the priest. 'But what really matters is faith, and that's something that must come from within. Yes, Gemma?'

'Yes, Father.' Gemma hung her head low, not because she felt like she was being reprimanded, but because she could see, in his X-ray eyes, that the priest had her number all right. She had no faith; no faith in God; no faith in herself. How was it he could tell so well, when he'd only spoken to her twice before (albeit those two talking-tos had lasted a very, very long time)? Once he got going, the man could talk for England. As he opened his mouth, he looked set to impart his wisdom once more. Third time lucky, perhaps? Maybe he'd just make a quick comment on the weather and take Diya aside for a private chat about fundraising. Gemma drank her brew, hoping it might prove apotropaic, as well as milky. But no.

'Have you heard me do my sermon on purgatory, Gemma?'

She shook her head, helplessly.

'I rather think your soul is in a sort of purgatory.'

His musings on purgatory and its uncanny likeness to Gemma's soul lasted for twenty – almost uninterrupted – minutes. The only occasional butt-in came from terrible tea lady who attacks people with pencils.

'Yes, yes, Father, but tell her about Hell's eternal damnation, already!'

Mercifully, Father Tom ignored the heckling, and finished. 'I run a few WhatsApp groups. Would you like to join the "Undecided" one?'

Gemma could think of nothing worse than joining a club full of people like her. 'No thanks.'

'Okay.' He shared an "I-tried" smile with Diya. 'Hope you feel better now, at least. I must go mingle, but all the best. I'll pray for you; that you might find happiness. And faith. And a boyfriend. Lovely as always to see you, ladies. Dee.' He kissed Diya on the cheek, letting his hand linger on the small of her back for a fraction longer than it should.

Diya blushed again.

*

'Isn't he lovely?' cooed Diya on the cold walk home.

'He is. Does drone on though, doesn't he?'

'I could listen to him all day.'

Gemma pierced Diya with a teacher's stare. 'It's so obvious you fancy him.'

'What? No I don't!' Diya was glowing red, too good to be a good liar.

'Admit it.'

'You shouldn't talk about a priest like that. Anyway, he could never… we could never…' She left it there.

They were at the junction. A carer had come to shepherd The Conductor home. 'Come on, love,' they heard her say. 'You haven't even had breakfast yet.'

The Conductor was distraught. Throwing his head in his hands, he began to sob. The carer managed to settle him down, and then he followed her, meek as a lamb, scrunching his eyes and blocking his ears as he went. When the terrible crash happened, the one his absence was responsible for, he didn't want to know about it.

Loath to address the distressing scene, Diya said, 'Are you converted yet?'

'Not really, no. I mean, apart from anything else, what if I believe in Him, and He turns out to be a falsehood? I'll have wasted a whole lot of time and emotional energy – and I'm currently suffering a severe shortage of emotional energy. My Year Nines and Paulo have drained most of it.'

'And that about sums it up!' said Diya, triumphantly. 'The root of all your unhappiness. If only you would stop what-if-ing and dive into life, wonderful things would happen to you.'

'I guess. I mean, if I'd ordered chips when I wanted to,

instead of worrying about what would happen if I did, Paulo and I would still be together.'

'I was thinking more along the lines of opening your heart to God, but yeah, chips too. And if you really can't commit to Him, at least change your mind-set and think positively.'

Here it comes, thought Gemma.

'Always remember, you're not an orphan in Bangladesh whose orphanage has been flooded.'

'I will, thanks.'

'Who knows? Tomorrow you could be walking down the street, minding your own business, and bump into The One.'

'You mean I might accidentally bump into Paulo, and he'll realise he made a mistake, and take me back, and we'll get married and have three kids?'

Diya sighed. 'Sure.'

'Not that I buy into soulmates, but in a world of seven billion, if you ranked all potential partners, someone would have to come top.'

'Spoken like a true mathematician. You seriously think Paulo would be number one?'

'Yes.'

'You're crazy.'

A baby in a pram went past, and Gemma felt a familiar longing deep inside. 'I'm in love.'

'You need help.'

Gemma caught sight of her hair in a shop window. Limp was the word. 'What I need is new shampoo.'

*

It was another week before Gemma's hair was voluptuous and glossy. It happened on the day she won sixty thousand pounds on a TV quiz show. Or rather, she had in some parallel universe, where she was the contestant, instead of the flummoxed person on the other side. It was a shame she'd been stuck shouting the answers from the wrong end of the screen. Her bank account could do with an injection like the one Beryl's from Dundee had received. Gemma's cheeks flushed with pride as she gave herself a good talking to in the mirror.

'See? You are not stupid.' (Saying it aloud was comforting). 'You've got a Cambridge degree, for God's sake. If a quizmaster asked you "What is Fermat's theorem?" you'd be able to answer, like that.' She clicked, before her fingers morphed to a passive-aggressive point. 'Stupidity is not your problem. Your problem is where there are no black and white answers, where it is a question of *judgment*. Dee's right. You constantly worry that doing this means you cannot do that, and *that* is that something wonderful you've been waiting for your whole life. If only you'd stop second guessing everything, you'd be much happier.' She shook her head at herself in a very pitying manner. 'Now stop crying over him every day, wondering what you could have done differently, and go with the flow.'

She wasn't sure where she was meant to be flowing to, exactly, but wherever it was, for once, she was going to flow there decisively.

Inspiration struck. *If I head off now, there's a chance I'll catch him going home.* The impulse to leave the flat took hold - she felt its hand on her back, pushing her out.

'Wait!' she told the impromptu bouncer. 'Let me fix my face first.'

A dab of lip gloss, a touch of concealer, and Paulo's favoured "au naturel" look was complete. Grabbing her stuff, she left.

Before the mirror therapy, she'd have spent ages in the hallway, killing herself with internal crossed lines: *What if he rejects me again? Better not risk it, better stay where I am… On the other hand, my hair's looking so fab, it could change his mind. As Uncle Tony used to say, "fortune favours the brave, and blow-dried".* Then, after she'd left the flat, she'd have spent the whole time wishing she'd not left, or at least had chosen a different coat. But there was none of that nonsense today. The lack of dilly-dally over both the decision to go, and the choice of coat, was liberating.

Muttering like a master ventriloquist, so passers-by wouldn't think her mad, she said, 'Okay. So I'm not the only woman on Earth who has "Should I? But what if…?" wonderings. The thing is, others have those thoughts when the decision is "Should-I-marry-this-man-or-not?"-life-changing, whereas I've always crippled myself over small questions like "Should I order chips or not?". It's a form of neurosis. Well, no more, my friend.' She wasn't sure who this invisible "friend" was. Probably her neurosis.

Wind slapped her face like a sassy bitch saying, "Watch it, girl. It's getting dark." Gemma raised her collar against the warning, pausing briefly in front of the miniature clothes in a boutique window which, as usual, made her womb salivate. *My baby would look so cute in that sailor's outfit.* Whenever she saw her still-to-be-born son, he was the spitting image of his father.

She passed the charity shop. Yesterday, she'd spent half an hour there, agonising over a pair of five-quid earrings. She'd decided against them, because she was supposed to be saving for her own place, when a customer had jumped up behind her and purchased the pair on the spot. Gemma had begged to buy them from her – even offered twice the price – but the damn woman had refused. Something about how they resembled her dead mother's favourite jewellery. Gemma had doubled over outside the shop and cried at her loss.

No crying now. This was a new her, striding with a conviction so alien, it took her breath away. Devoid of worry and regret, her head felt light as a Chinese lantern released on New Year's Eve.

She was brought down by a sudden sense that she'd left her keys behind. Checking her bag, she found them, halfway between a used tissue and some lip-gloss. A car and its blaring music cruised past. Her phone! Her music! Ah, well. There was always her childhood game.

'*Songs to Party to*, number fourteen,' said Gemma to herself. The CD player in her head started pumping, and an exuberant Diana Ross sang "I'm coming out".

Growing up as an only child, Gemma had often faced boredom and loneliness. To ward off those two unpleasant playmates, she had either done complicated sums, or grouped her favourite songs into "mood" compilations. (Her mother had banned her from owning a personal stereo. "You don't want to be cut off from the world like your father. So much in his own world, he forgets to do his trousers up half the time."). Thanks to Georgia, whenever Gemma was out and phoneless, there was a musical catalogue to count on, up there, in the shelves of her mind.

Gemma couldn't bring herself to move with the times. In the age of Alexa and Spotify, her brain hadn't yet gone digital. This was partly for nostalgic reasons, so she could continue a childhood game way into adulthood, and partly because she found it a fun challenge intellectually to remember the exact place and number of every song she'd ever loved, or self-penned. It would be cheating to turn her brain into a device that played anything she named, on demand.

Songs to Party to hadn't had a much of a hearing since Paulo had left her, unlike *Songs to Cry to*. Tunes from the latter were a mix of well-known ballads, plus her own song-writing attempts, which were basically rip-offs of Tammy Wynette tracks (whenever she had envisaged herself as a singer, she had pictured a '70s country music star in a full-sleeved sequined gown, complete with sad guitar and Marie Antoinette hair). *Wish I Hadn't Eaten That Cake* was one of the self-penned classics from *Songs to Cry to*. Recently, Gemma had adapted its lyrics: *Wish I hadn't eaten Paulo's chips. Now the chips are down. I can do nowt but frown. The greedy gambler, she is down.*

'Stop,' ordered Gemma.

Diana Ross obliged. Exterior rush-hour street noises flushed through her ears, like a rush of freedom. Acting with impunity, it turned out, was bliss. So this is what it felt like to leave past decisions made, in the past. So this is what it felt like to be spontaneous; to be the sort of person who could pack a suitcase and jet off to Lanzarote on a whim. Okay, so she wasn't jetting off to Lanzarote, she was only going to (hopefully) accidentally-on-purpose bump into Paulo, but still. It was wonderful to be living without a care in the world, and with something resembling confidence. A streetlight switched itself on as Gemma approached, and it felt symbolic. She was a woman reborn, close to the church, at the junction. The Conductor wasn't present to grant her safe passage, but no matter.

There he was! It was fate!

'Paulo!' she screamed, like a crazed fan at a gig. 'Paulo!'

Her rock star waved.

With a smile that went on for miles, Gemma crossed the road, and was hit by a bus.

CHAPTER THREE

Dust danced in the air beneath a strong, synthetic spotlight. The room she was in had an unnatural sheen to it, on account of the walls, which were covered in a tin foil substance. The only furniture was a long table with Bunsen burners and metallic instruments upon it. These silver objects were so polished, they acted like bulbs, bathing the room in glows they reflected. In her daze, Gemma half expected Roz, one of her closest friends, to ask for some after-school club cover. Rationality set in. Wherever she was, she was not in the school's Chemistry Department.

God, it was bright. The source of the abundant light was a mystery. No blue flames emanated from the Bunsen burners. There were no fittings on the ceiling. Indeed, there seemed to be no ceiling at all. The tin foil walls stretched as high as Gemma could fathom, and the illusion was that they met at a singular point in some distant centre. Looking up made her dizzy, so she closed her eyes, and looked back.

The machine smashed into her, catapulting her to concrete like she weighed nothing. Pain all about her; different manifestations of pain, all vying for her attention with the screams of witnesses and blazing headlamps. Her limbs were arranged in strange angles, in ways she had never thought possible. Her skull had ruptured, and the blood it had contained so effortlessly till now was in free-fall. Shards of bone had punctured her chest – at least, that's what it felt like. The bone in her lungs and the terror – the rising, rising terror – made it hard to breathe; hard to scream. A man had spoken, and he had comforted her. The next thing she knew, she was. Wherever this was.

Heart pounding, breaths racing at the horror of the memory, she calmed herself down with logic. Clearly, her perception – that she'd been there, blinked, landed in this room – was wrong. She must have fallen into a coma, and this must be a hospital. For how long had she slept?

She was about to call out, but stopped herself. Questioning and thanking saviours could wait. Right now, she wanted to make the most of the solitude, gauge her condition and get a bearing on things. Let the doctors come later. Tentatively, she jerked her limbs. To her amazement, everything moved, and moved freely. One more once-over to confirm the room was vacant. As she removed her clothes, she thought, *how funny. How funny that undressing doesn't hurt one jot.* Naked, Gemma body-checked for signs of trauma. No blood. Nothing broken. No discomfort at all. As far as she could tell, there wasn't so much as a cut. Judging by her pristine state, she'd been unconscious for weeks, and any wounds had long since healed.

She could do with a mirror, but there wasn't one, so she searched for a reflection in one of the table's silver implements. Nothing but shine stared back at her. The wall would have to do. It showed her up as a pale, abstract painting, broken up into inhuman shapes. Staring at a self she didn't recognise, the confusion was overwhelming. It felt like someone had laid out her timeline and cut off the bit between past and present. Her missing part would've endured pure hell – she should be glad it was misplaced. Yet it didn't feel right. It felt like she had cheated at life.

Recalling what she'd lost on the road, Gemma prodded her flesh. *Perhaps,* she thought, *medics mined my stash of red gold?*

After all, she was a regular donor, so it was possible they'd found what had once been hers, and pumped it back in. Maybe, unwittingly, she had saved her own skin? Wouldn't that be something? The smile was sardonic. Proof, when her dad asked for it, that she was responsible, and was able to save for a rainy day. Of course, he'd been thinking in fiscal, rather than bloody terms, but still, it was vindication of sorts.

Gemma traced the blue up her arm, confident at first, but as she went on, her fingers became more and more shaky. It was improbable she was wholly herself anymore. Every time she had volunteered blood, it had ceased to be her property, and become an impersonalised (0+) number in a plastic bag. Then, like everyone else's gifts, it had been randomly distributed. It was more likely she owed her life to a stranger's actions, than her own. It was more likely she had the blood of a stranger running through her veins, than not. The shock of this realisation – of the crash; of her strange surroundings – was too much to bear, and she started to cry.

Crying and naked, Gemma was forced to acknowledge the absence of dressings, of scars, of any evidence she'd ever been accessed. She fought to remember more. It was dark, and her coat was black. The bus had tried to brake; she'd seen it in the corner of her eye, too late to do anything about it. Too late, even, to have time to worry about the inevitable. There had been pain – yes, great pain – but no need to dwell more on that.

There had been a man. In the darkness she heard him say "stay with me", and it had felt like she was being asked to come home, which had been a welcome respite from the urge to die.

Try as she might, she had no recollection of kind nurses or sobbing bedside parents. It occurred to her there was no bed, and the air was quiet. Hospitals were hives of activity, alarms and dinner tray smells – weren't they? Maybe she had caught a contagious virus, and was being held in isolation? Still, no noise at all wasn't right… Unless the accident had left her deaf? *Deaf* – it sounded like that other word, but that couldn't be.

'Hello?' said Gemma. It was quiet, but audible. She covered her ears, and the sound of the sea surrounded her. Taking deep breaths to quell the fear, she shouted. 'Hello? Hello?' The room echoed her cries, but no one came. This was no hospital.

Forcing herself to breathe slowly, she gave her brain space to work things out. All it did was offer swear words. Then, after the fifth "fuck" came a genuinely helpful, lightbulb moment. *Gem*, said one of her inner voices (the Diya-esque one that favoured the bright side), *don't you understand? This is a dream.* Gemma grinned from ear-to-ear. Until "Amber" piped up with the caveat, *or a nightmare.*

'Wake up! Wake up!' screamed Gemma.

Nothing changed. A door! Thank goodness there was a door. Hastily, she re-dressed. Baby steps at first. As it became apparent she wasn't collapsing to the floor, or vanishing in a puff of smoke, she picked up pace. Mid-run, "Amber" made another contribution. *Check out these instruments. They look like they belong to a lobotomist.* Gemma didn't particularly want to be experimented on, even if this life was illusionary. Swallowing down her "Amber" panic, Gemma turned the handle, and laughed.

The best case – that this was a *good*, non-dissecting dream – was confirmed, and relief soaked her to the core. Now she could relax and appreciate the jaw-dropping beauty of where she was, which was outer space.

'This is bloody brilliant!' she said, walking and talking like she owned the place.

There was no Earth beneath her, only a blackness broken by a thousand stars. Running her hands through the see-through platform underfoot was like disturbing a tranquil sea. Surfer-like, she rode the vacuum as it wavered and waved, before settling back to its state of transparent stillness. It appeared particles that made up dark matter were bending the rules, in order to support her. Gemma grinned goofily. Who doesn't want to feel like God, master of the universe, from time to time? Even in their own head?

The majesty of the scene took Gemma's breath away. Scattered about in every direction were stars more dazzling than any she'd ever seen back home. In her eyes, Earth's sky dots had transformed from distant, twinkly things, into fist-sized balls of white gold fire. Running rings round these comparative giants were colourful clouds of gas that swirled with a boundless energy. The stars and their living, breathing auras were so close, she could touch them. Stretching out her arms, she grasped nothing. She marginalised her disappointment with the rationale that it was a privilege just to *see*; to see the stars this close, without going blind. An apple from the tree of knowledge had been offered to her, and there was no punishment for accepting the gift. Gemma put on a "humble prophet" face, because that felt like an appropriate expression to adopt. She, Gemma Higgins, was New Eve, surveying a new world.

'I am most humbled, and give thanks,' said Gemma solemnly, in case there was someone higher listening. No reply came.

Gemma was very impressed with herself for concocting such a profound universe. As far as she was aware, until now, her dreams had either been completely nonsensical, or else had featured six-pack hunks desperate to sleep with her. Let's rewind: until now, all her dreams had been completely nonsensical. She perused space once more, in case she'd missed any dashing, sex-starved astronauts heading her way.

A dumpy Chinese woman in tweed came out of the closest star; just came out of it, like it was nothing. It wasn't quite what Gemma had hoped for but still, it was cool.

The woman marched towards her, looking frazzled and clutching a clipboard. *Frazzled-looking people often have clipboards*, thought Gemma. She wondered if the world would be a happier place if there were no clipboards in it.

'No, no, no,' said the woman, when she was close enough. 'This is all wrong.' She pointed at Gemma. 'You're all wrong. What are you doing here?'

'Well, that's a bit rude.' Gemma squint-glared at the woman's name badge, which read: MARGE, HR MANAGER in bold, indisputable capitals. 'I know you're a figment of my imagination, Marge, but that's no excuse to—'

Marge interrupted, rudely. 'How did you get here?' She flipped through forms on her clipboard, intermittently glancing at Gemma and shaking her head.

'Dunno. I just woke up in that room there.' Gemma turned around to indicate where the room had been, but there was nothing behind her, only more space. 'Oh. Well. There used to be a room there. Last thing I remember, I was hit by a—' Gemma whistled. What if this dream went back before space and the tin foil room? What if she hadn't been hit by a bus after all? What if – Gemma squealed – what if Paulo hadn't broken up with her either? Why stop there? What if she could travel back in time even further? Maybe most of her life had been a dream, and when she woke up, she'd be twelve again, before the start of the *Songs to Cry to* years.

'Woke up, pah!' Marge stopped at a particular paper. Her face turned white. 'Ah. I see.' She squatted and hit herself on the head with the clipboard.

'Um, can I help with anything?'

Still down and under the clipboard, Marge raised a cynical eye. 'That depends. Do you know much about physics?'

'Er…'

'Cosmology?'

'Um…'

'Quantum mechanics?'

'Even less.'

'General relativity?'

'As in Einstein's theory?'

Hope dawned on Marge's face. 'Yes.'

'E equals MC squared?'

Hope died on Marge's face.

Aware she was coming across as a bit thick, Gemma added, 'But I do really well on daytime game shows.'

Marge sighed.

'And I teach maths at secondary school so, you know, if you want to quiz me on quadratic equations, go for it.'

That did the trick. Marge sprung up. 'Of course!' she cried, leafing through the papers again. 'It says so here! Sorry, I was getting you muddled up with one of the other Gemmas – the one who joined an investment bank. Don't ask me why, but we can't send anyone back who works for an investment bank if they don't have a comprehensive knowledge of physics.'

'What?'

'I think it's maybe the universe's way of limiting the number of investment bankers on Earth.' Marge laughed like a gentle ding-a-ling-ing bell. 'Sorry. Everything's so chaotic, I don't know whether I'm coming or going. What with the maintenance work being carried out and—'

A million questions fought for prominence in Gemma's mind. Some spilled out. 'What the hell are you going on about? What maintenance work? What do you mean "other Gemmas"?'

The answer to all those questions was, 'Aha. It says so here. Yes.'

'Give me that!'

Gemma tried to snatch the clipboard but its owner ducked. Spiralling her finger as if teasing a bigger hole, Marge slipped the clipboard through the void, and it disappeared.

Gemma blinked. 'Okay. I've had enough now. Wake up! Wake up!'

She slapped herself on each cheek. The hurt of the hits didn't match the applied force. It merely felt as if she'd tapped herself lightly. Trying again, she employed harder and harder blows, until she lost balance and fell to the ground. Which was, of course, not there. Gemma wobbled on the vacuum until it steadied.

Marge rode the unseen current, cool as a cucumber. When they had stopped moving, she patted Gemma on the shoulder. 'It won't work, you know. The classic rules don't apply here.'

'Right.' Gemma punched herself in the stomach.

Marge, taking pity on Gemma's futile acts of self-harm, said, 'Would you like to borrow my gun?'

'Sure. Why not?'

Marge removed a hand-sized one from her pocket and placed it in Gemma's trembling fingers.

'How come you carry this around with you?'

'It's my stress ball. Childish, I know, but there you go.'

Gemma examined the object. It didn't strike her as being remotely childish. Pressing the cool metal against her right temple, she screwed her eyes tight, said, 'Goodbye, then,' and fired.

Nothing. Wearily, Gemma prised the gun from her head, and a single bullet limped out, into Marge's waiting hand.

'Maybe now you'll stop trying?'

'I want to go home.'

'Pete will do his best, but no promises,' said Marge, brusquely. 'He's done something similar before, but that was donkey's ago. It may no longer be feasible…' She faded out, because Gemma's lip was too wobbly for her liking. Clearly, what this one required was motivation and mollycoddling. Realistic pessimism with a dash of gentle disdain was more Marge's style, but she was an HR manager who took pride in the fact she could adapt according to her personnel's needs. Taking a deep breath, Marge channelled a more can-do persona, and said, 'I mean, don't worry! Pete can get you home! Things will work out just great!'

'Great?'

'Sure. Or at the very least, tolerable.'

'Great.'

'Would you, er, like a hug?'

'No thank you.'

Marge tried not to look too relieved. 'All righty then. Come with me, dear, and I'll take you to Pete.'

'Who's Pete?'

'He's our fixer.'

'Cool. And where will we find this Pete? Saturn? Mars?'

'Don't be daft. The Problem Room.'

'The Problem Room?'

'Yes. It's where all people with problems go.'

'I see. So The Problem Room is where we'll find a solution?'

'No, no. For that, you need the Solution Room.'

'Well why can't we skip the Problem Room and go straight to the Solution Room?'

'Because you need to go through the one, to get to the other, you dodo!' She paused for thought. 'I mean, come on, my dear.'

'I've seen this film before. If I want to wake up, I've no choice but to do as you say. Right?'

Marge sighed. 'I've no idea why you keep going on about *waking up*.' With that, she turned on her heels and, with swinging hips that showed she meant business, led the newcomer on.

Contemplating the cosmos beneath her shifting feet, Gemma said, 'I never knew I could dream up something so wonderful. And so terrifying.'

Marge shook her head. 'For the last time, this is no dream! You need to improve on your grip of reality. Can I have my gun back, by the way?'

Gemma handed the thing over and, aiming ahead, Marge pulled the trigger. The bullet trundled through space. If she'd wanted to, Gemma could have overtaken the slice of silver. As it was, she followed the woman and bullet in a trance, whilst cursing Diya for last week which, now she thought about it, probably explained everything. Last week, rather than taking her mind off things with a rom-com, Diya had suggested they "branch out", and watch sci-fi instead. There had been alien planets and binary numbers and gravity overcome, and Gemma hadn't been able to make head nor tail of it through all the tears. Maybe the film's high concepts, sensing a lovelorn woman on her period, had figured it prudent not to penetrate their viewer upon entry. Like soldiers biding their time in enemy territory, mind-boggling ideas of *interstellar travel* and *physics* had buried themselves deep in her subconscious, so that they might strike at a later, more impactful date. It seemed they had chosen now as their time of attack. In short, if it weren't for last week's Diya, Ryan Gosling would be declaring his infinite love for Gemma right now, and she wouldn't be following an HR manager and an unsettlingly slow bullet through space so deep, the laws of physics were warped beyond all comfort. Talking of comfort…

Perhaps it was because there'd been too many other things to consider, but only now did it hit Gemma: she was a comfortable temperature. She suddenly remembered that in every dream she'd ever had in her life till now, unrealistic as they might have been, the fundamentals of nature had always applied. She had never been able to fly, unless she had been in a plane. If she had fallen off a cliff, she had always stayed asleep long enough to hear the crunch and witness the splayed, blood-splattered body for confirmation. Gemma's breathing became uneasy. So far, there were a thousand reasons she should be dead here, even without accounting for the fact she had shot herself at point blank range. Radiation should have blitzed her. Lack of oxygen should have suffocated her. Lack of gravity should have sent her floating into oblivion. Heat should have boiled her alive, or coldness should have frozen her to death – she wasn't sure which.

Gemma hopped, making the invisible ground beneath them tremble.

'What are you doing?' asked Marge, slipping up, keeping a lid on her voice so irritation didn't leak out.

'Nothing,' mumbled Gemma, once the trembling died

down. She didn't feel like explaining she'd wanted to summon an earthquake, even though there was no earth. She wanted to fall; fall as she had every right to expect; fall into a state of wakefulness.

There was one possibility, of course, that Gemma had refused to acknowledge properly. Ever since she had found herself in that strange, tin foil room, a pestering child had popped its head in her brain every now and then. Before the child could fully ask the question, she had told it to "go away, go away". Gemma was ready to give the child voice now.

'Am I dead?' she asked.

'Yes.'

'Oh. Are you sure?'

Marge puffed out her chest. 'As HR manager for section 1735 XB of the universe, it's my job to know these things. Yes, you are dead. Dead as a dodo. Extinct. Finitoed. Caput. Dead. Well, don't give me that face, there's no point beating about the bush, is there?' Surveying Gemma's silent tears and streaming nose, she realised, perhaps there was a point. Scolding herself for neglecting to baby the thing, she asked, 'Tissue?'

'I'm never going to see Turf Fen Mill again.' Gemma wasn't sure what made her say that, of all things.

The bullet bounced against something unseen. Its path took a downward trajectory.

'Ah. Here's the door,' said Marge, thankful to change the subject. She pushed against the place that had forced their guide to change course.

'I thought our destination was a star?'

'Don't be ridiculous.'

'How come that thing can fall, but I can't?' asked Gemma, jealous of the tumbling bullet.

'Because it brushed against a new reality, of course.' Marge turned her exasperated tone down a notch. 'I mean, come on in, my dear.'

CHAPTER FOUR

With a shrug of her apparently dead shoulders, Gemma went through a wormhole. Or was it a black hole? If she'd been a physicist in life, she might have known what it was she was doing. For now, it was enough to know that whatever she was doing was fucking weird.

Performing a three-sixty, she saw the universe had left her, and she was where no one in their right minds would want to be: the world's biggest waiting area. Even the chairs seemed reluctant to be there, strapped as they were to porridge walls, in case they made a run for it. Rope barriers formed a maze to the far-off promise land of counters. They seemed miles away, those counters behind Perspex screens. None of them were manned. Gemma squinted. Maybe there were people there, only presently, due to the vast distance, they were scarcely perceptible blobs. Grainy, circus-style music crackled from sound speakers. Far from cheering Gemma up, the jaunty notes made the already depressing scene seem more depressing.

'I suppose we'd best play along, then.' Marge picked up a fresh clipboard from a table and set off for the maze.

Gemma was on her tail, and madness was on her mind. Was she really experiencing death or was she, in fact, insane? And which of the two options was preferable? 'Please, Marge. Can you explain… everything?'

'I'm getting there,' said Marge, winding this way and that. 'Oops! No I'm not. Dead end. Back the way we came.' Marge barged past her.

Gemma tested the rope out, and it was light as, well, rope. 'You know, we could just cut through the middle,' she said, arcing the barrier.

Marge tutted. 'Cutting corners won't work here.' Turning back, she carried on her convoluted path.

'But why?'

'Because you'll upset Pete, and that's not very nice. Not when he works so hard to make the Problem Room a fun, interactive experience for all you unfortunate people with problems.'

'So, I'm one of the unfortunate people?'

'Yes. Whenever a person dies who shouldn't have, they become a problem. It's Pete's job to get them to other side of the Problem Room, through to the Solution Room.'

'Wait – so you're saying I shouldn't have died?'

'Exactly. Oh blast it!' said Marge, confronted by another twine line. 'Back. Back again.' She flapped her clipboard in Gemma's face. 'According to my notes, you shouldn't have died at all. In fact, right after the accident, which was only supposed to rough you up a bit, you were due to meet the man of your dreams, win the lottery and generally have a tip-top life.'

A symphony of swearing played from Gemma's mouth, with a grand finale of, 'Who's fucked this up for me, then? Whose bloody fault is it?'

'Probably Bob's. Though I'm sure he didn't mean it. Look, sometimes, things just go wrong.'

'Bollocks! Who's Bob?'

'There's no need for all this f-ing and blinding.'

'Well, you'd swear too, in my shoes!'

Marge looked down at Gemma's shoes. 'Touché.' Then she remembered it was her job to keep people happy. 'I mean, they're great on you, but I couldn't pull them off.'

Gemma shook her head. 'Whatever. Look, back to the me-being-accidentally-dead thing: it's easy to fix, yeah?' Much to her dismay, Gemma saw that Marge had the helpless air of a customer service agent, faced with a bloke and his faulty product, one day after a guarantee has expired. More in hope, than in expectation, Gemma added, 'You can just… put me back?'

'HR's my department. Reinstating people on Earth doesn't fall in my remit. Terribly bad luck that you died, you know. Your type of glitch has only happened thrice since the dawn of humanity.'

'What happened to those other glitches?'

'One went back and became a pope. The other two joined a cult.'

'So, it will be possible for me to return, then?'

'Fingers crossed. Pete will provide access to the Solution Room, at any rate.' She stopped before another barrier in the maze. 'Sorry, wrong again.' Marge zigzagged left instead. 'We're close now. I can feel it.'

Dazed beyond measure, Gemma blindly followed. 'This maze is impossible.'

'We'll get there eventually. You should be grateful there's not a sphinx on site anymore. We used to have to answer its riddles to get to the other side. I don't know about you, but I was never one for linguistic conundrums.'

'Was it a real sphinx?'

'Don't be daft. Pete wore a costume. I remember when he went through a Sudoku puzzle phase – that was a nightmare. I was stuck in this place for five hundred years.'

Gemma wasn't exactly feeling reassured. 'But why do we have to go through all this, just to reach the counters?'

'It was my idea,' said Marge, proudly. 'As an HR manager, it's my job to keep people happy. Pete complained he was getting bored with problem-solving: in two hundred thousand years, he'd only had three shouldn't-be-dead-dead people to deal with, and some broken machines. So – and here's my genius – I suggested he should make his office *part* of the problem. Give him something to do.'

'Right.' Gemma's head was swimming.

'He's since been much happier at work, spending all his time coming up with new problems for people with problems to solve so that he can solve their problems.'

'Makes perfect sense.'

'Doesn't it? It makes my life harder of course, having to escort others through whatever he's dreamt up, but I'm selfless like that.'

She wore a pious look that Gemma hadn't the heart to puncture with the observation that, in placating Pete, Marge had likely doubled everyone else's stress levels.

'And,' continued Marge, 'I also advised him to build a store cupboard for the broken machines he couldn't fix, so he didn't have to look at them and cry. That's where you found yourself, before I found you.'

'The tin foil room?'

'Yes. It is rather aluminium-heavy, isn't it? Well, whatever you do, don't tell Pete I said that. It took him seven thousand years to complete, and I'm never one to hurt one's feelings. Oh, hallelujah! The end is in sight!'

As they got closer to their destination, it was apparent Gemma's first impression had been a correct one: there was no one at the desks. This didn't seem to deter Marge though, who carried on with her purposeful marching. They reached the front of the non-existent queue, and a bell appeared out of nowhere. *Sure, why not?* thought Gemma. There was a time when rabbit-from-the-hat magic tricks had invoked in her a sense of childhood wonder – back when she knew the rules of the game.

The conjured bell wasn't one of those dingy little things used to call someone's attention, but a great, big, church-tower bell, with a thick rope strong enough to hang a man. Marge tugged with all her might and a mighty clang sent its vibrations flying round the room with the crazed zeal of a knife-thrower. Gemma herself felt the ring had slashed her. Or maybe her heart hurt because she was still coming to terms with the fact she might never see her parents again. And she had almost won the lottery. The infuriatingly upbeat music that had played throughout the maze run, stopped.

'Congratulations for completing the maze, which we hope was a fun experience for you!' said an automated voice from above. 'You are number twelve million, eight hundred thousand, seven hundred and sixty-three in the queue.'

Marge hit herself on the head with the clipboard.

'Your query is important to us. An available agent will be with you as soon as possible.' The music picked up where it had left off.

'I don't understand,' said Gemma. 'We're the only ones here.'

'That you can see,' said Marge, mysteriously. 'You may be both alive and dead, but you haven't mastered all the dimensions yet.' She slumped to the floor and beckoned Gemma join her.

'Why don't we go sit in one of the chairs on the side?'

Marge gaped at her. 'And lose our place in the queue?'

'But you said Pete rarely had anything to do?'

'In normal times, yes. But not when there's building work

going on. Meteorite mining spells the death knell for many a drill, I can tell you. Poor Pete's probably got quite a backlog of drills.'

'Argh!' Gemma found herself ground down. She slumped to the floor. Nothing made sense here, and she was just going to have to get used to it. She grappled for some order in her mind. Okay, so what did she know? That she was in outer space where traditional laws of physics didn't apply; that she had died when she wasn't supposed to and ended up in a storeroom for unfixable things; that the universe was run by Marge and this Pete, and maybe others. There were a thousand questions to be asked, so she made a start: 'Marge, is this place a sort of purgatory, like they have in the Christian tradition? If it turns out I must stay dead, do I have to be cleansed of sin, before I can enter Heaven?'

'Um…' Marge consulted with her clipboard.

'*Is* there is a heaven? Because if there is, I'm sorry for all the things I did, and all the things I didn't do. I'm sorry I didn't believe in Him. I should have paid more attention to religion. Maybe if I had done, I'd understand what was happening now. Maybe I'd have heard of… Saint Marge, the HR manager?'

Marge put down her clipboard and laughed. 'What a thing to call me! No, I am no saint. And I don't know if there's a god, or gods. Plenty of others around here have faith of one kind or another, though. Pete himself is a scientologist, I believe. For my part, I think God is beyond us… another imperceptible layer in a multi-layered universe.'

Gemma was tiring of metaphysical answers, even though, to be fair, she had been asking metaphysical questions. 'Okay. Now please can you explain to me, in black and white terms, what's going on?'

Marge considered her for a moment. 'Yes, I see that I need to. But it is hard to know, when speaking to someone so ignorant – I mean, *inexperienced* – where to start.'

'How about, in the beginning…'

Marge sighed. 'Very well. In the beginning…'

Clasping her knees to her chest, Gemma hardly dared breathe. She didn't want the slightest sound interrupting the secret to life. Unfortunately, the sound system didn't get the memo. A juggler's theme continued to scratch against her eardrums – da, da, dada, dada…

'There's no such thing as free will – not in the way you understand it.'

'There isn't?'

'No. Every time a person has a decision to make, however small, the universe splits. This split is imperceptible, so no one ever senses it.'

In the silence, Gemma digested, then said, 'So if, in my life, I ever had a choice to go left or right, you're saying reality would branch off the two ways?'

'Yes.'

'But then how is it, from my perspective, I ended up stepping in one direction?'

'Your consciousness is part of reality, so that split too, in perfect unison with the universe. A version of you ended up going both ways, only each Gemma was ignorant of the other's existence.'

'So how come I – my consciousness I guess – knew which Gemma to occupy?'

'It didn't, as such. Where you experienced yourself ending up was completely random. It was always equally probable that you'd wind up in a different Gemma body.'

'So you're saying no decision I ever made mattered

because somewhere else, I'd made a different choice? If I'd got it wrong in one place, I'd have got it right in another?'

'Exactly.'

'I see.' Through the brain fog, one thing was suddenly abundantly clear: living life as an angst-ridden human being had been a complete waste of energy. She had been a mathematical permutation like everyone else, and there had never been any way to change that. She might as well have spent her whole life as the number one, desperately trying not to be an odd number, when she couldn't help but be an oddity because it was an unchangeable part of her nature.

Then again, it was comforting to think the load of living had always been, unbeknown to her, shared. She felt grateful, like she wanted to thank and shake the hand of everyone in her sorority. If only she could know them.

'What are us Gemmas to each other, then? Sisters? Distant relations? Clones?'

'You are strangers who will never meet.'

'Ah.' On the other side of the coin, it was sort of sad, to think Chesney Hawkes had got it wrong. She was not the one and only. 'I suppose there are hundreds of me. In hundreds of universes.'

Marge laughed. 'I thought you were a mathematician? There are millions upon millions of you! And an infinite number of universes! Think back on your past, on all the times you could have acted differently.'

Gemma thought what might have been if she'd stayed at home, and thus avoided being run over by a bus.

'And then, when you take the others into account, the size of the numbers become boggling. We are dealing with infinities, here. Can you imagine? Each time one of the seven billion has the slightest choice to make – even one as small as choosing salad over chips – they drag a copy of the world and all its inhabitants with them in a completely new direction.'

Gemma's head was struggling to wrap itself around the information she was receiving. On top of the knowledge she was accidentally dead, it was all getting a bit much. She wanted to cry again. 'Is there any way a person could leave the world behind? Find themselves completely alone?'

'No. Humans and realities, they are made up of the same quantum stuff, and so are attracted together by a force not yet understood by man. It's kind of like magnetism, but a bit more complicated.' Marge referred back to her trusty clipboard. 'According to my notes,' she said, 'your existence alone is responsible for the creation of eight million and twelve whole other universes.' Gemma couldn't help but feel a bit proud – important, even – until Marge said, 'Of course, someone like Queen Elizabeth was responsible for over a billion.'

'Ah.'

'On the other hand, one American president has destroyed over six million Earths via accidental nuclear warfare, so you're not doing too badly, all things considered.'

'Right.' Gemma thought for a second. 'Does that mean there is no reality where I have become an important world leader?'

Marge masked her laughter with a cough.

The music that had been playing while the world was explained, stopped – "Thank you for waiting. You are now number five thousand and two in the queue" – and started again.

'Blimey, that was quick!' said Gemma, perking up a bit.

'Was it?' said Marge. She thought better of saying "any time spent with you, trying to make you understand, is too long". 'I suppose it was. Well, after all, time works differently here.'

'It does?'

'Oh yes. We're in the fourteenth dimension.'

'We are?' Each new revelation felt like a hole punch in her brain. She could feel her old understanding of reality leaking out through the freshly formed holes. 'Wait a second – how come my life is mapped out for me on your clipboard? How can you know what choice I am *supposed* to make, before I even make it?'

'Basically, each human is assigned a group of writers whose job it is to document every life an individual will lead. We often call these writers "monkeys".'

'Monkeys?'

'Yes.' Marge laughed her tinkle laugh. 'On account of the fact that, as they type, they sound uncannily like mating apes.'

'Right. But I'm not sure that answers my question.'

'Hello-ooo?' called a man from on high.

Marge and Gemma leapt to their feet.

'Pete!' cried Marge, feigning a kiss through the plastic screen.

'Marge!'

Pete was a seven-foot black man who had more beard than face. His eyes looked like two chunks of granite, he wore a plain robe and, to top it off, he held a staff in one hand. All in all, he gave off a Jesus disciple vibe. Gemma whispered in Marge's ear.

'Are you sure he isn't *the* Peter?'

'Oh yes,' she whispered. 'He just loved Middle Eastern fashion back in late B.C. I have a soft spot for 1950s Britain, myself.' She brushed some dirt off her tweed jacket and spoke more audibly. 'Open the gates, will you Pete? We've had a bit of a mix-up here.' She scanned Gemma. 'Well, if I'm being honest, a monumental, ten-on-the-Richter-Scale cock-up.' She filled Pete in.

'Excellent!' he said, his sandaled feet hopping on the spot. 'Finally, something more interesting to deal with than Lucifer's fungal nail infection.'

He banged his staff on the ground three times. The parquet tiles, which until now had rested against each other in neat little chevrons, opened up like birds spreading their wings. Suddenly, it felt for all the world like the floor was taking flight and was eager to shake dead weight off its back. As the cosmic plates shifted, Gemma clung to the counter for support. Tremors made the great bell chime and, as debris rained down, it seemed to ring for the end of time, so deafening was its call. Lumps of plaster and brick and glass began to strike – but for all their impact, they might as well have been feathers. Gemma's body could feel no hurt. A brick collided with her skull and bounced off. With that brick, Gemma remembered that in this place, the pains and restraints of her body were a thing of history. She was free. Gemma grinned. It really was wonderful, not to feel fear in the eye of destruction. Marge looked a little green.

'Are you okay?' asked Gemma.

Marge scrunched her eyes and bulged her cheeks, like she was trying desperately to hold something in. Pete gave Gemma a conspiratorial wink and began whistling a familiar tune. Gemma joined him, warbling all over the place, because she was being shook like a tambourine. Pete began an absurd shouting match.

'Didst thou like my maze?'

'What?'

'I said, didst thou like my maze?'

'It was great, thanks!'

'Didst thou find it a pleasant distraction?'

'Oh yes!' A chair catapulted into Gemma. 'Thank you so much for the experience!'

'My pleasure! Tis what I'm here for! Well, nay, tis not. I'm here to fix things. But I might as well have fun along the way, eh?'

The background had finished falling apart. Exhausted by their violence, the parquet birds went to sleep, then vanished, taking their destroyed load with them. The bell was the sole remnant of the old room. Its cry rang on, though it had nothing left to cling on to, and was plummeting, plummeting towards some unfathomable depth.

'Sorry about your Problem Room,' said Gemma.

'Oh, there's nothing wrong with it,' Pete replied. 'Its total annihilation was merely an illusion. Tis far more exhilarating to believe thou hast survived the apocalypse than to walk out a back door, eh?'

'Um...' Gemma wasn't sure what she was more confused by – Pete's hybrid language (a strange mix of modern and ancient) or his warped logic.

'And after surviving my apocalypse, people tend to realise their problems aren't so titanic after all.'

Gemma thought her problem still seemed pretty titanic. They were back in the vastness of space. Where the counter had been were people with drills and hard hats, quarrying the great belly of a meteorite. The sound of the distant bell was drowned out by the commotion of diggers.

'Sorry about the racket,' shouted someone scruffy, leaping off the rock and landing next to them. He was holding large plans in his hand.

'I should think so,' said Marge. She seemed to have

recovered enough to sniff out words, if not say them. 'That was a dreadful transition. I nearly barfed all over my new suit. And now you're giving me a headache.'

Gemma wondered about her own bodily functions. If she stayed dead, would she ever need the toilet again? Or sleep? Would she still feel hunger? Since the tin foil room, she had felt no urge to eat or drink or go at all. Maybe, if she cut herself open, she would find she'd become a cavity, and there was no longer anything in her body that needed filling or emptying. No lungs, no kidneys, no stomach. Perhaps all the inconvenient bits that used to cause desire, or urination, or defecation, had been scooped out. Maybe that was why, since the tin foil room, she had remained steadfastly, unflinchingly comfortable. Although… hadn't she cried earlier? Yes, she had, upon discovering she was dead – which was perfectly understandable. Well, it was good to know that if nothing else, a person could carry on expressing misery after they'd snuffed it. Gemma pinched her torso and found it still set around muscle and bone.

'Universe maintenance is a complicated, sometimes noisy job, Marge,' said the builder, waving his generous plans in their faces.

Gemma's eyes swam with equations and diagrams that looked like something from a nuclear power plant disaster film.

'We're going as fast as we can,' the builder continued.

'I know,' said Pete. 'And we appreciate all thou does, Bob.'

Gemma's ears pricked up.

'Do we?' added Marge. She waggled her finger at Bob. 'It seems every time you lot get your diggers out, something goes wrong.'

'Does it?' said Bob, blinking.

'Yes. Things run tickety-boo across the reality board — okay, there are genocides and famines and wars and what have you, but it all pans out as one expects… until *essential maintenance work* gets carried out, and suddenly, Gemma dies when she's not supposed to.' She put her arms around her charge's waist, and Gemma didn't know where to look. 'Look at this poor, innocent woman. It's your fault she's dead.'

Bob hung his head. 'Sorry, Gemma.'

In a battle versus her indignation, Gemma's Englishness won. 'I'm sorry, too. Don't worry about it.'

'Now, now,' said Pete. 'We can't prove this mess is the builders' fault.'

Marge begged to differ. 'They were around the last time it happened with the pope and the cultists. Coincidence? Me thinks not.'

Bob looked like a man who couldn't take anymore. Gemma felt desperately sorry for him and thought, not for the first time, that for someone who worked in HR, Marge wasn't much of a people person. A spotty woman with a hammer lumbered up.

'Sorry boss,' she said, shaking her head at Bob. 'It's more polonium.'

'Not more bloody polonium!' Bob rolled the plan up and shoved it in his back pocket, before proceeding to have a minor breakdown. 'Why is it always polonium? Why?' He pointed an accusing finger to the stars above. 'Is this your idea of a joke? How can you expect us to facilitate new life with radioactive poison, huh? Why can't you give us something more useful? Like oxygen or carbon or gold? Come on! Give us something to work with here!' He started crying.

'It's all right,' said the young builder, putting her arm

around the boss. 'Why don't we stop for a tea? Things always look better after a tea break.'

The boss wiped his eyes and nodded. 'You're right.' Talk of tea had given Bob strength. He bellowed, 'Okay lads and lasses! Tools down! Time out!' Checking his watch, he faced Marge again. 'Latest estimate for work's end... standard time... twenty thousand years.'

It was a good thing he was wearing a hard hat because Marge looked like she wanted to whack him on the head with her clipboard.

'Very well, Bob. We're just off to the Solution Room now. Fare thee well.'

Pete dragged Marge away, as she hissed, 'Where's their sense of urgency? We don't want any more Gemmas.'

The giant laughed and Gemma joined in, slightly hysterically. It had been a funny day. If indeed it had been a day at all, and not a night, or a week, or a century. She had left her sense of measurement behind long ago, roundabout where she had started walking on vacuums. Jetlag: that's what changing realities and dimensions felt like.

Shepherded by the huge, disciple-dressed man and the woman in tweed, Gemma stole a glance back towards the builders. They were sat on the rump of the meteorite where glittering rock formed a natural ledge. There were about twenty of them there, drinking, looking extremely ordinary for people who, if Gemma wasn't very much mistaken, were responsible for the upkeep of the universe. Boss of them all, Bob, was looking longingly at his tea, as if he wanted to shrink to the size of an ant, jump in the mug, and drown.

CHAPTER FIVE

Swirling his staff before him, Pete formed a hole in the fabric of spacetime, so the three wanderers could step into a new place. The Solution Room had the ring of a staff room, with its foam-filled, royal blue seats and kitchenette on one side.

'Coffee?' offered Marge.

'Tea please,' said Gemma, sinking into something frothing at the mouth.

'You need to sew that rip,' said Marge, with a sideways glance at Pete.

Pete rubbed his eyes wearily. 'One problem at a time.'

'It's fine,' said Gemma, shoving the seat's stuffing back where it belonged. 'If you don't mind me asking, what are you guys? And Bob, and the others? Are you humans? Or aliens?'

'That's a bit rude,' huffed Marge, dumping a teabag in a mug with a pun on it ("I am building a universe – can you help me planet?").

'The child has a right to ask,' said Pete. He looked upon Gemma with his solemn, holier-than-thou face. 'We are humans from another age, who have become something else. We have mastered most known dimensions, and can bend spacetime to our will. We call ourselves...' he paused dramatically '... The Dimension Masters.'

'No we don't,' said Marge. 'That's just the name you and a few other nut-jobs insist on using. Most of us know ourselves to be humanish.'

'For thy information,' said Pete, puffing out his chest and parting his beard to reveal a badge with the letters "DM" on it, 'we are no tin pot movement. There were two billion of us at the last protest.'

'I remember,' said Marge, grimly. 'Getting around the galaxy that day was a nightmare. Total gridlock.'

Gemma used her reply as a linguistic travellator, elongating the word so that it might carry her from a place where she was mentally floored, to a place where she wasn't: 'Rrrr-iight.' It didn't work. She was still baffled by the end of her reply. On to the next question. 'How come the humanish Dimension Masters speak English?'

Marge served the drinks. 'Don't mash us up – we are one or the other – the other being wrong. And please, once you've conquered spacetime, multilingualism's a breeze. As well as English, we also speak Mandarin, Spanish, telepathy and Thai, don't we, Pete?'

'Châi.'

'Furthermore,' said Marge, boasting a little now, 'us humanish have ditched the old inconveniences of our species, like needing sustenance, or sweating, or falling ill—'

Pete, who was sipping from a mug that read "World's Best Problem-Solver", burst the bubble. 'Alas, we've yet to conquer fungal nail infections.'

'Yeah, they're a real bugger. But apart from that, we've come on loads, haven't we?'

'We've come on so much, we've evolved into a different animal.'

'Oh, not this again.'

'Marge, I wish for thee to recognise me as a Dimension Master.'

'And I wish for you to recognise me as Medusa, but that would be rather spurious, wouldn't it? Seeing as how I'm not an ancient Greek monster with snakes for hair.' The HR manager toyed with her gun like she was tempted to use it. 'Now, Pete. The law defines you as a humanish man; I strongly suggest you embrace this identity.'

The part of Pete's face that wasn't beard turned puce. Slamming his staff against the floor like an angry Moses, he shouted, 'The law is wrong! Hast thou read the part about penises? Why should my penis define who I am? My penis is completely defunct!' To prove his point, he considered flashing his adversary. Eyeing Marge's gun, he thought better of it. 'Enough talk of my penis,' he said, his pacifying voice at odds with his complexion. 'Marge, we shouldn't have fallen into a political debate about who we are and are not. It only turns us against one another.'

'Which is so very humanish.'

Throughout the heated discussion, Gemma had been drinking her tea, which from the start had been disconcertingly tepid. She had witnessed the kettle boil. Wishing to change the subject not only for her own sake, but for the sake of Pete's facial blood vessels, she said, 'I didn't burn my tongue.'

Pete and Marge stopped bickering and looked at her quizzically.

'And it's been a while since I've, you know, *needed to go*. Am I turning into one of… whatever you guys are?'

There was a strained silence before Marge remembered, as HR manager for section 1735 XB of the universe, it was her job to keep workers happy. Instantly, she switched herself to conciliatory/fawning mode.

'It was the same with the pope and the cultists, wasn't it, Pete? You… you wonderful man!'

Pete offered a half smile and looked a little less crimson.

Marge continued. 'It seems anyone who enters our realm

assimilates to become like us, but our scientists need to do more research in the area. Isn't that right, Pete?'

'That's a good point,' he said. 'We can't let Professor Zinglebard get his claws on the child, or he'll insist on taking her away for questioning.'

'Not to mention the probing and dissecting,' said Marge, a little too excitedly for Gemma's liking.

Even if such things could no longer hurt her, the thought of being pulled apart didn't particularly appeal, and it showed on her face.

'Calm, child,' said Pete, back to his soothing, godly-mannered best. 'All will be well.'

'Have you come up with the solution to Gemma, then?'

'Not yet, Marge, but I'm sure I will by the time I've finished my coffee.' The world's best problem-solver (according to the mug) took a sip of his drink and stroked his beard pensively.

As a sometime exam adjudicator, Gemma was aware how distracting it is to have desperate eyes trained on you, so she tried to focus on something other than Pete and his grooming. A tatty poster on the wall had a quote beneath a mountain. It read: Mediocrity is not climbing mountains.

Great. Now, on top of everything else, Gemma was sad that, back when she'd been alive, she'd never tackled anything more vertically challenging than a hill. Oh, all the things she hadn't done, but wished now she had! Her heart ached with remorse. Then came a consolation of sorts: even if she'd never done a million things, somewhere out there, her carbon copy was rocking life. There existed a Gemma Fernandez, mother of three and Governor of the Bank of England who hiked in Snowdonia at weekends. Boy, she really wanted to be her.

Hankering for something stronger, Gemma downed her tea. Then she whispered to Marge, 'How come we still drink, even though we don't need to?'

'Old habits die hard. Besides, it's not that unusual for species to have redundant traits. Men have nipples, don't they? The pope showed me his when he was here. I must say, they were rather lovely. All smooth – not a nodule in sight.'

'I've got it!' Peter banged his mug down. 'We are going to do for Gemma exactly what we did for the others!'

'What? We're going to examine her nipples?'

'No, no, Marge! We will go to thee's Writing Room, where we will beg the monkeys let this Gemma overtake the consciousness of a Gemma still alive back in one of the alternate realities.'

'That sounds complicated,' said Gemma, dispiritedly. 'So the Solution Room isn't where the solution actually happens?'

'Oh no,' said Pete. 'It's just a nice place to think over a cup of coffee.' Picking up his staff, he thrust it towards the exit like a sword. 'To *do* we must venture. Onwards!'

*

They travelled through space again. It seemed to Gemma that since she had died, life had been a journey from one tedious room to another. The stars between destinations were starting to lose their sparkle. Marge was bored too and playing with her gun. Taking aim at Pete's head, she cackled when it grazed his scalp and trickled down his back.

'Marge!'

'What? How many times have I had to put up with your stick poking me?'

Pete stroked his staff, clearly offended. ''Tis a staff, not a stick.'

Gemma addressed him now because she thought he might be more conducive to philosophical discussion than Marge, who had started firing bullets at far-off Bob.

'So let me get this straight: every time a person has a choice to make, all eventualities happen. The person's consciousness, and the universe, splits in sync with the eventuality, and no one ever experiences this phenomenon?'

'Well put.'

'And it's completely random – which life a consciousness ends up living?'

'Right again.'

'And Marge also mentioned, that when a person is born, every possible future is recorded by their personal writers.'

'That is correct. Though some of us favour the term "monkeys", on account of the fact—'

'Their computers sound like mating apes. Yeah, Marge told me.'

Gemma thought back on her own history and wondered if, even accounting for the fact that there were millions of her living millions of lives, she could have predicted that one of them would have won Year 8 Sport's Personality of the Year (Gemma's PE teacher had said, before announcing the winner, that whilst this pupil might not be the fittest, or the fastest, or the most talented sportsperson, they always "gave it their all". Gemma had tripped up walking to the stage).

The former Sport's Personality of the Year shook her head. 'It's impossible. How can writers match real life? I mean, I guess they could theoretically fluke the odd prediction, given we're dealing with infinities, but still—'

'Who said anything about predictions? These monkeys are

in fact *time travelling* monkeys.'

'I've heard a lot of weird sentences since I died, but that tops the lot.'

'I thank thee. Anyway, the monkeys can accurately record the future, because they've already seen it happen. *Humans* may not be able to manipulate time, but Dimension Masters can. Each monkey simply follows their branch of person to the end of his or her line, then returns to the writing room and documents all they have witnessed.'

'But I never saw my writer.' Or maybe she had? Hadn't she once spotted a guy in shades and a mackintosh, scribbling in a notebook as he tailed her through Camden? Diya had dismissed him as one of the area's standard psychos, but Diya hadn't known about Dimension Masters, had she?

'Of course thee could not see them! When on Earth, the monkey exists in the quantum world, and is smaller than a quark.'

'And *how* do they follow their person, exactly?'

'The monkey and their individual are connected by certain particles. One cannot go without the other.'

'So the writer is like a person's guardian angel?'

'That's a nice analogy – if a false one. The monkey has no say in thy person's life; they cannot advise, or change, or save a person's fate. They're just there to take notes, from cradle to grave.'

'So you're saying, my whole life, I've had a tiny biographer on my shoulder? Only I didn't see them?'

'Essentially – yes.'

'Who? Who is my ghost writer?'

'Thou means, who *was*.'

The past tense was a kick in her stomach.

'Thee will find out, soon enough.'

She thought about it, then said, 'Pete, if the writers cannot affect change, how are they going to help me?'

'Ever since the pope incident, monkey computers have been re-programmed so that in the unlikely event of a non-death death, they can relocate the innocent party. I'm only sorry it took me a cup of coffee to remember that fact, but in my defence, I have had a lot of broken drills and fungal infections to deal with lately.'

Despite his explanations, she was struggling to find sense in it all. 'Pete, would reality stop working if the writers didn't produce their books?'

'Oh no. It would all plod along just the same.' He eyed Gemma. 'And there would still be the occasional glitch.'

'So why must the writers do it? Why must they write?'

'Why do any of us do anything? Because we must all do something with our lives.'

'But theirs is a pointless task — yes?'

'I suppose. But don't tell them that during our discussions. We want them to do thee a favour, not tell thee to do one.'

'It's all so stupid.'

'Perchance. Still, isn't it nice to think that somewhere, all possible futures have been observed, typed up and saved? Isn't that a satisfyingly tidy thought?'

'I suppose.'

Marge cleared her throat. 'Not only have I been trying to shoot Bob, I've been listening to the pair of you.'

'And?' said Pete.

'Well, just so you're both aware, all writers think the fate of the multiverse depends on them.'

If it weren't for his staff, Pete would have keeled over.

'What was I supposed to do?' said Marge, defensively. 'I had all these whiny, sensitive types telling me they were unhappy because no one ever wanted to read their stories, and as HR manager for section 1735 XB of the universe, would I read one?'

'Er, thee could have read one?'

'Don't be daft, Pete. I'd die of boredom. No, no. I thought it far better all-round if I convinced the writers they weren't redundant; that they were valued members of society. That without them doing what they did, the multiverse would implode.'

'I wondered why the monkeys seemed more jittery than usual.'

Gemma interjected, 'Pete, what if you and Marge and the builders were not around to do your jobs? Would the alternate realities still play out?'

'Yes,' snapped Pete. They carried on in discontented quiet for a while, before he added, 'Thou didst like my maze back in the Problem Room, didn'st thou?'

Gemma mumbled something reassuring, but her guide was rather muted by the time he formed a fresh hole in the fabric of spacetime, which took them to the entrance of a large office. It reminded Gemma of a 1940s newsroom. There were rows upon rows of red-lipped, pencil skirt-wearing clerks on typewriters. The sound of monkeys mating was deafening. Dictators, pacing the floor behind the typists, had to holler their plotlines to be heard over the *ooo, ooo, ahh, ahh*s. The dictators all had a similar look – like they belonged to one mafia family. They were squat, square shouldered men with braces, rolled up sleeves and fedora hats. Gemma honed in on one of them. Like the others, he spoke with a Chicago twang.

'Then Steve decides to silence his right-hand man, see? Which means Bruiser gets promoted, and bam! Bruiser's in the inner circle! He'll have all the dirt he needs in a month, and then the feds swoop in, and bam! Steve gets life!'

'Brilliant,' said his clerk/monkey, punching away on her typewriter. 'Much better than the plot where Steve realises the error of his ways, attends rehab, and starts working for the UN.'

'I agree,' said the bored-looking typist next to her.

Pete tapped his staff on the floor three times, and everyone stopped. There was quiet as a thousand fedora hats tilted their way.

'Sorry to interrupt,' said Pete. 'Is this Gemma Higgins's Writing Room?'

'Look at the door, would ya!' shouted one of the mob.

On a gold plate it read: Steve Maloney's Office.

'Sorry,' said Pete, sheepishly. 'Can thee direct us?'

'Five doors down the corridor,' said one of the clerk/monkeys, and the hoo-ha started again as everyone returned to their work.

'Knew it didn't look right,' said Marge, shaking her head.

'Hey, you!' said one of the mafia men, menacingly limping towards them. One of his feet had a shoe on, the other didn't. 'This fungal nail infection still hasn't cleared up.' He raised his foot as high as it would go, which was up to Pete's ankle. 'What are you gonna do about it?'

Pete sighed, and Gemma wondered why it was that all the problems of the universe were laid at Pete's feet. It was a heavy load for anyone to bear – even a seven-foot giant.

'Make your way through the Problem Room,' said Pete, 'and I will attend to thee then.'

'But I've already been through that maze twenty times! I'm a busy man, you know.'

'Patience is a virtue. Farewell.' Pete waved his staff, and they were gone.

*

The corridor stretched for miles. Gemma peered through the windows of the offices they passed, so that when they reached the door with her name on it, she had an idea what to expect. All the same, it was a shock when they knocked, and entered. The feel here was more collaborative than 1940s newsroom. Instead of typewriters, there were modern computers that still inexplicably sounded like monkeys mating. You could barely see the floor for beanbags, and there were scores of round tables with pot plant centrepieces.

The décor wasn't the shocking thing; the shocking thing was that every person in here looked like variations of her family. Even those who weren't exact replicas of relations, still seemed akin in some way. They had similar hair to her, or the same shaped facial features. It was like she'd stepped into a room of long-lost relations. She wanted to run up and hug one of them, so she did. The nearest person was a guy in a black turtleneck. Even without a Norwich shirt, he was the spitting image of ten-years-younger Uncle Tony. His eyes popped out of their shell at the stranger's embrace. Gemma let him go and, after giving her a funny look, he scarpered.

For some reason, Pete and Marge decided now was the time to revisit their old argument via passive-aggressive whispering.

'Stop referring to the writers as Dimension Masters. They are no such thing.'

'Well, whatever the monkeys are, they're certainly not humanish.'

Whilst Pete and Marge did that, Gemma eavesdropped on a nearby meeting. The attendees were doppelgangers of her mum, her dad, her grandma, and Aunt Rose – although, there was something different about her… That was it: she was holding a pen, instead of a roast chicken. Next to the poultry-free aunt were two women about Gemma's age. In another life, they could have been her sisters.

One of them said, 'I *think* that in my story, Gemma agreed to go ice-skating with Paulo.'

'What do you mean, *think*?' said the other.

'I'm struggling to remember what my Gemma did in her twenties, but I keep visualising her face-down on an ice rink. I reckon that might mean something.'

'It means you're a numpty,' said Dad, rolling his eyes as he adjusted his fly. 'Have you gone and lost your notes again?'

'Yes,' said the woman, hanging her head in shame.

'Can you at least remember the gist of Gemma's life? Where she winds up?'

Gemma's could-be sister thought for a moment. 'No.'

'Wow,' said the other sister. 'She must have been really dull.'

'You'd better go back to the beginning, then,' said Mum. 'You can't rely on memory and get it wrong, or the universe will blow up.'

The woman left hastily.

'I know where my Gemma's going,' said Dad, shaking his head in the hapless writer's direction. 'And it's not bloody ice-skating with Paulo. In fact, in my plot, the doughnut gets run over by a bus, so that's the last we have to hear of him.'

'Joe!' scolded Mum. 'He's not a doughnut, he's a nice investment banker.'

'Don't shoot the messenger. What's your spoiler then?'

Mum looked round the table like a poker player revealing a straight flush. 'Gemma makes enough money to pay for a lifelong gym membership. And she lives to be a hundred and three.'

'Boring,' said Grandma. 'Since she broke up with Paulo, my Gemma's slept with forty different men.'

Dad started retching.

'If you want my opinion,' said Aunt Rose, patting Dad's back, 'all your girls have gone down the wrong path. Mine is with this doctor son of my friend, and…'

Gemma was listening to all this, open-mouthed. Of all the unbelievable things that made up reality, this really took the biscuit. Even in another dimension, her family dictated her life. Then she remembered that actually, they were not in control of her fate, any more than she was. Or should she say fates, plural.

'By the way, does anyone know a better word for blue?' asked Mum. 'In my latest chapter, I'm trying to describe Paulo's eyes.'

'What does it bloody matter what word you use?' asked Dad. 'We're only supposed to be documenting the facts, not submitting an entry for the Nobel Peace Prize.'

'You mean Nobel Prize for Literature, you uncultured buffoon.'

'Just so you know, no one who ever won a book medal dedicated a whole chapter to the sugar-free muesli its protagonist ate for breakfast.'

'Look, my only purpose in this world is to write about one life. I might as well make my work as beautiful as I can, muesli and all. Now – blue? Anyone?'

'What about azure?' suggested Grandma.

'Perfect!' Mum scribbled the word down in her notepad

so hard, she made a hole in the paper. She looked up. Suddenly, she was aware that someone was observing them. 'Er, who are you?'

She felt weird saying it, like "Gemma" no longer belonged to her; like it belonged to someone she once knew, long ago… 'Gemma. Gemma Higgins.'

Silence everywhere.

Gemma flashed her audience a shy wave, wondering if they would hail her like a celebrity. They didn't.

Marge and Pete stopped arguing, and remembered why they were there.

'All right!' bellowed Marge. 'Whose Gemma is this?' She raised one of Gemma's limbs, like she was a farmer auctioning her cow at a cattle market. 'This Gemma is dead, when she shouldn't be.'

Eventually, a woman who bore a suspicious resemblance to Amber put her hand up, and Gemma thought, *of course.*

The office filled with groans and admonitions.

'I'm sorry, okay,' snapped Amber to everyone. 'Now get back to work!' Abandoning her desk, she trotted over to Gemma. 'I was having trouble with my computer that day. It kept crashing and restarting itself.' The writer gave Pete a dirty look.

He twiddled his staff and murmured something about how the computer had been fine that morning, after he'd fixed it.

She rubbed in salt. 'Perhaps if I hadn't had to waste God knows how long in your stupid maze, Gemma's life wouldn't have been cocked up.'

'Amber, there's no need to play the blame game,' said Marge, sanctimoniously.

'And you!' said the writer, switching target. 'I told you I

was close to burnout. And what did you do? Point your gun at me and tell me to pull myself together before the universe imploded!' She glared at Gemma. 'You are the result of poor HR management.'

'Let us not fret over things that have passed,' said Pete, back in wise disciple mode, 'but rather focus on things still to come.'

'Can't you just, like, say she's supposed to be dead and take her to the place where all the dead people go?'

God, thought Gemma, *even* pretend *Amber is a bitch.*

'I cannot do that,' said Pete, gravely. 'Only those who are meant to have passed can pass through those gates. You know that.'

'Well, can't she like, just stay here with you?' said Amber, trying again. 'Maybe she could be your assistant, Pete? Or boss. Yes – that'd be far less misogynistic.'

'I can't stay here!' said Gemma. 'I take ages to come to any decision. I'd be the worst universe problem-solver ever.'

'That's true,' agreed Marge.

'It would be cruel to make her endure more time with us,' added Pete. 'Especially when none of this tis her fault.'

Before she could stop it, a point flew from Gemma's mouth. 'Wait a sec, Pete, didn't you say things would play out, with or without the writers' input?'

Both Pete and Marge were shaking their heads madly. *Remember their fragile egos,* mouthed Marge. Luckily, Amber was scowling into the middle distance, paying no attention to anyone whatsoever.

Gemma continued, 'If that's the case, how come Amber's actions, or computer, or whatever, stopped me from living as I was supposed to?'

'Like we said, it was *a glitch*,' hissed Marge. 'We cannot

explain it, okay? But if you really want to get to the bottom of it, we can always volunteer you for Professor Zinglebard's experiments.'

'No thanks.'

'Fine then. You'll just have to accept that, for some unfathomable reason, temporarily, your writer was able to play God.'

Amber took a sudden interest in the conversation. 'God,' she sighed, like she was in love. 'Yes, I was a god for a while, wasn't I? Able to snatch life away with the click of a finger; change the course of a whole universe.' She looked down at Gemma. 'I had absolute power over you.'

'And you liked that?'

'Oh yes.'

'Glad you made one of us happy.'

'You have a way of making me happy. Your break-up with Paulo over chips had me in stitches.'

'Yeah, I can picture you with your little proton friends, knocking back the popcorn and laughing at my failures.'

'Protons aren't my friends. And they can't laugh.'

'No, but they are positive, to be fair,' said Marge.

Whilst not so cleverly charged as the last comment, Gemma still felt her follow-up had power: 'Yeah. And you're a bitch.'

The bitch smiled. 'Oh, come on, Gem. I've been watching you from when you were sucking on your mother's breast...'

'That's not at all weird.'

'... to when you died an old woman in your sleep. And I know you're nicer than that.'

'You're right.' Gemma took a breath. 'Sorry, I'm just getting a bit frustrated.'

'Sorry, I'm just getting a bit frustrated, God.'

'For fuck's sake, Amber! I'm not calling you God!'

'Children! Children!' cried Pete, flourishing his staff. 'Cease this strife!' He faced Amber. 'We none of us shall be referring to thee as God, monkey. That would be blasphemy.'

Animosity drained from Amber's face – it ran down her shoulders, making her shrug. 'Sorry, Pete. Didn't mean to cause offence.'

'That's quite all right. Now, I propose thee allowest this Gemma's consciousness to override another, living Gemma's consciousness.'

'Sure. Whatever.'

Despite getting off on the wrong foot, Gemma thought this Almighty wannabe might not be so bad after all.

'As long as we can convince the relevant writer.' Amber addressed her distant relation. 'So, which life d'ya want? You've got six million and two options. You're dead in the rest already.' She flicked through her fluffy notepad and glanced expectantly at Gemma, like she was a jaded waitress, waiting to take an order.

'You mean I get to choose?'

'Derrr.'

A familiar fear bear-gripped Gemma. She used to take half an hour to pick a dish from a menu. How the hell was she supposed to select a whole new life from a contemptuous mock-up cousin? Her first thought was to ask for a life where she'd be rich and meet The One. Then, with a sigh, she realised what she should do.

'Is there a life where the world lives in peace, and there is no poverty?'

Amber snorted. 'No.'

'Oh. That's a shame. Well, if I can't go for that, please can I have a life where I'm rich and meet The One?'

Amber shook her head. 'That's the reality I was working on, but then you went and died prematurely, so no, sorry.' She flicked through her notepad. 'I can give you rich, or The One?'

'The One,' said Gemma, without hesitation. 'Although, just so we're both on the same page, we're talking about the person I'm most compatible with in all my realities, right?'

'Yeah, yeah, yeah,' said Amber, impatiently. 'I've got two options for you—'

'Two?' squealed Gemma. 'Out of six million and two?'

'Yep,' said Amber. 'Of course, it would have been three, but…' She glared at Pete, who was refusing to look away from his staff, and Marge, who was twiddling with her gun.

'So, what exactly are the two different options?' asked Gemma.

'Not allowed to go into detail.'

'But Paulo's The One, isn't he?'

'Sorry. Brief overview, only. In one of your options, you meet the love of your life straight after the bus hits, and live to be ninety-seven. In the other, you meet the love of your life straight after the bus hits, and die of cancer at forty.'

'Well, the second option sucks, doesn't it?'

'Yeah, sucks to be you.'

'I'm obviously going to go for the first. I thought I remembered Paulo being there. Turns out I was right.'

'Yeah, great. That storyline belongs to Tony.'

'What? As in Uncle Tony?'

'Don't know what you're talking about. Tony!' Amber shouted his name, but he didn't hear over all the monkey-mating computer noises. With a frustrated click of her tongue, the writer led them to where a man in yellow and green was making his keyboard grunt. The situation was explained to him.

'So,' concluded Pete, 'we just need thee to authorise this Gemma taking over thy Gemma.'

'But won't that make the multiverse explode?' asked Tony, anxiously.

'Er, not on this occasion.'

'Oh, good.' Tony gave Gemma an encouraging smile. 'No.'

'Oh come on!'

'Sorry, but I'm swamped as it is. I'm trying to formulate the reality where Norwich City win the Champions League. Have you any idea how hard that is?'

'Please. I'm begging.'

'No! Apart from everything else, that Gemma's my baby. I've been by her side since she took her first breath. We've come so far together, I can't abandon her. Would you swap your child for someone else's?'

'I hadn't thought about that,' said Gemma, quietly. 'Um, theoretically speaking, if you were to do this for me, what would happen to your girl's consciousness? Would she die? Would I displace her completely?'

'Oh no,' said Tony. 'She'd find a cosy spot in your brain, curl up and go to sleep.'

'That sounds all right.'

'It's not exactly the rich life I had planned for her. And us writers, we're never supposed to get involved. Never.'

'Ordinarily, tis true,' said Pete. 'However, there is a precedent for this situation. Remember the pope?'

'Yes, I've done my pope training.'

'So why don't you—'

'The last word lies with the writer. And I'm sorry, but what you're proposing doesn't sit right with me.'

Marge looked like she wanted to throw up. 'My friend, if you give this the go-ahead, I'll read your finished book.'

The writer's eyes lit up. 'You… you will?'

A staff nudged Marge into responding, 'Yes.'

'Then what the heck! Deal!'

Gemma showered Tony with kisses. He flicked her off.

'So, what do I have to do to go home?' she asked.

'Click your shoes together and sing *Somewhere over the Rainbow*.' Amber slapped Tony on the shoulder. 'I mean, nothing. I've just got to enter the password. If I can remember it.'

'Is it "Norwich City"?'

'Oh yeah, it is.' He typed the Canaries' letters, and Gemma couldn't believe the key to her best life was a mediocre football team.

'Fare thee well then,' said Pete, holding out his wok-sized hand.

Gemma ignored it and hugged him instead. 'Thank you so much! You're exactly what your mug says.'

Pete looked puzzled.

'The world's best problem-solver.'

Pete blushed.

'Although, you know, maybe it wouldn't hurt for you to employ some more people to help you do your job. So it doesn't all rest on your shoulders.'

'Alas, the burden is mine, and mine alone to bear. So it has been foretold, and so it must be done.'

'Okay. Well, all the best with that. Marge, I couldn't have done this without you.'

'I know.' She planted fake kisses on Gemma's cheeks. 'Say hi to the pope for me.'

'Will do. And thank you, Amber.' To make up for the not-calling-her-God thing, Gemma bowed.

That action went some way to pleasing Amber, who grinned, despite herself. 'Yeah, whatever.'

'I'm about to press enter,' declared Tony. 'When I do, you will wake up from being hit by the bus, and live what I write. Comprendez?'

'Comprendez. Wait — will I remember all this?' Her hand swept the room, encapsulating the family writers, the monkey noises, the HR manager and the fixer.

'No idea.'

'But if I remember it all, won't it affect my actions, and therefore my future, and therefore change all that should happen to me?'

'Maybe. If it does, I can hold a staff meeting. We can re-write the future. It's fine. Writing makes us happy, even when it makes us miserable.'

'Well, on behalf of the people on Earth, a big thanks to all the writers out there.'

Tony grinned. 'I'll pass it on.' Channelling his inner NASA controller, he said, 'And we're go in five, four, three, two, one.'

CHAPTER SIX

Gridlock surrounded her. Horns sounded. People abandoned their cars to shout at a culprit, before shuffling back, ashen-faced, mumbling, 'Hope it's nothing too serious.' A human chain encircled the spread-eagled woman. The chains told the curious to back off, give the poor girl some privacy. In the heart of the protected ring was the bus driver, shaking uncontrollably on the first step of his bus while passengers tried to console him; an old lady who'd been adjacent to Gemma at the traffic lights; a doctor who'd been on the other side when the bus hit; and Paulo.

The doctor, with his broad build and dark, expressive eyes, was almost too handsome to be believed. Not that Gemma could see him. Bowed next to her on the floor, he calmly directed Paulo. 'That's it. Keep the pressure against her head. Careful not to move her neck, now. The ambulance will be here soon. Can someone check her bag for ID?'

Pottering about in the ring, trying not to look too thrilled to be caught up in a drama, the old woman repeated the doctor, 'Someone should check her bag for ID!'

'Over there!' said one of the chains, kicking fake Chanel towards her.

'Lucky it was zipped,' said the lady, absolutely delighted that she had the moral authority to go through someone else's bag. 'Oh dear. This make-up's had it. Crushed powder everywhere. I'm going through her purse now. I'll have you all witness that I'm stealing nothing! Gemma Higgins! Her name is Gemma Higgins. Oh, what a pretty thing she is. I do hope she doesn't die.'

Sirens. There was chaos as everyone told everyone else to get out of the way.

'Don't you worry, Gemma,' whispered the doctor. 'You're going to be okay.'

Gemma blinked. 'Thank you,' she managed to croak. She smiled at him, and he jolted, as if shocked by static.

'She blinked and said something!' shouted Paulo. 'Hello? Is your name Gemma? You've had a little accident, but I've been here to help you. My name's Paulo, and I'm an investment banker.'

She tried to say "I love you", but there was too much blood in her throat. Then the paramedics came and took her away.

*

Someone had wiped the past clean, and a smell of disinfectant hung in the air.

After the haze of waking, came clarity, and Gemma remembered. Starched, sick-person's bed sheets hemmed her in. To gain a better perspective, she tried to inch herself out. It was quite an effort – she'd been tucked in well as a baby, and had all the strength of one. Still, she managed to loosen her covers enough to earn an improved view. Everything was as it should be. There were oat-coloured blinds on the window, a vase of flowers, and get-well cards. None of these objects violated the laws of physics. She was in a humdrum hospital room, and the banality of it was a warm bath for her soul. Final ratification, that's what she could do with. Her eyes searched, but there was no mirror. No matter. Already, she was tired of the new world.

In the dark, she lay on a chaise longue. Sigmund Freud was there, with his trusty goatee. 'Thank you for describing your experiences to me,' he said, in his thick Austrian accent. 'You have slept for a long time and had many drugs pumped through your veins. Dreams can feel very real.'

'I've told you,' replied Gemma. 'It was no dream. I really *did* travel to another dimension. I *did* used to live in a different body. These new, hospital bones are achier than my old ones – but I suppose that's my injuries talking.'

'And you say the woman who used to fill your mind, she is lying dormant there now?'

'Exactly. My consciousness has usurped her. I hope she's not capable of resentment, otherwise there's a silent enemy within. Creepy – right?'

'So you share your body, your most private space, with a potentially hostile woman?'

'Yes.'

'I see.' Her head's psychologist paused for thought. 'And how would you describe your relationship with your mother?'

'Erm. Not that I see what that has to do with anything, but it's complicated. There's my aunt as well, you see, and for most of my life it's felt like I have two mothers, and I'm an only child but I have two cousins who are like my sisters, and I love one of them to bits but the other one— I see what you're getting at! That's not what this is about!'

'What is this about, then?'

'I dunno. I just need you to help me figure out how freaked out I am.'

'Okay. How *freaked out* are you?'

'Well, to be honest, I'm nearer the "oh crap. I've locked myself out of the house and I'm in my pyjamas" end of the freaked-out scale, rather than the "I died, then came back as a different version of me in a different life, and now I've no idea what my past is" end. Probably because giants and guns are a thing of history now.'

'This is good. But I fear you may be repressing your emotional response, and if you carry on doing so, you could succumb to hysteria.'

'So, what should I do?'

'You must confide in someone.'

'I'm confiding in you, aren't I?'

'I don't count. I'm merely something your unconscious has conjured up as part of your coping strategy. Also, you're high on painkillers.'

'But no one will believe me. They'll all think I'm mad.'

'Bottle this up, and you will go mad. You must find, as we Victorians like to call, a *confidante*.'

'I guess I could try talking to my mother. Or my aunt.'

'Dear God, don't do that.'

*

That was the last piece of advice she heard before she woke up, grateful to be back in a sensible world – even if it wasn't quite her one. At least that's how she felt at the moment. There was still time for her to have a total meltdown – or succumb to hysteria, as Freud put it.

Behind the cards was a jug of water, but upon trying, she found it impossible to lift. Her arm was held back by a manacle drip, the cast on her leg was dead weight and her body protested when she moved.

A flush and fast-running water – music to her ears. 'Dad?'

'Gem! Gem!' called her mum's voice. A portlier, replica Georgia came dashing from an *en suite*.

The patient had to bite her tongue; her birth mother had never been a pound above perfect. It was lovely to feel this woman's hug and shower of kisses. Still, there was sadness as Gemma understood who she'd never see again. A torrent of explaining poured from the surrogate's mouth:

'You were hit by a bus! Eyewitnesses say you ran into the road like a madwoman – nothing the driver could do. Silly girl. What were you thinking? Thank goodness it wasn't worse. I mean, you've been badly bruised. Cracked ribs. Broken leg. But apart from that, you're going to be fine. No don't cry, darling. I know it's been traumatic, but some good has come of it. A nice investment banker helped save your life! His name's Paulo. He's sent you a card with his number on it. Which reminds me, I must ring your dad!' She dialled. 'Ergh. He's not picking up. Joe? Why are you not picking up? Gem's alive! I mean, she's awake! Call me when you get this!'

Gemma attempted to sit up again and her stomach hurt. 'Can I still have babies?'

'Yes.'

'You sure?'

'Yes, yes. Now rest,' said Georgia, rearranging pillows and dragging her daughter to a more comfortable position. 'There. Better? Blow your nose. Have some water.' She helped Gemma to drink, just like Aunt Rose used to in times of trouble.

'Ow.'

'What's wrong? Where does it hurt?'

It had struck her: she had no way of knowing which of her memories were still valid, and which were not. 'Nowhere. I'm fine.'

Suddenly, Gemma was jealous of the sleeping woman in her head, and all the secrets she kept. Had Aunt Rose ever spoon-fed her? Did she have the same friends? Had she ever been the victim of financial fraud? The green ruminations threatened to set the patient off again. Luckily, there was a distraction she could cling on to.

'So, this investment banker,' said Gemma, blinking back tears. 'You said he gave me a card?'

'Oh yes – and these beautiful flowers,' said Georgia, drawing Gemma's attention to the roses, like she was selling a prize in a game show. She proceeded to rustle through the cards. 'Not this one… that's from the driver, bless him. Told him we didn't blame him. Police will come get a statement from you soon, I expect. This one's from school. All the staff and pupils miss you, of course. They bought you vouchers. I've spent them for you, your flat looks much better now. Roz got you this pink gin bottle.'

'Roz as in Roz Roz?'

'Yes, Roz Roz! This card's from my sister…' It had a button on it, which she pressed. A love-song played, assuring the recipient she would always be loved. Gemma could have cried with relief. 'Here's the one from Paulo!' Georgia selected a plainer "get well" and handed it over.

It was his handwriting all right, wishing "the pretty woman" better soon, telling her he was an investment banker, and that when she felt up to it, he'd love to take her to this awesome steakhouse: here was his number. Gemma wished her best friend would walk through the door, so she could say "Told you so". Only, she was too scared to ask after Diya directly, in case Georgia's answer was a blank look.

'I saw Paulo when he dropped the card and flowers off for you. Well done for getting run over near such a handsome man.'

'Er, thanks. So, I'm having a bit of trouble remembering.

Can you tell me everything, please?'

'What do you mean? I've told you what happened already.'

'Yeah, I know. But I mean, what's happened with my life? Can you go back to the beginning? Like, back to when I was a baby? Do I have any sisters? Am I still a maths teacher? Is Turf Fen Mill still there?'

'Oh, my darling,' said Georgia, losing colour. 'The doctors did a scan. Said you'd suffered no brain damage.'

'I haven't,' said Gemma, hastily. 'I feel a bit dazed, is all. Will you tell me? Please?'

'Of course I will, sweetie,' said Georgia, kissing her hand. 'But first, I must tell a nurse you're awake. And I should ring Diya too.'

'Of course,' said Gemma, high on the name-drop.

Whilst the nurse made her checks, and Georgia made some calls, the patient thanked God she hadn't lost her best friend. Even so, her heart beat fast, drumming to the fear that a loved one was irrevocably missing, or changed beyond recognition – even more so than her mum.

'Take this,' said the nurse, plying Gemma with drugs.

As the patient swallowed, it was all too easy to slip into an old habit…

What if she was teaching at a different school, and her students and co-workers were all wrong? What if Roz had tipped over to the wrong side of fun-loving, and was now a raging alcoholic unable to spell chemistry, let alone teach it?

Muttering something about a fast pulse, the nurse left, and it got worse, because Gemma recalled the wider world, and geopolitics. *Oh, Lord. What was Russia, here?*

It felt like she was committing some sort of betrayal, calling this copy "Mum", but she had to bite the bullet at some point. She took a deep breath.

'Mum, is there Internet? I need to check the news.' At her mum's bemused face, Gemma said slowly, like a native addressing a foreigner, 'Do you know what the Internet is?'

'Um, yes. Would you like me to fetch the laptop?'

'Please.'

'Okay, sweetie. Long as you don't dwell too much on what's happening. It's all so upsetting.'

'Oh no. Is it Ukraine?'

Georgia patted her daughter on the head. 'No, the laptop's not in Ukraine.' She checked the cabinet drawers. 'Must have left the thing in the car. Won't be a sec.' She inundated her daughter with kisses.

'Please don't tell me you're going to treat every goodbye like a Hollywood ending from now on.'

'Of course not,' said her mum, tears in her eyes. 'I just love you so much.'

'Love you too. The laptop?'

'On it.'

A few more kisses later, Gemma was alone, remembering that, actually, she wasn't alone. She envisioned a tiny Tony, sitting on her shoulder, quietly note-taking.

'Uncle Tony, can you tell me the life story of the woman sleeping in my brain? The one you used to follow?'

The writer put down his pen. 'No. That information is strictly confidential.'

'Right.' She paused, and the drugs got to work a bit more. 'Uncle Tony, what's that theory called? The one where a butterfly flaps its wings in Brazil, and triggers a hurricane in Fiji?'

'Chaos theory.'

'That's it! That's what explains the interconnectedness of life.'

'What of it?'

'I was wondering… What if the woman sleeping in my head, through some innocuous action or non-action, accidentally caused some terrible global catastrophe, back when she was alive? What if she inadvertently stopped crops from growing? And if she did, should I feel guilty, seeing as she's so much a part of me?'

'Nah. You guys are separate entities. Even if she did trigger seismic disasters – which I'm not at liberty to confirm or deny – that's her bad. Not yours.'

'Okay, great. But wait: what if *I* go on to cause death and destruction, in a way she might not have done? Will it be my fault for bringing pain to this world, like a tourist with baggage?'

Her uncle thought for a moment. 'Nah.'

'Okay, great. Just one more thing: can you tell me if the Gemma I took over was born to exactly the same parents as me, and we're like sisters? Or was she born to parallel parents, and we're more like cousins?'

'How the hell do I know? Why does it matter how you're related to my girl, anyway?'

'Because, if I now have parallel parents, who in turn were born to parallel parents, who in turn… I mean, Jesus! The number of macro and micro changes possible in *my own* ancestry, let alone in the ancestry of the seven billion others – it blows my mind. What if the whole history of the world is different? What if—'

'Not that I'm meant to intervene in your life in any shape or form, but aren't you supposed to have quit the what-if-ing? Now you know about multiple realities and the fragility of life, you've realised there's no point stressing so much, haven't you?'

Gemma sighed. 'You're right. New world, new start, new me.'

'That's the spirit.'

'I might just worry a little longer, depending on what *Mail Online* says.'

Her mum returned, phone against her ear, and the tiny writer was gone. 'It's your dad.'

Gemma spoke to him for a bit, and was relieved to hear him sound exactly like he used to. 'Soon as I've had a dump I'm coming,' he concluded, before she hung up, and turned her attention to a different screen.

'Don't let the news upset you,' repeated Georgia.

Navigating the Web with trembling fingers, Gemma wondered what terrible event was being referenced. More war? Widespread famine and suffering? And, the million-dollar question: was the woman in her brain to blame? Front page of *The Mail* was: *Prime Minister Apologises for Misleading Parliament*. Gemma showed her mum the headline, and questioned with her eyes.

'Yes,' said her mum, shaking her head. 'Really upsetting, isn't it?'

For a few precious moments, Gemma dared hope that might be the worst of it. But it wasn't. The more she scrolled, the more sadly familiar the news became.

'Climate Change is still a thing.'

'Not for us, Gem. We've got an electric car.'

The Diya of Gemma's mind spoke. *'At least any shared tragedies between the old place and this mean you'll understand where you are.'*

'True,' said Gemma, before widening her search to other sites. Not that she was an expert on global affairs, but from what she could ascertain, this world was in the same boat as the last one – with two notable exceptions. There was tension between Finland and New Zealand (Gemma thought she probably wasn't to blame for the international squabble, but still couldn't help feeling slightly guilty). On the bright side, Norwich City had been taken over by Saudi Arabian oil barons, and were currently favourites for the Premiership.

Once she was up to speed with the present, Gemma crossed her fingers, and confronted the past. It was just as she remembered. Mind you, it had been a while since her last history lesson. Relief washed over her, swiftly followed by a fresh wave of guilt. Was it right to feel glad old horrors had come to pass, just so she could know the foundations of her new home? She didn't have the strength to answer that one, so she focused on France.

France was the one place she had picked up a discrepancy in the world's timeline. Napoleon had failed to show up in the eighteenth century. Apparently, a bulbous-eyed man called Emperor Lecretin had ruled the country, post-revolution. As it turned out, the identity of France's leader was neither here nor there, as according to *Wikipedia*, Lecretin had followed the same path as his Bonaparte counterpart – i.e. he had tried, and failed, to conquer all of Europe, before being exiled to a distant island, where he had spent his remaining time writing love-letters to his mistress, lamenting "the good old annexing days".

*

When the police came to ask for her take on things, Gemma stated she didn't remember much, only that the accident had been her fault, and the driver was innocent.

'Eyewitnesses and CCTV concur,' the officer said.

'So that's that?'

'That's that. Unless… you're sure you don't recall *why* you ran into the road?'

'To get to the other side?'

He didn't laugh.

'Sorry. It's my head. It's all a bit blank.'

*

Over the next few days, her mum filled the blankness in, and Gemma formed a picture of her alternate life. Like the wider world, it was similar to the one she'd known. She could have cried with joy, that her story was more or less her own – minus one vital detail: officially, she hadn't yet met Paulo. She wanted to ring him and hear his voice. The thing was, she couldn't trust herself to play it cool, and not act like a psycho who knew everything about him. Better by far to do the initial *getting to know you* stuff via text, so that when they spoke, or met up later, her familiarity with him wouldn't seem quite so freakish. Her opening message was to the point: "Hi there, it's Gemma. I just wanted to say, thank you for saving my life".

The reply was instant – as was the scream.

'What is it?' cried a nurse, running in with a defibrillator.

'He got back to me! He wants to know how I am!'

'Is that it?' The psyched-up expression on the nurse's face was replaced by one of crushing disappointment. 'I've come back from basic life-support training. Thought I was about to put my skills to good use.'

'Oh. Sorry.'

'That's all right. I'm glad this boy likes you. But do me a favour?'

'Yeah?'

'Don't scream like that again unless you're witnessing a cardiac arrest.' No sooner had the nurse left the room, than she popped her head back in. 'You've got a visitor.'

*

When a much-loved person walked through her door, first came relief because they were alive, then it was a nerve-wracking game of spot the difference. Gemma vowed to love everyone in her orbit just as much, if not more than before – no matter how much they'd turned. Psychologically, it was easier to pretend that everyone she knew was still precisely the same person, but things happen, people change. Gemma whipped up enough hypotheticals to explain everything:

Her mum was slightly fatter than she used to be because she had been introduced to a food support group and could now follow a normal diet without having a breakdown. As for her dad, a savvy investment had facilitated early retirement, so he could spend his days volunteering his accountancy skills to local charities, and his golfing skills to local golf courses.

'Oh,' said Gemma, when she had found out she was in the hospital's private wing. 'I'd assumed public healthcare was better funded and managed in this world, and that every long-stay patient in the country was afforded their own suite.'

Her parents had laughed at her, then gone to get coffee. Diya walked through the door.

Gemma cried into her arms, which triggered her best friend too. 'Oh, hunnnn!'

They hugged for the length of the "hun".

'Tell me everything! Mum says we still live together, right?

Did we meet on the first day at school when you told me you loved my fluffy pen? Do you still work at Amnesty?'

'Steady on!' said Diya, half-laughing, half concerned. 'Are you sure you're okay?'

'I'm fine! Just tell me! Please.'

'Okay. Oh,' she pulled out Gemma's favourite chocolates from a bag. 'Tom got these for you, by the way.'

'Tom?'

'Yes, Tom. You know – my boyfriend?' She said it like it was obvious, and was shocked by Gemma's reaction. 'Your mum said you'd been asking questions, but I didn't realise… and the doctors say you're okay?'

'Yes, yes,' said Gemma, impatiently. 'They're monitoring me because I seem a bit confused. But they don't think there'll be lasting damage.'

Diya exhaled. 'Good.' She took out her phone. Proudly, she showed Gemma a thousand photos of her with a man on a ski slope, her with a man on the London Eye, her with a man at a birthday party. It was Father Tom.

'But he's a priest!' gasped Gemma.

Diya snorted. 'Where'd you get that idea? We're both proper Catholics, yeah, but he's not a priest. I met him at work six months ago, remember?'

'Oh yeah,' said Gemma, her smile wilting. Diya was happy – happiness was radiating from her like heat. Gemma couldn't put a finger on her own coldness. Was it because she hadn't been there to share her friend's joy? Or was it because back in the real world, she knew what her friend was missing? Gemma shook her head. She had to get it into her skull: *this* was the real world now. Diya misunderstood her reaction.

'Don't worry, Gem. I know you've not exactly had the best luck with men, but things will change for you.'

'You mean Paulo?'

'Um…'

'I have a really good feeling about him.'

'So does your mum. She won't stop bloody talking about him.'

'We've exchanged a few messages.'

'That's nice,' said Diya vaguely, fiddling with her scarf. 'I bumped into him a few days ago, when you were still out of it. He was dropping off flowers.'

'And?' said Gemma, rising up the bed in excitement.

'And what?'

'How was he? Gorgeous, right?'

'Um… yes, I suppose, if that's your type.'

'Did you get to talk to him?'

'Not much, to be fair. But he was a bit… I dunno.'

'Oh no. Not here too.'

'What?'

'Is there nowhere you two can like each other?'

'I don't know what you mean. We were chatting in the corridor. I don't think that was the problem, though?'

'Never mind. Forget it.'

'How come he hasn't visited you now you're awake?'

'I asked him to wait till I look less like a bus crash victim.'

'Oh, huuuun. You look beautiful.'

'I look like shit.'

'Okay, you look like shit. But at least you're *alive* shit.'

*

The day after Diya came Aunt Rose and Uncle Tony and Amber, all together, like one lovely family bundle. Gemma had gone mad for them all – especially her uncle and cousin, whom she kept thanking, over and over again. Uncle Tony had laughed at her and called her a sweet girl and said, as soon as she was better, he was going to take her to watch Norwich City. Amber had called her a weirdo, but said she was glad the bus hadn't killed her. Aunt Rose was acting strangely.

'Didn't you like the card I sent you?' she asked Gemma.

'Of course, Aunty. Thank you so much.'

'Well, really then,' said Rose, folding her arms, barely bottling her glare. 'You could have sent me a thank you card to say thank you for the get well card.'

'Mum,' said Amber. 'You've always been too hard on Gem. She's just woken from a coma – give the girl a break.'

'You know I only hold you to high standards because I love you, don't you, darling? As the card that you didn't thank me for clearly states.'

'Er, yes,' said Gemma, grateful when a nurse came to shoo away her visitors, so she could rest her head. On the pillow, she whipped up another of her explanations: her aunt had early onset dementia, only she hadn't told the family yet. Perhaps she didn't even know there was something wrong, and Gemma was the first one to notice. In no time at all, the pillow was wet.

CHAPTER SEVEN

A feeble glow broke the darkness, but it wasn't the bedside lamp that had disturbed her. No – she had been summoned to wakefulness by a sense of her own senescence. Since her school days, she had known the biology of herself, known her cells aged and died, but she had never before been able to *feel* this process, like she was, simultaneously, each and every cog in a watch, being turned. With absolute clarity, she felt her time ticking away to the day the cogs stopped. This unexpected appreciation of her body's minutiae, of its mortality, was lost, almost as soon as it was found. Like a dream, soon forgotten.

Gemma tried to remember what had stirred her. Then muffled a scream.

'Sorry!' said the source of her fright, springing from the armchair and raising his hands in peace. The stranger, tall and well-built, wore a white and slightly translucent shirt that teased at what lay beneath. 'I didn't mean to scare you,' he added. 'I thought you were sleeping.'

The patient felt lightheaded. She must've sat up too quickly. Lying down again, she fell back on humour. 'If you're trying to convince me you're not a serial killer, you're not doing a good job.'

'I could try and convince you I'm not a serial killer, but—'

Gemma completed the sentence with him '—that's exactly what a serial killer would do.'

They shared a smile.

'Come further in,' said Gemma, beckoning him over.

The man started shuffling near the half-open door. 'Maybe, in a bit. Are you comfortable enough?'

Gemma rearranged herself on the bed. 'I am now, thank you. Sorry, but I suffered a bang to the head. Do I know you?'

'No.'

'Oh.' Inexplicably, she found herself surprised and disappointed by his response. 'So who are you?'

The man moved his mouth up, but it wasn't a smile. 'That's quite a question.'

'It is?'

'Mmm.'

'But surely you can tell me your name?'

'Josh.'

'Nice to meet you, I'm Gemma.' She offered her hand, and the machine alarmed.

'There's a kink in your line. If you straighten it out and press—'

'Yeah, I know,' said the patient, going through the motions, 'I've seen the nurses do it before.'

Silence returned. Josh was hesitant, like he wanted to come closer, but daren't.

Gemma wished she didn't like the way his hair curled quite so much. 'Why are you here?'

'I don't know where to start.'

'Very mysterious, aren't you?'

'You've no idea.' He started pacing the floor. 'I've spent ages trying to figure out what to say; how I'm going to put it. And I still haven't decided.'

'You remind me of how I used to be.'

'I do?'

'Yeah. I used to get in a flap about everything, second-guess all I did, and all that everyone else did. I'd feel jealous of things I hadn't done. It was a nightmare.'

'Sounds like you used to be very anxious.'

'Yep.'

'And you're not anymore?'

'Oh no. After being hit by a bus and… other stuff, I've decided life's too short. I'm not going to spend it worrying. Plus, I've got this *intuition* that I've met the love of my life, and we're going to be happy.' Gemma blushed. Something about Josh had made her say too much, and she wished she could be a Dimension Master just for a second, so she could step back in time, and shut her stupid mouth.

'I'm flattered, but I—'

'Oh no! I wasn't hitting on you.'

'You weren't?'

'Absolutely not!'

'Okay, cool. Though I'm not sure your denial needed to be quite so emphatic.'

They both grinned.

'Actually, I was referring to the man who saved me. We have a thing.' That wasn't strictly true. Technically, she hadn't even spoken in person to Paulo. All they'd done was exchange a few flirty texts.

'I'm happy for you. He seemed like a nice guy. Very calm and collected and keen to tell everyone he was an investment banker.'

Gemma froze. 'You were there, too?'

'Yes,' said Josh, quietly. 'That's why I've been visiting you. To make sure you're okay.'

'But no one ever mentioned you,' said Gemma, her shock thawing into fury. The bus crash was her Big Bang moment; when this world began; when she met "The One". How dare others keep Josh from her? It would be like giving Diya a

Bible minus Day One in *Genesis* and telling her that was the whole story.

With dark eyes, Josh looked upon her, and she could feel tiny, invisible hands burst from the hairs on her skin. Somehow, this man was drawing out of her what she did not know she had. As millions of her hands reached out for him, she wanted to shout at them: "Come back! You've made a mistake! He's not Paulo!"

'People didn't mention me,' said Josh, with slow, deep breaths, 'because they couldn't see me.'

'Oh. Was it quite dark?'

'Yes. But that's not why… Oh, heck.' Josh ran his hands nervously through his hair. 'The truth is, I'm a ghost.'

Gemma began a laugh, but stopped it halfway through. 'You're serious?'

'Yep. Well, as far as I know, I'm a ghost. Can't think what else I could be. I can walk through things like a ghost.'

'Prove it!'

'Okay. But only if you promise not to freak out.'

'I promise.'

Josh walked through the armchair, and Gemma had a panic attack. 'Paper sick bag next to you!' said Josh. 'Breathe into one. Normal breaths, now. That's it.'

'Why not? Why not? Once you know there's a multiverse with millions of parallel worlds; once you know there are Marges and Petes and Dimension Masters; once you know there are fourteen dimensions; once you know your family spies on your whole life, then turns it into a book – why should you be surprised if hot ghosts are real too? Sure! Hot ghosts! No biggy!'

'What are you saying?' asked Josh. 'I can't understand you because you're talking into a paper bag. Are you okay?'

'Sure! Fine!' said Gemma, slowly removing the paper, and scrunching it in her hands like a stress-ball. 'So, er, just so I know, are monsters and vampires and Bat People real as well?' *And are they as handsome as you?* She didn't say the last sentence out loud.

Josh laughed. 'Not that I know of.'

'Oh, good.'

'I've not met any other ghosts either. I think I'm an anomaly.'

'Right.' Gemma closed her eyes, with the pretty notion that she might be able to go to sleep, and wake in a place where normality reigned. After several minutes, she realised she might as well fly to the moon. She turned to her paranormal companion. 'You're still here?'

'Yeah, sorry.'

'Um… so, I was wondering… how do I phrase this?'

'You want to know how I died?'

'Yeah. God, I can't believe I'm asking someone that question.'

Josh smiled in a sexy-sad way, and Gemma braced herself for something heroic, but tragic. Like "I threw myself in front of a train to save my puppy".

Instead, he said, 'I don't know.'

'You don't know how you died?'

'No. To be honest, I don't know how I lived, either. All I know is one day, out of nowhere, I found myself walking to work in the dark. I knew my name was Josh, and that I was a doctor, and that I needed to get to my shift. I knew exactly where I needed to be. But before I could get there, the bus hit. I ran to help. I soon realised, none of the others could see me. I tried to touch you…' Josh moved towards Gemma's bed. He leant over her. If he'd had breath, she'd have felt it on her skin. 'May I?' he asked, softly.

She nodded, heart pounding. Josh tried to brush her cheek with his fingertip, but fell right through her and, on the surface, she felt nothing.

'I tried to touch you, but I couldn't. So I shouted instructions. None of those present acknowledged me, but they seemed to be able to follow what I was saying, like I was a voice in their head. But then you…' Josh stared at Gemma in awe. 'For the briefest moment, you saw me and heard me as I am. And I knew you were the answer, somehow. That I had to make sure you'd be all right.' Suddenly realising how close he was to her, Josh backed off. 'I've kind of checked in on you, ever since. Not during the day, when all your visitors come, but at night. I'm sorry if that's a bit… weird. I couldn't pluck up the courage to talk to you, till now. Also, you roused and saw me. Sorry.' He looked at her anxiously. 'How am I doing, by the way? At this conversation thing?'

'You're doing fine.'

'Thanks. It feels like so long since I've talked to anyone. I've kind of got used to being invisible.' He smiled. 'It's been really nice, this.'

'You're welcome,' said Gemma, faintly. 'You know, up close, I can see you're a bit more transparent than the average person. I'd thought it was a trick of the light, earlier, but just now, I could almost see the blinds through you.'

Josh looked embarrassed; like Gemma had confessed she'd seen him naked.

'So what do you do all day? Float between walls? Moan at people?'

'I try and make myself useful. Stick around the junior doctors to give them inspiration.'

'And they can hear you?'

'Yes. Just not properly. I think to them, I sound like a brainwave.'

'You seem pretty sure of yourself. What if you're ever wrong?'

'Doubt it. I'm a consultant.'

'Cocky ghost, aren't you?' Gemma heard what she said and shut her eyes tight. 'Freud was right. Everything's a dream.'

'You're not dreaming. I'm real. I don't know why, or how, but I am. And since you're the only one who can see me, I'd like to… become better acquainted with you. If that's okay?'

'Oh. You don't want to become better acquainted with me.'

'Why not?'

'Well one, I'm not an eighteenth-century maiden, and two, I'm probably a lunatic. You'll never guess what I think I've been through.'

She told him everything – everything she hadn't dare tell her family and friends – and afterwards, she felt free of gravity. For a second, she worried the laws of nature were letting her down again, but no. Confiding in Josh only gave her the *sensation* of lightness, not the real thing.

The doctor listened to her intently, eyes wide, saying nothing to interrupt. When she finished, he paused for thought, then said, 'That's a lot to take in.'

'Yup. I'm not really sure how I've managed to keep it together. It probably helps that nothing seems too changed. At least, it didn't until I met you.'

'It can't be coincidence, can it? That you access this other realm, and suddenly you're the only one who can see me?'

'I guess. So you believe me?'

'I do.'

'Really? You're not just humouring me?'

'As a ghost, I'm not in a position to dispute the existence of an alternate reality.'

'Fair point.'

They sat in silence for a while, both considering the whys and hows. Josh spoke first. 'I have three initial theories. One: that ghosts have always existed but are incredibly rare. That's why I haven't met another. Only those who have visited this fourteenth dimension are able to see us.'

'Sounds credible enough. What's your second theory?'

'The second relates more to my purpose. I believe I am meant to save you.'

Gemma spluttered on air. 'Save me?'

'Yes. There are many stories, aren't there? About a loved one, or family member in trouble, and the hero cannot rest until he has ensured their safety.'

'You need to get your ego in check. I am not your lover. And we're not related. Um, are we?' The only thing worse than fancying a ghost, would be fancying the ghost of her cousin.

'Some genealogical research wouldn't go amiss.'

'Fine. But for the record, I *do not* need saving.'

'You needed saving after the bus crash.'

'Apart from that.'

'Are you sure no one's plotting to murder you? Or frame you for a murder you didn't commit?'

'Not that I know of. Mind you, I've only recently woken up in this Gemma's body, so I guess I can't be a hundred per cent sure. None of my visitors have expressed concern about my life direction, though. I'm still just an ordinary maths teacher. And I haven't been accosted by any gangsters since I've been here, or anything.'

'Good, good. Still, we cannot rule out the possibility that someone wants to murder you,' said Josh, rubbing his chin.

Perhaps this ghost wasn't so attractive after all. Suppressing her annoyance, Gemma asked, 'What's your last great theory, then?'

'I was wrongfully killed and must now bring my killers to justice.'

'So basically, you're saying one of us isn't very popular.'

'Yup.'

'I suppose you want me to uncover the truth, so you can rest in peace?'

'That's it in a nutshell. Yes please.'

Gemma suddenly felt very tired. 'This is all so weird. I thought I'd left the great unknown behind. Now here you are, shaking me up again.'

Josh's face twisted in frustration. 'It's not exactly how I want things to be either.'

'They were considering sending me home tomorrow.'

'I understand. Sorry for disturbing you. I'll—'

'Screw it, I'll help you.'

'Oh.' A shy grin replaced his tension. 'Thanks. That's… that's great. I'll, er…' He browsed the floor, as if what to say next was engraved upon it. 'I'll leave you to get some sleep now.'

'Okay. It was nice meeting you, officially.'

'Ditto.'

Josh had the decency to leave through the open door, rather than the solid wall, and Gemma felt thankful for that. In his absence, it was easy to wonder if she had imagined him. The idea that he wasn't real was a troublingly heavy thought.

'Paulo,' she whispered, hoping his name would act as a crane, and lift the load. It did the trick.

*

Georgia tidied as she whirled from one end of the suite to the other, like a useful hurricane. 'They've given the all-clear! I'm taking my baby home!'

The plan was for Gemma to crash at her parents for a couple of weeks. This was because, aside from charitable work and golf commitments, her dad had ample time to fuss over his daughter. Not that she wanted to be fussed over, but Georgia had insisted on someone fussing.

'I'd do it myself,' she'd said, 'But the Norfolk HEAD branch won't run itself.'

Gemma had hit the laptop. Established during the Cold War/rise of fast-food outlets in the eighties, HEAD stood for Healthy Eaters Against Disinformation. A sample from their manifesto read as follows:

*"We will not stand idly by as world leaders strain to control the masses via scaremongering! Burgers are not the enemy! We will not rest until every man, woman and child, whatever their race, religion, or sexuality, can eat a burger without feeling guilty about it! **

**Providing they also eat their five-a-day and are not obese."*

'Don't you just love our values?' said Georgia, leaning over her daughter's shoulder.

'I guess. Although, they're rather exclamation-mark heavy, aren't they?'

'Nothing wrong with that! It gets across our passion! And the importance of our work!'

'Sure. I don't know – I always saw you as more of a

doctors' surgery receptionist.'

'How very boring.'

'Yeah. And if you were a doctors' surgery receptionist, you'd probably be disciplined for dishing out multivitamins over the counter.'

Then Dr Raj had come in, and her mum had whispered, 'I wouldn't mind being *that* man's receptionist.'

*

'Why so glum, Gem? Thought you'd be over the moon.'

'I am, but… the thought of the outside world suddenly seems scary – big. What if I don't recognise it anymore?'

'It's not surprising you're scared after what happened. But remember, not everything on the outside is as big as a bus. And not everything is going to run you over.'

'Right…' Her mum's pep talks had never exactly been Churchillian. At least she didn't round off speeches with an offer of more multivitamins, these days.

'It might take you a while to find your feet. No pun intended,' said her mum, indicating the crutches. 'But we'll help you. Your aunt has made enough chicken soup to last a month. And your uncle's secured you a disabled spot for the Norwich game.'

'I don't know that I'm ready to leave, let alone visit a football stadium.'

'Oh dear,' said her mum. 'You've got that syndrome, haven't you? The wotsit-called syndrome. You've become so institutionalised, you think you can't cope without doctors and nurses.' She paused. 'Have you fallen in love with one of your captors? That Dr Raj is rather handsome, isn't he?'

'No. I mean, yes, he is handsome, but he doesn't really do it for me.'

'He does for me,' sighed her mum, like a teenager in love.

'You have a husband, remember?'

'Just because I love your father, doesn't mean I can't fancy other men.'

'True. Guess that explains—'

If her mum had been on a seat, she'd have been on the edge of it. 'Yes?' she prompted.

'Nothing. No one.' Through the window, she saw him, and her heart soared with the birds. She hadn't been hallucinating last night. The sun had arranged itself around Josh's head like an aura. It reminded her of the stars. 'Can you help me get some air, Mum?'

'Of course, sweetie.' She handed Gemma her crutches and towed the attached machine. 'This window only opens a fraction,' she said, as she let in a thin line of air. 'So as to discourage jumpers.'

'I'm not suicidal. Far from it,' said Gemma, absorbing the pastoral beauty through the frame, the tangerine sky, and him.

They were very close; only glass between them. With a coy smile, he pointed to his feet on a ledge; at all that was fuelling the feeble illusion of support.

'I'd move back,' he said. 'Only I don't want a repeat of last night's performance. If you can't handle me walking through objects, I doubt you could handle me walking on air.'

'Darling, why are you grinning like a goon?'

'Dunno, Mum. Maybe I'm happy to be going home after all.'

'That's the spirit! Now then, I don't know where that nurse is. She said she'd come unhook you. I'll go chase her up. Be back in a sec!'

'Close your eyes,' said Josh, when they were alone. 'Okay, now open them.' He was in her room, hands in his pockets. 'I gather they're chucking you out?'

'Apparently so.'

'Brilliant news.'

'Yeah, it is. And soon as I'm settled back home, I'll look you up.'

'Thank you. Sorry you don't have much to go on.'

'You're Doctor Josh and you're a consultant in, what?'

Instinct told her the answer before he confirmed it. 'I'm a paediatric consultant, based downstairs in the children's ward.'

'Of course you are. Well, I'll do my best. Maybe you could visit me in a few days?' She blushed. 'To discuss any findings, I mean.'

'I'd like that very much.'

It felt illicit, giving a dead man her address, and making arrangements to meet – 'Do you know Turf Fen Mill?' – but she was sure, if she could find the words to explain, Paulo would understand.

CHAPTER EIGHT

'Not another one!' said the driver, banging his head on the wheel.

'I've missed the tractors,' said the passenger, as they made a snail's progress down the road. 'And the fields. Just look at the pumpkins, Dad.'

Joe grudgingly glanced sideways. 'Yes yes. Very nice pumpkins.'

'Thank God. I thought it might all be gone.'

'What might all be gone?'

'I dunno. Autumn. Norfolk.'

Joe stared at his daughter suspiciously. 'Are you being… *poetic*?'

'No,' said Gemma, winding down her window so she could taste manure-cum-rainwater scent.

'Good,' said Joe, as he beeped a tractor.

'The Duke of Wellington!'

'Yes, it's still there.'

'Thank God. I thought it—'

'Might all be gone?'

'Yes.'

'Can you do us a favour and not talk anymore? No offence, love, but I'm getting a bit sick of your gratitude for life and pubs and that. Especially when we can't BLOODY GET ANYWHERE!' He beeped a tractor again.

'Sure. Sorry, Dad. I know you want to get home for the golf.'

The more they inched forwards, the more Gemma saw

landmarks unchanged from her past place. The snatches of farms, woods and streets caught en route put a huge smile on her face. Her childhood home was same-enough to be appeasing too. The most glaring discrepancy was the lack of an exercise bike in front of the TV.

Gemma turned to her parents. 'Is the gym equipment upstairs?'

'You mean my golf clubs?'

'How many times, Joe. Golf is not exercise. And your clubs are not weights.'

'Yes they are, Georgie. You try lugging them round a seven-thousand-yard golf course.'

'*You* try lugging them around a seven-thousand-yard golf course. I saw you that time, in the buggy.'

'I did that once! Because I'd twisted my ankle.'

'Guys, stop! I meant the exercise bike. I thought I remembered…' She blinked at their faces. 'Never mind. I'll head up to my room now.'

'We discussed this, sweetie. We converted the office for you.'

'Sorry, Mum. I forgot you want to keep me on ground level.' Once in her designated area, Gemma sat on the sofa bed, hugging a cushion like a comforter. 'Maybe I could take a peek upstairs, for old times' sake?'

Her mum looked horrified. 'And tire yourself out? No. Joe! Make sure she doesn't make a break for the stairs, until her cast is off.'

'What kind of operation you running here? A prison camp?'

'I'm warning you, Joe. If I come back from work and discover she's been up there, I'll—'

'It's all right, Mum. I won't try and escape. Although you

know, I'm going back to work soon. I won't be able to avoid stairs forever.'

'I've written a note to your headmistress. I've demanded all your classes take place on the ground floor. I can put the note in your bag for you.'

'Mum!'

'And have you messaged that lovely Paulo yet to tell him you're home?'

'No,' said Gemma, sulkily. 'I only came through the door ten minutes ago.' It was coming back to her why she'd left home in the first place: a little thing called sanity.

'Joe, make sure she messages Paulo whilst I'm gone.'

'I'll do no such thing,' said Joe. 'What is this? Guantanamo for singletons?' He wandered off to the kitchen and returned with a beer. 'Want one, Gem?'

She grinned, hugely appreciative. This was the dad she knew – not a retired golf enthusiast, but a man who offered food and drink so late, he was rarely in danger of being taken up on the offer. 'No thanks, Dad.' Her mum had started unpacking her things. 'It's all right, Mum. I'll do it.'

'But—'

Gemma snatched her knickers from her mum's clutches. 'Thanks, but I got this.'

'I really think that—'

'And as soon as I'm done, I'll message Paulo. Promise.'

'Out, Joe! Out! Give Gem some space!'

Joe dished out an eye roll for his wife, and a wink for his daughter, all while receiving an earful.

'I don't know why she's so reluctant,' hissed his wife. 'These investment bankers, if you don't snap them up, someone else will.'

The bell rang. Craning her neck, Gemma witnessed her

mum answer. A bewildered-looking man was holding a bunch of roses. 'Um, these are for Gemma,' he said, sounding flustered. Then he dropped the flowers like they were burning and legged it.

'Are they from *him*?' asked her mum, excitedly.

Gemma scanned the note. 'Yes.'

'Can I see?'

'No.'

'Oh well,' said her mum, amiably. Clearly her delight in Paulo sending notes was greater than her ire that she couldn't read said notes.

When she was alone, Gemma went over the message again:

Hope you don't mind, I met this guy at the petrol station, and inspired him to give you flowers, and write a note that made no sense to him whatsoever. I'll reimburse him sometime. Congratulations on being home. See you tomorrow. J

The jolt of feeling was unexpected. It frightened her. To counter it, she whipped her phone from her pocket, and told Paulo she was ready for that date now. Unless he wanted her in heels, in which case, he'd have to wait a little longer. Did he like a woman in heels?

'Yes,' came the swift reply. 'And not much else.'

Glad there was a lock to her interim bedroom, Gemma touched herself in a way she hadn't for a very, very long time.

*

In childhood, the golden reed marsh had been her land of make-believe. Now, she pretended it wasn't him, making her

113

heart spin with excitement. It was the windmill, and the joy she felt to be back in her favourite place in all the worlds.

'Not a bad spot,' said Josh.

Gemma nodded as she breathed in the smell of overgrown grass and sweet, muddy water; the smell of happy memories. A boat floated past, carefree as the breeze. On the other side of the bank, was Turf Fen Mill. Abandoned and unmoving, its sturdy brick trunk and jaded white sails were a frozen monument to another time.

Tossing aside her crutches, Gemma lowered herself onto a blanket. 'I've always loved it here. Other kids go through a dinosaur phase. For me, it was Ancient Greece. My nine-year-old self was forged on gods and monsters. One day, during a family outing, I was gripped by a terror. I was sure that Hydra, with her many heads, would burst from the River Ant, and swallow us whole. I cried to my aunt. She pointed to Turf Fen and told me he was a sleeping god, who would awaken if ever I was in danger. The windmill was my protector, and his blades were swords that could kill an enemy with one swipe. As long as I kept him in sight, my family and I would be all right.'

Josh watched her massage her arms. It seemed to agitate him. 'Your aunt sounds like an awesome woman.'

'She was – *is*. Roast chicken and comfort, that's her.'

'All the same, it must have taken a lot of effort for you to get here. Are you sure you're okay?'

'It's fine, I grabbed a taxi, wasn't a long walk. We needed somewhere we could talk in peace. Somewhere I feel safe – I mean. Not that you make me feel unsafe. It's just the whole situation is so disquieting, I almost need the Broads to stroke my hair, tell me everything's going to be okay.'

'Well, I can do one, but not the other,' said Josh, so

cheerfully it wasn't cheerful at all. 'It's going to be okay.'

'I know. I trust you.' The smile was too much, so she hid it beneath her scarf.

'Are you warm enough?'

She didn't know why a gently concerned expression, from someone she barely knew, tied her heart up so. She nodded.

'Tell me if it becomes too uncomfortable – you've been through the mill enough as it is already.' Josh pointed towards Turf Fen. 'No pun intended.'

'Who are you kidding? It was totally intended.'

'All right, you got me.' There was a slightly hopeful look in his eye. 'Maybe I didn't use puns in my past life? Maybe I was, you know, less geeky?'

She wished she had better news. 'I'm sorry, Josh. My online searches have come to nothing.'

He put on a brave face. 'Not to worry. It was a long shot anyway. Perhaps – when you're fully better – we could visit my ward together? Question a colleague or two?'

An absurd image broke into her brain. She and Josh were bent over a hospital bed, gazing lovingly at a child with his hair, and her eyes. The child's leg was in a cast, but he was tranquil, drawing stars on the plaster. Gemma shook her head.

'Of course. I understand why that would make you uncomfortable.'

'Sorry, I wasn't shaking my head at that. I'm up for it.'

'You are?'

'Yes.'

His whole body relaxed. 'Thanks.'

Just then, Gemma's phone rang. She answered it with a, 'No. Yes. No. No. Love you too, Mum. Bye.' Then hung up and struck an Edvard-Munch scream-pose.

'So it's going well?' asked Josh, sympathetically. 'Moving back in with your folks?'

Already, she felt too close to this stranger. Disclosing yet more of herself was the last thing she should do – but the compassion in his eyes melted her resolve, making her do the last thing. She opened up about her parents, her family, how she missed her old life (not that she wasn't very grateful for the new one), how religion might be wrong – then again, how it might be right. She poured her heart out, until it was empty. Only, no sooner had she done that, than he looked at her, and it became full of something else. She couldn't bring herself to name what was filling the space. Oh how she wished Josh wasn't such a good listener! Or quite so handsome. Gemma curled up under her blanket.

'I dunno. I'm okay, Josh, but I'm not there yet. I still need to wrap my head around all the things that have happened to me.'

'I understand. Let's do nothing but watch Turf Fen sleep for a while.'

'I'd like that.'

All the morning, they were easy in each other's company. The spell was only broken when, quite unconsciously, Josh began whistling something famous.

Gemma started. 'Is that the *Doctor Who* theme tune?'

'Who's Doctor Who?'

'Wow. So ironic.' Gemma explained about the time-travelling Time Lord.

*

There were other cab rides to where he was. Until there weren't. Her mum insisted on waiting with her.

'You got the sandwiches I made? And the bottles of water?'

'Yes, Mum. Although why you've given me a packed lunch for a thirty-minute bus ride is beyond me. Especially when I've just had lunch.'

'In case anything happens.'

'Nothing will happen.'

'How do you know?'

'Who gets caught up in bus-related near-death experiences twice in their lifetime?'

'What about a really incompetent bus driver?'

'Yeah, well, I'm not one of those, so it's fine.'

Georgia sniffed disapprovingly. 'You've been spending a lot of time at the Broads lately. You sure you haven't been secretly rendezvousing with any investment bankers? Because Paulo's always welcome to ours. I'll tell your dad not to use the downstairs loo.'

'It's got nothing to do with that. I just like the peace, okay?'

Number Fourteen rumbled into view.

Gemma felt her arm being grabbed.

'Don't go!'

'I'm sorry, Mum. I need to do this. I need to know that fear won't rule my actions anymore. Plus cabs are expensive. I'll message when I'm safely there. Promise.'

The disabled doors opened, and Gemma hopped on.

'Goodbye!' screamed her mother, waving her used tissue like a mother packing her child off to war. 'I love you!'

'Love you too.'

Because she didn't want to hear *Mum's right – we're all gonna die* every time the bus jerked or braked too abruptly, the passenger found a distraction. On the back seat, through the headphones, came the haunting notes of Kate Bush's *Wuthering Heights*. The music of impossible love, between a ghost and a mortal, spoke to the listener. When it ended, she played it again, and again, until she reached her destination. Josh greeted her by the water.

'Made it!' said Gemma, hobbling along excitedly, like she wanted to propel herself off her crutches, straight into his arms. *If only…* 'Ah, bloody hell, my crutch is stuck in the mud.' She wrestled it out.

Josh laughed. 'I'm proud of you.' Noting her blush, he switched topics. 'So… how was school this week?'

'The same. They're being so well-behaved at the moment. So attentive and diligent. I wish Ofsted would schedule a visit now.' As she spread herself out, furry reeds brushed her arms like purring cats, welcoming her home. She stroked their backs, and Turf Fen slept on.

'Maybe prior to their next visit, the teachers should arrange a near-death experience en masse, so that the students feel sorry for you all, and act like angels.'

'Good idea, doctor. I'll suggest it at the next staff meeting. Talking of near-death experiences, just got to message Mum, tell her I arrived in one piece.'

'Was she a mess, seeing you off?'

'Yeah. I'm still not used to it. The old her would have shoved me some multivitamins and told me to knock myself out.' Josh was lying on his side, staring at her contentedly. Gemma put her phone away. 'You as well,' she said. 'I'm still not used to you, making the world disappear.'

'What do you mean?'

'Even though you're a ghost, I can't see the earth through your image. There is only you.' Reaching out to where Josh was, she grasped brown leaves, damp from earlier rain. 'I have to try and touch you to remind myself you're a phantom, because you look so… solid. I swear you were more transparent when I first met you.'

'I've felt less like an outsider, since I've had you to talk to. It's as if you make me more real.' He mocked a look of disgust. 'Ugh. That came across corny, I take it back. I haven't changed at all, the hospital just had shit lighting.'

Gemma laughed. The ghost and the woman shared a glance, and she tried not to see parallels between their story, and the story Kate Bush had told her. She was being absurd. Cathy had never hobbled across the moors in a plaster cast, and she had spent most of her life knowing Heathcliff. Gemma had known Josh for, what, five minutes?

Yes, but time is relative,' she heard Marge say.

'Gem, is everything okay?'

No! she wanted to shout. *No, because we've only just met, but it feels like you're my oldest friend. No, because talking to you puts my mind at ease, even as it wreaks havoc in my heart. It's not right. Because I was promised a perfect life with Paulo. Paulo.*

'I'm okay. It's the cold, making my eyes watery.'

'Where were we before it all went downhill?'

'My work.'

'That's it! So you're happier with it than you used to be?'

'Yes. It's not because the children are being so considerate. It's more like, I feel confident I made the right choice of career, now.'

'What was the alternative, back in the old world?'

'Investment banking. I was offered a placement at a major firm, but I turned it down to teach, because I wanted to make a difference. Only, I spent my teaching career worried I'd made the wrong choice – especially on days I fancied a holiday home in Monaco.' Otters darted by on the sky's reflection, which was rippling in the river. 'Who needs Monaco when you've got Norfolk, anyway?'

'Investment banking,' said Josh, quietly. 'Isn't that Paulo an investment banker?'

'Yes,' said Gemma. Josh was looking particularly handsome, so she added, 'As soon as I can wear heels again, we're having our first date.'

'Why do you have to wear heels before you can meet *The One*? Does *The One* have a foot fetish?'

'Shut up. I want to be back to my best, before he sees me.'

'Why?'

'Because he's a perfectionist.'

'Maybe this version of him won't be?'

'Oh trust me, he is. There's not a world in a million he wouldn't be the best, demanding the best.'

'Sounds exhausting.'

'It's not exhausting at all. It's refreshing, actually, to be with someone so self-assured when you yourself are…' She faltered.

'Yes?'

'Not so much.'

Josh frowned. 'No one can be the best version of themselves twenty-four seven.'

'There's no excuse not to try. Paulo taught me that.' Gemma smiled to herself. 'I used to set my alarm before his so I could apply make-up in secret. Then I'd go back to bed to wake up again with him.'

'That's ridiculous.'

'It's called "living your best life".'

'It's called "ridiculous". You're not wearing anything now, are you?'

'No.'

'And you look…' Josh didn't know how to finish what he'd started. Instead, he made his gaze meet hers. 'Don't shy away. Listen. The person who loves you should love you in sickness, and in health.' For a moment, Josh looked like someone who wanted what he couldn't have.

'Why are you staring at me like that?'

'Like what? Like I see you?'

Silence fell, and she heard him say an unsaid thing. Suddenly, she was bothered by an itch she couldn't scratch. Relief – this was something real to discuss.

'Only a couple of days left, and I can get this bloody cast off!' She stared at Josh defiantly, warning him to keep the conversation on this new, neutral track.

'Yes, that's great. Gem, I—'

He hesitated, and Gemma cut in, in case he took her where they couldn't go. 'Mum might actually let me go home, and I can finally have something that isn't chicken soup for dinner.'

Josh sighed. 'You'll only be dispatched to the flat with more chicken soup.'

Thank goodness. He'd decided to follow her lead. She smiled. 'I dunno. Aunt Rose is pretty offended I haven't written to thank her for all the chicken soup, so the supply might dry up.'

'Has Rose got back to you about any Joshes in the family, yet?'

'There was my great-great-granddad Joshua. He was a soldier. Fought in the Boer war. But Aunt Rose showed me photos, and there's no resemblance.'

'You're sure?'

'Yes. He's got a funny moustache that twirls at both ends.'

'Maybe I shaved it off the day I died.'

'Do you have any great urge to restore the British Empire and invade South Africa?'

'Not particularly.'

'Then you're probably not my great-great-granddad.'

'Yeah, seems unlikely, given my corduroys too,' said Josh, feigning a kick in the long grass. 'I doubt such an excellent choice of trouser existed during the Boer War. And nothing on your dad's side?'

Gemma shook her head and rubbed her shoulders.

Instinctively, Josh tried to put his arm around her, and looked angry at his stupidity. 'Are you sure these outings haven't been too much for you? Especially since you're back at work.'

'No, it's fine. I'm not an invalid.'

'I could meet you in your bedroom. Your parents would just think you're talking on the phone.'

Gemma had reddened at the word. 'Don't underestimate my mum's capacity for eavesdropping. Besides, it wouldn't be… private enough.'

Josh grinned boyishly. 'You make us sound like a couple of teenagers sneaking around.' He broke eye contact so he could watch the coots soaring overhead. 'If I'm honest, I'm glad you insist on this place.'

'I remember, as a girl, I used to think this land was haunted.'

'When it wasn't being Ancient Greece with gods and monsters?'

'Are you laughing at me?'

'No.' Josh smiled fondly. 'I love the way your mind works. And I agree. The Broads do give off otherworldly vibes. Maybe that's why I feel so comfortable here, with you.'

In the dying light, they shared a lingering look.

Josh realised what it meant. 'It's getting dark earlier now, Gem. You should be heading home.'

She nodded. 'There's a bus due in twenty minutes.'

'Cool. I'll walk you to your stop.'

'You mean, you'll pretend to walk.'

'Yeah. Unless you're ready for me to start floating?'

'I'd rather you didn't.'

'Okay. I shall respect your feet-on-the-ground wishes.'

Gemma struggled in the terrain, and it seemed to pain Josh too.

'Not long till it's off, Gem.'

'Two more days. And then we can visit the ward.'

'I've got so many questions.'

'Me too.' Like why was she doing it? Why was she falling for him?

CHAPTER NINE

Used-gum-coloured walls became a forest of monkeys.

'Wish their expressions weren't so sceptical,' whispered Gemma as they made their way down the corridor. 'It's as if they know we're up to something.' Tipping back her head, she stared at the heavens, which were presently a bar of light, and a suspicious, asbestos-like stain on a ceiling. 'Wonder if the monkeys are up there, typing this as we speak?'

'Probably,' said Josh. A groan from the pipes, and he shook his head. 'What kind of sicko sticks a children's ward in a basement, anyway?'

'I know what you mean,' said Gemma. 'I can almost feel a thousand sick above us, and all the weight of what they need to stay alive – the beds, the ventilators, the operating tables. It's hard not to feel buried underneath it all.'

'And that,' said Josh, 'is a sadly accurate metaphor for the NHS. On the bright side,' he said, pointing to the last animal before the door, 'I like that monkey.'

'What? The one shoving a banana up its mother's bottom?'

'Yeah. Cracks me up every time.'

'That would *appeal* to my three-year-old cousins, too.' Gemma grinned like she was proud of herself, pressed the buzzer, and spoke into the intercom. 'I'm here to see Matron.'

'What's it regarding?' enquired the voice at the other end.

'I need to ask about a doctor who used to work here.'

The speaker crackled, then: 'Sorry. Can't let you in. I suggest you try emailing her.'

'I did, she didn't reply. Hello? Hello?'

Josh shrugged. 'Worth a try. Plan B it is, then.' He scanned the corridor for a potential thought host. Spotting the perfect candidate, he pounced on the young man, who had fluffy chin-hair, and a student badge that revealed his identity. 'Hey, Minesh! Why don't you tell this lovely lady here where you're going?'

Minesh stopped in his tracks, flashed Gemma a grin and said, 'Hi! I'm just on my way to a lecture on eczema.'

'Oh, thank goodness,' replied Gemma, cottoning on. 'I'm on my way there too. Left my ID at home.'

'Haven't seen you on rounds before,' said Minesh, suspiciously.

Josh leant into his target. 'That's because she's the guest lecturer, you numpty!'

Minesh slapped his forehead and couldn't stumble out his apology fast enough. 'I'm so sorry! What an idiot! I mean, I'm the idiot, not you. You're Professor Grayson, the greatest authority on eczema in Europe. Sorry. Can I, er, escort you to the lecture hall?'

Gemma adopted her most distinguished voice. 'Thank you, Minesh. That would be most gratifying.'

The student started heading down the corridor.

'There's a leaky ceiling that way,' hissed Josh. 'Cut through the children's ward.'

'Ah. Actually we'd better take a different route,' said Minesh, looking really confused as he changed direction. 'I've heard there's a leak down there.'

A tap of his card, and they were in. Near the nursing station, Josh fed Gemma an excuse. 'Tell Minesh that you've got urgent business to attend to, so you'll be late.'

Gemma passed the lie on to Minesh.

'Okayyy,' he said, unconvinced, but leaving nonetheless.

'Can I help you, madam?' said the ward clerk, crisply.

'Yes. I'm looking for Matron, please.'

'Didn't we just talk on the intercom? How did you get in?'

Her mouth was on the verge of the word "security" but Josh interjected. 'It's all right. This woman is genuine. And she won't need Amanda for long.'

The ward clerk softened. 'Ah, what the heck. If you can't bend the rules for letting complete strangers into a children's ward for no good reason whatsoever, when can you, eh? Matron's office is down there, on the right.'

'I don't know why you couldn't do that from the start,' whispered Gemma, 'instead of involving Minesh in our web of deceit.'

'What's the point in being dead if you can't have a little fun along the way?'

Echoes of wheezy coughs. Through windows, Gemma saw pale little faces in translucent green masks and tired-looking parents huddled at bedsides. As she passed them by, her maternal instinct wept for them all.

'Respiratory season,' said Josh, shaking his head. 'In winter, children can't breathe; in summer, they break bones.'

'In a way, you're lucky to be a ghost. Being human is hard work.' Gemma knocked on Matron's door.

'Come in!'

Policy and procedure posters everywhere and instantly, Gemma thought this was a bad idea. What if Matron was a Nurse-Ratched-stick-to-the-rules-or-I-will-humiliate/drug-you type? One with a mind not so pliable as Minesh's or the ward clerk's? *Piss off, what-if,* said Gemma angrily to herself. *You're part of the old me. Anyway, she can't be all bad… look!* She directed her attention to centre stage above a desk, where there was a break in the "what-to-do" flow charts, in the form of an '80s boyband poster.

A woman with a perm on her head and a smile on her face swung round on her swivel chair. 'Can I help you?'

'Yes! Hi! My name is Gemma.'

'Nice to meet you. I'm Amanda. Are your hands clean?'

'I gelled them when I came in, but I can wash them if—'

Matron nodded towards the little sink in the corner.

Gemma assured herself it was perfectly normal – nay, diligent – for a nurse to hold high hygiene standards; not psychotic at all. *She likes Bon Jovi; she must be okay.*

'It's okay,' whispered Josh. 'Amanda is wonderful, and I'm here.'

Feeling her shoulders slacken, Gemma pulled it together as she scrubbed off traces of the outside world, and old-school doubt. 'Um, sorry if this is upsetting but… I was wondering if you knew of a Doctor Josh who used to work here, before he died?'

At his name, Amanda's eyes welled, then glassed over. 'Surname?'

Drying her hands, Gemma shook her head.

Before she could be reprimanded for barging in so ill-prepared, Josh spoke soothingly, and Amanda changed her mind. 'Can you describe how he looked?'

'About six foot. His muscles aren't showy or anything but, I dunno, he just gives off this impression of strength. Thick, dark, curly hair and borderline black eyes. Mediterranean skin. Dimples when he smiles…' She stopped abruptly. He was looking at her funny. They both were.

'You talk about him like he's still with us.'

'I do?'

The matron opened a drawer, rummaged around, and

took out a photo. 'This him?'

The man she knew had shed a layer of corduroy and smart shirt skin. Josh of the photo was tanned, in nothing but khaki shorts. There was sand in his feet, and his hair, which had been made frizzy by the sun. Less toned than his ghost self, a slight belly was on show.

'Yes, this is – was – him.' She stole a glance at the real thing. Or rather, the unreal thing. In his face, she could see he was being pulled in all directions – in the way of fury, of sadness, of frustration. He was pacing the room, unsure which way to turn. Gemma longed to touch him; to experience what it felt like, even for a moment. 'May I?' she asked.

'Of course,' said Amanda, handing over the photo.

He was glossed over. She stroked him, before gliding her fingers over the others – over the linked, bronzed arms either side of Josh, over Amanda in a swimsuit, over all the unbearably white grins.

All too soon, Amanda whisked the past away; stuffed it back in the drawer. 'Handsome, wasn't he? Everyone fancied him. Even me, and I'm a lesbian.'

Gemma's laugh wasn't much.

'That was Majorca. Great holiday. The year before he…' Amanda couldn't finish that sentence. Taking a deep breath, she started something else. 'Such an incredible person. Bit arrogant, of course, but that's doctors for you.' She chuckled at some private recollection. 'At least he wasn't an arse with his arrogance, you know? Always willing to laugh at himself. A funny guy. Yeah, that was him. A funny guy who liked to save people.' Her eyes were glistening. Josh looked away. 'His real name was Doctor Jeremy Cohen.'

'*Jeremy?*'

'Yeah, but he hated that, so he went by his middle name
– Josh.' A smile crossed her face, then left, like a fading
memory. 'He passed three years ago, now. His fiancée got
swept out to sea. Josh went in after her, tried to rescue her
and, well…' Amanda couldn't carry on.

Gemma felt like crying for him too – and for that word:
fiancée. A term that had cut her heart. Josh was standing in a
way that concealed his expression. More than anything,
Gemma wanted to comfort – but there was no way to hold
him. 'I'm sorry I've upset you.'

'It's fine,' said Amanda, dabbing her eyes. 'You'd think I
might be used to it, eh?' She gazed reverently up at Bon Jovi.
'But we're all of us living on a prayer.'

'Um, yes. Look, I'd like to pay my respects to his family.
Do you have any contact details?'

The matron raised an eyebrow. Josh did some reassuring,
until she caved in. 'I don't know his family. But as it turns
out, Francesca's parents live a couple of streets away from
me.' She scribbled an address down and handed it to Gemma.
'That was the name of his fiancée – Francesca.'

'Thank you. I can't tell you how much this means.'

An alarm sounded, and everything changed.

'Excuse me! You can see yourself out!' barked Amanda,
bolting for the door.

Her old friend was way ahead of her. Down the corridor,
Gemma witnessed a child being rushed to ITU; a trail of
medics in his wake. Josh was in the thick of the action,
extracting fear from a junior doctor. With a silent prayer,
Gemma intended to exit silently, without fuss. Unfortunately,
out of nowhere, a breathless Minesh accosted her.

'There's a rumour circulating that you're stuck in traffic
and have cancelled today!' he said. 'Don't worry, though. I

told them you're here. Only I remembered you don't have a pass, so might get stuck. Thought I'd come rescue you, Professor Grayson!' Minesh was grinning like a hero. 'If you've finished your work, that is?'

Gemma couldn't think what to do, except stutter, as Minesh dragged her somewhere she really, really didn't want to go. In no time at all, she was stood on a podium, with dozens of intelligent eyes fixed on her.

'Er, hello everyone!' she said, tapping on the lectern, hoping to give off some air of authority. 'So, eczema. Yes. It's a really terrible condition. That, er…' Blankness – and then, inspiration. 'Eczema causes itchy skin!' announced Gemma, triumphantly. No one looked impressed, but she didn't stop there. In her panic, she decided her only hope was to talk herself out of trouble (one of her many teacher habits), so more speech tumbled from her mouth like rubbish down a chute. How long it tumbled for, she didn't know. It got to a point where she said, 'Also, there are lots of different creams you can buy. It's not a case of one-size-fits-all. My cousin has to use some every winter. I can't remember what it's called, but it has a hippo on the pot.' She stopped to look at the faces in the audience, and realised she never should have tried to talk herself out of trouble.

Someone was wetting themselves in the front. Gemma wanted to punch him. Josh straightened his face out and joined her on stage.

'A little help here?' said Gemma, like an angry ventriloquist.

'Oh, it's too late for that.'

It was true. Students were checking their phones, shaking their heads and audibly complaining. 'This isn't the woman on the profile.' They started to heckle, and Minesh looked like he wanted to do what a fourteenth-dimension Gemma couldn't and shoot himself in the head.

'Should I make a run for it?' whispered the failed lecturer.

'Oh no. You shouldn't run away from things. Just stay there. Try and look competent.'

Gemma did as he said.

'Less snarling, that's it.' Josh whizzed round the hall, muttering. Soon, the mutinous atmosphere was switched to one of pity. People exited the room, firing sympathetic glances Gemma's way, and chattering amongst themselves. At least, that's how most of the students exited. Minesh found himself flanked by women, all vying for his attention. Bemused, but happy, he had his arm around one of his admirers.

'What the hell did you tell them?' asked Gemma, when only her and Josh remained.

'Oh, nothing.'

'Spill!'

'Just something about your mental state. That the psych's were on their way to escort you back to the ward. And that Minesh is a legend in the bedroom.'

Gemma wished she could be more annoyed at him, for his role in her humiliation. She stifled a laugh. 'And what if Minesh can't live up to your hype?'

Josh winked. 'I can coach him.'

'Oh, you can, can you?' His bravado, and the wickedness in his eyes, made her skin burn, and she knew the only sensible thing to do was pour water on the fire. 'On a more serious note, how is that boy?'

'Stable,' said Josh, exhaling the word out, a sigh of relief. 'I'll go back there, soon as you're ready to head home.'

Despite all logic, Gemma's feet wouldn't lead her away

from him. Instead, she sunk into one of the auditorium's many seats. Josh took his place beside her.

'So… Jeremy Cohen.'

Josh winced. 'Don't call me that. It doesn't feel like me.'

'You have no recollection of that name at all?'

'None.'

'It explains why I never found you online. Now I've got your birth name, I can dig for more info. And it's good we got confirmation you belong to this world; that you once lived and breathed here. You didn't just appear, the day of the crash, a fully-fledged ghost from somewhere else.'

'I guess.'

'Did you recognise anyone in Matron's picture?'

'No.'

The next question she asked quietly, like a lower volume might equal a lesser hurt. 'Do you remember Francesca?'

Josh's face hardened. 'No.'

'Maybe you need to help her family in some way?'

'Maybe.'

'Well, whenever you're ready to meet them, just say.'

Josh nodded, staring blankly ahead. His hand hovered above their joint armrest. Without thinking, Gemma filled the gap. After a while, they both realised what it looked like. They shared an unspoken understanding that in normal circumstances they would kiss, and that kiss might lead to more.

Gemma's phone vibrated. 'It's Paulo!' she said, panicking, as if she had been caught cheating. 'Um. We're going out to dinner tonight.'

Josh slumped a bit. 'Your mum will be happy about that.'

'Ecstatic,' said Gemma, not so.

'You know you don't have to go, right?'

Just like that, she was angry at him. Angry at him for being a ghost, and not a real man. Angry at him for trying to control her, like he did the others. 'Don't tell me what to do! I'm not one of your puppets!'

Josh was rising, angry too. 'I only lend them my thoughts. They're free to ignore me, if they want.'

'Whatever! You love making strangers dance to your tune, don't you? Why don't you fuck off to parliament and tell them how to run the country!'

'Fuck off!' Josh shrunk into his collar. 'As it happens, I did suggest to the Prime Minister his law on expenses wasn't a good idea.'

'And?'

'He ignored me, and increased the amount of expenses MPs can claim.'

Their smiles were shadows of what they should be.

'I'm sorry,' said Gemma.

'Me too.' Josh had the look of a man resigned to his fate. 'I hope you have a wonderful time with Paulo tonight. I'd better get back to work.'

'Sure. Hope that kid's okay.'

When he was gone, she felt his absence, as she always did.

*

'Chicken soup for dinner!' said her mum, by way of a greeting.

'Can't,' said Gemma, hanging up her coat. 'Out tonight. Sorry, forgot to tell you.'

Her mum emerged from the kitchen with her hands on her hips and a scowl on her face. 'And here was me, slaving away to provide you with nourishment.'

'It's leftover soup, not a state banquet. All you have to do is stick it in the microwave.'

'That's not the point. Where are your manners?'

'I said I'm sorry, already. Stop treating me like a baby.'

Gemma lip-synced the retort, because she knew exactly what was coming. 'It's my house, I'll treat you how I want!'

'Don't worry, Mum, I'll be out of your hair soon enough. Moving back to the flat this weekend.'

Her mum looked horrified and started begging her not to go.

'Sorry, it's a done deal. Gotta get changed now. Date with Paulo.'

'Paulo? Well, why didn't you say? Don't you worry about the chicken soup. It'll keep for tomorrow.'

'Great. Can I borrow your laptop?'

'Why?'

'Mine's not working. Need to look something up.'

'You can have screen time when you've got yourself dressed,' said her mum sternly, reminding Gemma what it was like to be five.

In the office, between her dad's toilet noises, and her mum's excited phone conversation with Aunt Rose on the subject of investment bankers, Gemma felt trapped. Her mum had suggested, now she was cast-free, that it might be worth clearing out the old bedroom upstairs and setting up camp there. After perusing the piles of unwanted junk, Gemma had declared there was no point. She'd be back in the flat in a few days. She could deal with the inconvenience of living from a suitcase, on the other side of a thin bathroom wall, till then.

She rummaged through said suitcase, and when the flush pulled, hollered, 'Dad, where's the outfit I asked you to pick up for me?'

Her dad, fly undone, poked his head round the door. 'It's there, isn't it? I put it in the zipped compartment.'

'This?' said Gemma, incredulously, holding up a shiny black PVC mini, with gold hooks down the spine.

'Yes, that.'

'This is not my little black dress!'

'Yes it is. It's black and little, isn't it?'

'Yes, but. Argh! This is the wrong one! I told you to look in my wardrobe! Not in my—' She stopped there. She was not about to discuss her "sex drawer" with her dad.

'I couldn't see anything in your wardrobe. Maybe what you wanted was too black and too little.'

'You shouldn't have gone through my stuff!'

'Sorry, love. I thought you might have left the thing in your drawers by mistake.' Then he said, entirely innocently, 'Don't you like that dress, anymore? Should I have picked up the silky one instead? It was tangled up with some chains, that's why I didn't— ohhhh.' He nodded at the look of abject horror on his daughter's face. '*That's* the one you wanted. It was *supposed* to have chains on it! Well, sorry, love, but I never claimed to be an expert on women's fashion. Next time you need an outfit collected, send your mother, okay?'

'Okay,' Gemma managed to say, her eyes and mouth still wide with horror.

He turned to go. Gemma thought her father could traumatise her no further, but she was wrong. 'I put your pink screwdriver in the DIY box, by the way. You should always keep tools in their proper place. How much did that thing cost you?'

Gemma couldn't talk.

'Bet they charged a fortune, just because it's a pretty colour.' He mumbled darkly about "marketing" and shuffled towards golf highlights on the TV.

Gemma wondered how the hell she'd ever been conceived. Then she wondered why the hell she'd let her mind wander there, and poured herself a drink – and another, and another, until she decided that, in a straight choice between bland, dowdy schoolteacher, or sexy, give-it-to-me-now bitch, she knew exactly who she wanted to be. It had been far, far too long.

She had been trying to push Josh from her mind all evening, but he was like a box of heavy things, and would not budge. 'Mum! I'm dressed! Can I have the laptop now?'

Her mum looked her up and down approvingly. 'Yes, sweetheart. If those hooks don't secure him, I don't know what will.'

'Thanks.' Grabbing the laptop, Gemma searched for Josh's newfound name and found his story. There was no time to cry. Her mum's excited screech let her know that Paulo's Porsche had pulled up outside, so she closed Jeremy Cohen's window.

When she saw Paulo, she felt the old tremors in her stomach and the heat rush to her cheeks. She had forgotten, but of course – of course Paulo was handsome. Of course she loved him. What had gone wrong with her brain to have forgotten how gorgeous he was? Just because she had briefly fancied some other almost-man. What an awful girlfriend she was, to have flirted so strongly with the idea of – what, exactly? It wasn't as if Josh could touch her the way she wanted – needed.

Paulo's eyes popped at the sight of the woman striding towards him in heels, the epitome of desire.

'Is this too much?' asked Gemma, when their bodies were close.

'No,' stuttered Paulo, breath lingering in the cold, cold night. 'It's perfect. You're perfect.' He reached behind to where the hooks were, and Gemma pulled him down for a kiss.

They made it to the car, but never stepped foot in the restaurant.

*

Gemma came to in the light of a room she knew well. The décor was clean-cut and there was modern art on the wall. Only last night's discarded clothes and smudged mascara on pillows hinted there was such a thing as chaos in the world. With her back to him, she re-did her face, then browsed her phone for more reports on a past tragedy. Before long, shame clipped her ear and said, *"Oy! You're in another man's bed."* Quickly, she put her phone away and, to compensate for her behaviour, kissed Paulo. He snored on.

Gemma got up, instantly appreciating the soft pile between her toes, and its shampooed-carpet smell. 'I've missed you,' she whispered.

Touring the rest of the apartment, she ran her fingers along walls with the warm touch of a woman greeting an old friend.

'Nice to see you again, kitchen.' The appliances in Paulo's apartment had no time for old-fashioned concepts like handles. Everything was touch-operated and high-tech. Despite the slight throbbing of a hangover, Gemma remembered precisely how to work things.

'Incredible.'

She turned around. There was Paulo, leaning against the doorframe, wearing nothing but muscles and boxers.

'Women can't normally work that coffee machine.'

'And there are a lot of women, are there?'

'Oh no, babe,' he said, silkily. 'Just my mum.'

'Right.'

The man made his move towards her. 'I know we only met properly last night, but I haven't stopped thinking about you since the crash.' His arms enfolded her. 'Even through the blood, I could tell you were fucking hot.'

'Er, thanks.'

'It was kind of a turn-on, me saving your life – don't you think?' Kisses landed on her; stamps of approval. 'It's like we were meant to be.'

'I'm not sure I believe in that. Oh.' The way he was touching her. Did this make her happy? Yes. Yes, she was happy. This was what she wanted. That niggling voice at the back of her mind, the one that spoke of Josh, that was just a remnant of her old self. Josh was her doubt, and she had no room for that anymore. The old her had died the day the bus hit. Good riddance. She was glad of it. Oh, but her head hurt. She needed that coffee.

Paulo whispered in her ear, as his fingers circled her. 'Last night, it was like you instinctively knew… exactly what I like.' He reached inside, and she gasped. 'I think you could slot right into my life,' he said, as the last of the black liquid fell.

CHAPTER TEN

'Sorry, babe,' said Paulo, tracing her curves under king-size covers. 'Didn't mean to do that. I *meant* to ask whether you've always lived around Norwich.'

So we're doing this again? thought Gemma, *the getting-to-know-you-thing.* But she supposed that's what semi-strangers sharing beds should do. After explaining herself, he did too. Gemma paid close attention to the backstory, hypersensitive to any anomalies. There were none – no obvious ones, anyway.

'When a cub's mother is eaten… Gets me every time.'

'I love Attenborough too.'

'You do?' Paulo kissed her shoulder. 'That's what I'm talking about! Sexy *and* smart.'

Gemma felt like a fraud. Her phone lit up. 'Sorry, just got to get back to…'

Paulo watched her send the message. 'Diya. She that Indian chick who visited you in hospital?'

'Yes.'

'I bumped into her when you were unconscious. No offence, but on the prostitute-to-nun scale, she's too far one end. Offered me a fucking Bible.'

'Excuse me?'

He flashed a grin. 'Sorry. Didn't mean to be rude.'

'Ah, well. Maybe you'll be friends in the next life.'

'Ha!'

'So I'm in the Goldilocks zone?'

'Yup. Not too slutty… Well,' Paulo winked, 'not in public, anyway. And not too poncho-y preachy. In the line of women, you're in just the right place.'

'That's sweet, if a little simplistic. You can't rank a person in the way you describe. We've all of us got more than one dimension.' Saying that made her wonder how flawed her own ranking system was – the one that had put Paulo in first place. Then he kissed her, and she wondered a little less. 'So…' she sighed, when she managed to prise herself away, 'you mentioned earlier, you've got a place in London?'

'Yup. Chelsea. You'd love it, babe – it's got a gym. I'm guessing by your body you like going to the gym, right?'

'Walks on the Broads are more my thing, but yeah, sure.'

'Cool. Well, I split my time between London and here. Don't mind the commute cos I've got a Porsche. I like to stay true to my Norfolk roots, keep it real; know what I'm saying?'

Gemma had a twinkle in her eye. 'But you support Man City, don't you?'

'Yeah, how do you know?'

'Intuition.'

'Amazing. Amazing. Yeah, I support Man City. But the way Norwich are going this season, might have to switch allegiances, eh? I've been called a glory hunter in the past, but I don't give a fuck what other people say.'

She remembered how she used to drink in his confidence. But, like a recovering alcoholic, she'd come to realise you can't drink your problems away.

'I'd say I'm one of life's winners. Would you say that about yourself?' He took one look at her and said, 'Why not? You went to Cambridge, didn't you? Self-belief, babe, that's what you need. That bus knocked it out of you, but I'm gonna knock it right back in. I'm a good person like that. I once did a heptathlon for charity.'

'That's awesome. What charity?'

'Um, not sure. Domestic violence?' Paulo's work phone rang. Seeing Gemma discouraged, he apologised, 'Sorry, babe. You don't get to where I am in life without making a few sacrifices.' He answered the call. 'Yo! What's up? No, I didn't tell him that, the prick! What do you mean the deal's dead?'

*

It's hard to say "Dee, I'm home" when you've got keys in your mouth, but Gemma made a fist of it. 'Dee-ee! Dadome!' She dunked down her suitcases and shook out her arms.

Her flatmate surfaced, flushed and flustered, from the bedroom. 'You should've called. I'd have helped you.'

'Nah, it's fine. Look, hope you don't mind, but I thought I'd move in a day early. Parents driving me mad… I stay over at Paulo's one night and Dad refuses to make eye contact with me and Mum keeps asking if he's well-endowed and wants to join HEAD.' She could have gone on, but Diya was off. 'Are you okay? Is this a bad time? I can come back later if—'

'No. Don't be silly.'

Father Tom strolled out of Diya's bedroom. 'Gem!' he said, creasing his face into kind, warm folds, and hugging her tightly. 'So good to see you again! We've been praying for you.'

Too many things were weird. One, Father Tom wasn't in black and collar; two, the priest was hugging her, and they definitely didn't have that kind of relationship, and three, most disarmingly of all, he had just emerged from Diya's bedroom.

'Lovely to see you too, Father.'

He raised his eyebrows.

141

'I mean Tom. Sorry. Obviously I don't think of you as my father. You're my friend's boyfriend. Yep.' Through her eyes, she sent an SOS to Diya.

'He wasn't! We weren't!'

'We were just chillin',' said Tom, putting on a cardigan so woolly, it was probably a sheep farm's yearly output. 'Anyway. I'll leave you girls to catch up.' He kissed Diya on the lips. 'See you round, Gem!'

When he left, there was a strange atmosphere, and Gemma really didn't understand why. Although… she hadn't told Diya of the fourteen dimensions. Or Josh. Had her best friend guessed she was holding back? If she explained everything, would that mend the chasm that had snuck up on them, suddenly as a thief?

'Can we talk?' said Diya, gesturing through to the living room.

'Um, sure. I can unpack later.' *Was that a wince? Had Diya winced?*

The furniture was the same – though when Gemma studied harder, she noticed two fancy new vases. She supposed this was where her we're-sorry-you-nearly-died vouchers had gone. Annoyingly, the sofa still dipped like an inverse bell curve.

'I want Tom to move in.'

She had braced herself for something terrible, but this was manageable. Okay, so being a third wheel would be cringing at times, but hardly the end of the world. 'That's amazing! I'm so happy for you!'

Diya shook her head. 'You don't understand. We cannot share a bed. He'll have to take your room.'

'Oh.'

'I'm so sorry! Obviously, us being faithful, we cannot…

And there's talk of marriage, only I want us to live together first. I have to make sure we're compatible. I can't go through what my parents went through.' She looked ready to cry. Gemma was too shocked to say anything, but instinct guided her arms around her best friend. Diya carried on. 'I feel so awful. I'm sorry I wasn't brave enough to tell you sooner. I didn't expect you to bring your bags today. You're normally so last minute. I never thought you'd be packed already.'

'Don't worry. Truth is, I never really unpacked from the hospital.' Gemma cleared her throat to sift the hurt from her voice. 'Um, maybe you and Tom could hold off, until I find a new place to rent?'

'I'd rather not. My polycystic ovaries, you know?'

'Oh yeah.' This was the first she'd heard of it. She felt guilty for choosing a world where Diya's body was compromised.

'I can't waste any time. I'm going to find it hard to conceive.'

'Of course. Sorry, I wasn't thinking for a sec.'

'You're angry at me, aren't you?'

'Of course not. I totally get it. And I'm really happy for you.'

'You are? I don't want you to think I'm ditching you for some guy.'

'I don't think that.'

'I figured, at least you're settled at home already.'

Gemma's eyes flickered to the bags in the hallway. 'Exactly.' Her throat was dry. 'Shall I make us a cup of tea?'

There was a muted nod. Gemma engineered a smile and, with the gait of a sleepwalker, glided to the kitchen; boiled the kettle; selected her favourite mug from the cupboard; wondered whether she should take it with her, or leave it here;

removed teabags; hugged herself, searching for a comfort that didn't exist; shivered, because she'd been here before – déjà vu. Then through the window, she saw them, and screamed. Where there should have been a residential street, was space with its stars, and her two old acquaintances, perched on a piece of drifting rock – bickering, from the looks of it.

Diya came running in. 'What is it? Have you burnt yourself?'

Gemma flung open the tiny window. 'Pete! Marge!'

'No, hun,' said Diya, shaking her head. 'That's just a delivery guy.'

The two, who were no deliverers of fast food, quit their bickering. Their expressions were that of people pleasantly surprised, rather than flabbergasted.

'Hullo, Gemma!' boomed Pete. 'Having a touch of the old déjà vu, ist thou?'

'You what?'

'Sorry, dear,' said Marge, consulting her trusty clipboard. 'What with all the excitement, I forgot to tell you… Déjà vu occurs when a thing happens in two realities at exactly the same time, and in precisely the same manner.'

'But I was only making a cuppa!'

Pete stroked his beard magisterially. 'And just like that, something mundane becomes something profound. To think! Of all the million Gemmas that exist, two of thee should be doing an identical thing at once. Extraordinary!'

Marge looked at her companion like he was an idiot. 'As I was saying, Gemma, an act of déjà vu causes a temporary bridge to form between the involved worlds, which in turn causes Time to jar, slightly. This is why, to the person who is experiencing the phenomenon, it feels as if the same thing has happened before.'

'I don't see any bridge!'

'Can't you see the other you behind us, making a cup of tea?'

Craning her neck and straining her eyes, Gemma did indeed see herself beyond the stars, through a window. It could be a reflection. She shook her head. 'But I've definitely had déjà vu in the past! And I've never seen you guys when it's happened before!'

Marge smiled, like a mother losing patience with the constant "whys" of a child. 'Now you've visited the fourteenth dimension, you see things more clearly, don't you?'

Marge was fading. Pete was fading. They were growing fainter and fainter, and so was the space around them. Their scene was shrinking into the centre of Gemma's eye-line – an ever-decreasing circle. "How's life treating thee?" was the last thing she heard, before the tiny pair were shrivelled to nothing, and there were houses and delivery guys again.

'What was that all about?' asked Diya, wide-eyed.

'You didn't see anything?'

In the style of a psychiatrist talking to a schizophrenic, Diya said, 'No. Did you?'

If she was going to reveal her mind-blowing experiences, now was the time. But Diya's expression said, *please, don't go off the rails – not when I'm getting my life on track. Please don't tell me you're crazy. Don't make me feel guilty – any more than I already do.* She said all that, without saying a word, so Gemma said, 'No. I didn't see anything. I was just venting my frustration – not about you. About… Paulo. Yes… Paulo.'

'Paulo?'

'Yeah. We were supposed to hook up again tonight, but

he bumped it to tomorrow. Has to go to London. And I'm like, argh! I need to scream random shit about bridges out of the window because I miss him. Know what I mean?'

'Yeah,' said Diya, laughing like she didn't quite believe it, but wanted to. 'I totally feel like that sometimes. Only not so much, since I've been with *him*.'

Gemma's heart melted at Diya's doe-eyes. She hugged her. 'I am genuinely so happy for you.'

'I know, hun. Thank you.' She grinned. 'Shall we have that tea now?' Her grin became a bit forced. 'Can't wait for you to tell me all the goss! Sounds promising if you've already got another date lined up!'

Gemma explained to Diya, in the best way she could, how exciting and passionate her time with Paulo had been. How, in being with him, she had forgotten everything else. Well, almost everything else.

If Gemma were being honest, she would have said she felt like she was at a train station, anxiously peering down the track, searching for signs of the incoming train – the one that carried the old world's feelings. Once that train came in, her love for Paulo would arrive, she was sure of it. Only, the wait was made hard, because there was an impossibly handsome traveller next to her at the platform, with his self-deprecating smile, and warm bedside manner. She needed to stop; stop dreaming of the man, who wasn't a man.

'What's that article on your phone, Gem?'

'Er, nothing. Just some guy my dad knew. He mentioned it, so I thought I'd look it up.'

'Let me see!' She read over Gemma's shoulder. 'That's so sad. He was good-looking, wasn't he?'

'Yeah.' Shoving her phone in her pocket, Gemma resolved not to think on the doctor anymore. 'I really think

Paulo is the one.'

Diya uncrossed her legs, so she no longer held a yoga pose. 'Don't get too far ahead of yourself. It's still early days. And—' She looked hesitant to expand.

'And what?'

'Nothing. You know I only spoke to him briefly before. Hardly enough time to make a fair judgment...'

'Let me guess. You think he's too money, money, money for me?'

'Yeah, I kinda got that impression.'

'He thinks you're too hippy.'

'Whatever. I don't care. I just don't want you getting hurt, or wasting your fertile years on someone you're not compatible with.'

'Don't worry. For the first time in my life, I feel like I'm in the right time, in the right place, with the right person. I'm Goldilocks.'

'Your hand is shaking, Goldilocks.'

'No it isn't. It's... numb from all the schlepping I did.'

'Let me take your bags to the car, when you're ready to leave.'

Gemma sat on her hand to stop the tremors. 'If it's all right by you, I'm ready now.'

The staircase that led to outdoors seemed narrower than it ever had before. Gemma almost expected it to vanish into nothing – as space had an hour ago. Then where would she be? Throughout the descent, she pressed against the wall, grateful for its solidity and constant surface area.

When she got in the car, there was a wait for the engine to warm up, and the windscreen mist and her head to clear. *Okay, so I saw the fourteenth dimension in Norwich, I'm not head-over-heels for Paulo, and I'm desperately missing a ghost, but these aren't reasons to have a meltdown. Pull yourself together, woman!* Gemma displayed an assured smile, wound down the window, and told Diya to head back in. Her best friend shook her head, even as she shivered.

'Seriously, Dee! It's freezing!'

'Well, okay. If you insist. Call me if you need anything, yeah?'

'Will do!' said Gemma, as brightly as the Christmas tune blasting from her radio. As soon as Diya slipped from her wing mirror, she switched off the radio. 'Shut up, Slade!'

At last, there was enough visibility to move. Clutching the wheel with a vice-like grip whilst her brain and tyres spun, Gemma shouted for him. He didn't come. In desperation at the red light, she pressed her index fingers to her temples.

'Come in, Josh. Come in. Do you read me?'

Radio silence. The Conductor waved her forwards. She had no choice but to push on, alone. Of course Josh couldn't read her. He was not her guardian angel, or her spirit, with a direct connection to her brain. He was his own man-ghost, completely independent of her. Whenever they met, it was because it had been pre-arranged. Gemma ransacked her memory: "*Let me know when you're ready to find your fiancée*". Panic clamped her stomach. What if he was never ready? What if she never saw him again?

'I've told you before,' she said. 'Go away.'

Back at her parents, she saw Paulo had left a filthy message in her pocket. Though she didn't much feel like reciprocating, she supposed she should, if she were to bring in that love train. Once her fingers had done some dirty talking, she carried on with the business of moving backwards.

'Where are you going?' said her dad, as she dumped her

bags in the porch.

'Change of plans. Mind if I crash here for a few weeks?'

'Yeah, sure.'

'Thanks. Can you help me clear out my old bedroom?'

'On second thoughts, why don't you go to your aunt's?'

'Because Mum will blame you and make your life a living hell.'

'All right, all right,' he said, grumpily, hauling himself off the couch.

'Thanks. Your fly's undone, by the way.'

They spent the next few hours transferring a plethora of objects – including giant placards – into the garage. The signs contained such gems as, "We demand more accurate labelling on ready meals" and "More support for families to help them cook from scratch". Gemma had once timidly suggested to her mother that HEAD's core messages could be confusing and contradictory. Her mother had said she only thought that because she had been brainwashed by the sinister and powerful multivitamin lobby.

At least lugging wooden slogans about had worked off some of her nervous energy/fended off a breakdown. Gemma was about to traipse inside for the final time when she saw him, standing sheepishly by the frozen hawthorn bush. To whatever god there was, she gave a silent thanks, and to Josh, she gave a barely perceptible follow-me wave.

'You sure?' he mouthed.

'Yes,' she mouthed.

Josh nodded, and dully followed her inside.

'Thanks for your help, Dad!'

'No worries,' said Joe, flicking the TV back on and swigging from a bottle. 'Oh, do you want one too?' he said, pretending to get up.

'No thanks. I'll, er, just be on the phone to Roz so, if you hear anything, it's completely normal. I'm not talking to myself, or anything.'

'What was that?'

'Never mind.'

She could sense Josh shadowing her up the stairs, and it was schoolgirl thrilling. She sat on the bed and, without denting the mattress, he joined her.

'You're not quite yourself. What's up?' Josh asked.

She filled him in, and peace descended. 'Wow, that feels better. Thanks, I totally needed to get that off my chest.'

'No problem.'

'I imagine your patients were happy to tell you anything. You've a great bedside manner.' She tried to nudge Josh playfully, but her gesture fell through. Blushing, she moved on quickly. 'So it's crazy about the déjà vu thing, huh?'

'Yeah. It's cool, though. Never had it myself. Well, not as a ghost.'

He fell quiet, but Gemma knew how to interpret him. 'Did you want to know what I've found online?'

'Yes please.' He seemed relieved she had said it.

She grabbed the laptop and took Josh through pages she had visited a hundred times. She watched him read the tragic story of Jeremy Cohen and his fiancée, Francesca Cortez. The narrative, according to newspaper reports, was this:

Jeremy was a successful and very popular paediatric consultant. Francesca was a high-flying lawyer. They had been together four years, engaged for a month, when they decided to visit a great-aunt in Clacton-on-Sea. On the beach, Francesca had entered the water alone, but got into difficulty. Her fiancé had tried to rescue her, but in the end, both were lost.

'She was very beautiful, wasn't she?' said Gemma, nodding at the image of a Latino woman with sumptuous eyes and coal-black hair.

'Yes.'

She tried to gage Josh's reaction beyond that affirmation, but his expression was impenetrable. Or at least, it was intended to be.

'I'm so sorry, Josh.'

'It's hardly your fault, is it?'

'I know, but…' Unfolding the paper from Amanda, she said, 'I take it you want me to make contact with Francesca's family?'

'If you don't mind?'

They made a plan, and that was it. Josh had done what he'd come to do. Oh, one last thing:

'How was your date with Paulo?'

His stare made her stomach churn. 'Great, thanks. Really good. You know, just because it's going well with Paulo, it doesn't mean we can't… I mean… I'm the only one you can have a conversation with, right? You must get lonely. Anytime you want to talk – anytime – it's fine.'

'That's kind of you.' Josh's mouth wavered, like there was more to say. Reticent as ever, he turned to go.

Gemma wanted to see him out properly but, with horror, sensed her time had come. Crossing her legs tight, she rushed the goodbye. Josh had seemed disheartened as he'd left, but right now, she had more pressing concerns. She rummaged around her old drawers – nothing. Since her stint in the fourteenth dimension, she'd completely lost track of time, of what a month was. *If I was back home with Diya*, she thought resentfully, *this wouldn't be a problem*. Suddenly, an unlikely saviour called out:

'Love! I'm popping to the shops! Need anything?'

Gemma waddled to the landing to check the coast was clear of disheartened ghosts. It was. 'Yes please, Dad! Can you grab me some pads?'

There was a pause. Then a very unsteady, 'Okay.'

*

What she should have been doing with her day off was marking, or lesson planning. What she certainly shouldn't be doing was shoving chocolate in her mouth in an attempt to numb the pain – and the jealousy. It was stupid to resent a ghost's deceased fiancée, she should quit it. Maybe one last salted caramel…

'I'm back!' shouted her dad.

Practically crawling her way to his shopping bags, Gemma removed one of the items. 'What the hell are these?'

'Lady pads.'

'These are not the right kind of lady pads! I'm not incontinent!'

Her dad went scarlet with indignation. 'How was I to know which ones to choose? There were millions of the damn things! I asked at the store!'

'Who did you ask?'

'I dunno. Some young, spotty lad.'

'Dad!'

'Well next time you need a lady pad, don't ask me. Ask your mother.'

'Argh! Fine! Whatever!' Gemma stropped off to her room, because life was too much. She felt like a teenager again; angry at her parents; angry at the way the world was. Maybe she should do something rebellious and stupid. She hurled the empty box of chocolates onto the floor. Nah, that didn't cut it. Even her phone was shaking with rage.

Can't wait till tomorrow, read Paulo's text. *I've cut London short. Bring your sexy ass here, ASAP.*

Can't, she typed, *I'm on.*

On?

On.

A pause, then: *But there are still things you want to do to me, right, babe?*

Another pause. *Sure.*

She packed a few things and left. When Paulo was satisfied, she told him Diya and her polycystic ovaries had kicked her out.

Hazily, he said, 'There's plenty of room here. You already know how to work the coffee machine. Why don't you just move in?'

'Isn't this all going a bit fast?'

'Fuck it. I earned a hundred grand bonus this week.'

CHAPTER ELEVEN

Georgia made half-hearted noises about the unnecessary relocation of placards, but on the whole, she was delighted her daughter was moving in with the investment banker. As she escorted Gemma to the door, she stuffed some frozen chicken soup in her arms.

'Thanks, Mum.'

'And we'll see you at Rose's get-together tomorrow?'

'Yes, Mum.'

Georgia glared at her husband, who was clutching a TV remote in one hand and a beer in the other. He misinterpreted the glare. 'Sorry, love, did you want one?'

'No, Joe, I didn't! Come say goodbye! Your only child's leaving! Possibly for ever!'

'We're seeing her tomorrow.'

'She could have died!'

'After the golf.'

*

Though he winced as she pulled in, Paulo managed to pull it back. Greeting her like a suave car park valet, he assigned the decade-old Suzuki a parking space. They were both thinking it: sandwiched between a Porsche and a Mercedes, her green banger was very much out of place. Paulo handed over a key-card, and the physicality of the thing made it hit home. Gemma did a deep breathing exercise.

'You're struggling. Let me help with the bags,' said Paulo,

as the lift carted them up.

Leaning against the mirror, Gemma was struck by how much she'd roamed since the crash. She had become a nomad in the world where she was meant to be. *Well*, she told herself with a degree of certainty – only a degree, *now I have arrived*. In the apartment, she firmly set her bag down on plush carpet, and all its contents – mainly newly purchased tampons – spilled out. She swore.

'I'll get it,' said Paulo, down on one knee, probably a sign of things to come.

Why didn't she feel happier about it? Must be the exhaustion of the transfer.

'I don't want you paying rent,' he said.

'I'm paying rent, and bills.'

'But the mortgage is already paid off, babe. And I'm not taking no money off a teacher.'

'I'm paying. That's final.'

'Okay,' he said, with a resigned shake of the head, and an I've-got-a-good-one-here smile. 'We'll discuss rates later. I've cleared out a load of stuff. You've got half a wardrobe and a chest of drawers to work with.' The clothes he'd left behind, like his apartment, were bland and designer. Gemma began hanging her dresses next to his shirts which, upon being disturbed, gave off a whiff of aftershave. It amused Gemma to think they did this on purpose, in protest to the intrusion of femininity.

'I like this one,' said Paulo, fingering a low-cut number.

'Thanks. Got it from the Cancer Research shop in the High Street.'

'Nice.' Paulo rubbed her shoulders. 'I've booked a table at that steakhouse for lunch.'

'Great. I already know what I want.'

'Me too.' He nibbled on her ear. 'Why don't you hang up the outfit you're wearing right now?'

*

Later, Paulo ordered his meat with a post-blowjob smirk on his face.

'And for you, madam?'

This time, she was not going to be dumped. Gemma dictated without hesitation, ending with an irrefutable, 'And chips, please.'

Like a cat who'd got the cream, Paulo leant back in his chair. 'Some girls take hours to choose. Drives me mad.'

'That's not me. Well, it used to be. But now, I know exactly what I want.' *Josh*. Gemma told that voice in her head to fuck off.

'What?'

'Sorry. Didn't mean to say it aloud.'

'You're right, though. Doubters should fuck off. The world needs doers and decisions. Don't give me all that due process, regulation, consultation crap. All that does is delay progress.'

Gemma shuffled uncomfortably in her seat. 'Surely there's a time and a place for careful consideration? The 2008 crash for example—'

'Yeah, yeah,' said Paulo, cutting her off.

The cuts never used to annoy her. She used to think she deserved it, and that he knew best. She told herself again that Paulo was ranked number one out of all potential suitors in the universe, and that her ranking system was not flawed, and that he had rippling, azure eyes.

'I'm talking in general, babe, yeah? It takes balls, not

brains, to grab life by the balls.'

'That feels like too many balls.'

'Take me, for instance. There are plenty out there clever as me, but not so many with my balls.' He punched himself in the stomach. 'I have seconds to make choices where millions are on the line. Millions! Clever pussies would cry into their lactose-free milk facing that kind of pressure. But not me. I'm not scared to make the call. If I get a bollocking as a result of a choice gone wrong, so be it. That's a risk I'm willing to take. And that takes balls.'

Gemma gave him a well-done-you kiss, and when their meals came, ate her own, without touching his.

'Poor sod,' said Paulo, pitying next table's man. 'His missus nicked half his chips.'

In a blaze of clarity, Gemma saw a way to make amends. 'Paulo, I don't need all my chips. Would you like some?'

'I could fall in love with you.'

Over the course of their conversation, Gemma recalled Paulo's likes and dislikes, and pandered to him. She rounded things off with the truth, 'I see myself having at least three kids.'

'Me too!' Beaming, Paulo marvelled at how compatible they were; said he'd never met anyone so wonderful.

'I'm not sure I deserve—'

'I'm treating you exactly how you deserve to be treated, babe! How would you feel if I came with you to your aunt's tomorrow?'

'I'm sorry?'

'Wouldn't they love to meet me?'

'Mum will probably start doing somersaults. But… are you sure? Men don't normally want to meet the family so quickly.'

'I'm not most men, and I've just made the call. Because I've got balls.'

'Um, okay then.'

'And whilst we're at it, the old man's back in town. Let's pop round my folks' in the evening.'

'Your folks?' In her head, *Songs to Shit Your Pants to*, song number fourteen, started playing. *Stop being stupid*, Gemma told herself. *Okay, so I've never exactly* bonded *with his family, but his mum is perfectly nice, that's why he worships her. The* Psycho *theme tune is a huge over-reaction. Besides, you've never actually met his parents before, remember?* 'Isn't that a bit too much family for one day? I mean, both mine and yours?'

'Nah! That's what it's like this time of year, innit? All fun and games.'

'Okay. If you're sure.'

Paulo kissed her. 'You could look happier, babe!'

Gemma was happy. As happy as one can reasonably expect to be.

*

Upon hearing Paulo was coming, Rose went all out. There were balloons everywhere. On top of the seasonal decorations, it was all a bit much. Paulo had to duck and dive under the helium-filled tat as person after person introduced themselves.

'We met in the hospital! I'm Georgia! Gemma's mother! Did you join HEAD in the end?'

'Haven't got round to it yet, but—'

'I'm Rose. Gemma's aunt. Do you like the balloons?'

'Love them, I—'

'I'm Joe. Gemma's father. Pleased to meet you. Don't

worry, Gem's given me the pep talk, and I've done up my fly for you.'

'Thank you. Ow!'

From nowhere, a triplet had run into him. (That was the most significant familial difference in this reality. Instead of splitting two ways, Ruth's egg had split three). The triplet was now crying. Gemma scooped him into a hug, glad of an excuse to mollycoddle this brand-new miracle. Well, new to her.

'Thanks, cuz,' said Ruth, dog-tired as ever. One of her sons was using her shoulder as a stepladder.

'Baboon!' he said, stretching to pull at a string.

'Don't do that, darling. You'll—' There was a pop, a thud, and a fresh round of tears. His mother bent down to scoop him up. As she was doing that, a different child in another room started crying. 'Amber, would you?'

'Why me? Why not Uncle Tony?'

Rose went to the rescue instead, shouting something about how Father Christmas only visits good children.

Amber glared contumaciously. 'Just because I'm a woman, don't ask me to turn into Mum! Don't expect me to start cooking no roast dinner, either!'

Joe snorted. 'Well, that would be pretty stupid, seeing as how your mother has already made one.'

'Whatever.'

'This is my cousin, Amber,' said Gemma to Paulo, with a look that said it all.

'Ah. Nice to meet you.' He kissed her on the cheek.

Annoyed at herself for looking flattered, she made up for it. 'Next time, ask for consent before you do that, please. Excuse me, got to check a work email.'

When the coast was clear, Tony tipped Paulo off. 'Ignore

her. She's had a bad week at work. And she's a bitch.'

'Uncle!' scolded Ruth, covering her child's ears, though it was too late for that.

Tony ignored her, and started sniffing Paulo instead. 'Love the aftershave.'

'Thanks. Sorry Norwich lost.'

'Don't mention it.'

Dwayne whirled into the room, pointed at the newcomer, and laughed. 'You smell like poo.' He thumbs-upped his brother, whose balloon-popping tears were now tears of laughter, and ran away again.

'Marvin!' screamed Ruth.

'What?' came the dazed reply, as Marvin wandered into the room. 'Sorry, I was chopping the carrots.'

'Paulo's here,' hissed his wife, like Paulo wouldn't be able to hear her if she hissed. 'And your son's just told him he smells of poo! Do something!'

'Hello,' said Marvin, shaking Paulo's hand. 'Loo's just through there.'

'Arghh!' screamed Ruth, dunking her son down and marching off to help her mum in the kitchen, so she could have a break. Before dinner, two more cousins and a grandma arrived, and they all squeezed round the dining table to the delicious sight and smell of roast turkey, potatoes and gravy.

'Turkey! It's not even Christmas yet,' moaned someone.

'I thought there would be a shortage because of the Finland-New Zealand crisis, so I ordered six to be on the safe side,' said Rose.

'But New Zealand is lamb.'

'Yes, but I thought *some* people must eat lamb on Christmas Day, and if they all start ordering turkeys instead, we're done for!'

'Who eats lamb on Christmas Day?' asked Amber, through a forkful.

'People who don't like turkey,' replied her mum, gruffly.

Paulo was about to point out how the host's argument fell flat, but Gemma stopped him with a "say nothing" kick.

'Now I've got too many turkeys,' sighed Aunt Rose, as she carved up a breast. 'Got to get through them by the twenty-sixth.'

'You can freeze them?' said Ruth.

'Can't,' said Rose. 'The freezer's too full of chicken soup.'

'As is the whole family's,' said the uncle who wasn't really an uncle.

Grandma narrowed her eyes at Gemma, and cut straight to the chase; the chase being, as far as she was concerned, the matter of sex. 'What are your sleeping arrangements?'

'Gran!'

'I don't want you winding up one of those pregnant teenagers!'

'But I'm twenty-six!'

Rose waggled her finger. 'Don't talk back to your elders.'

'He's not sleeping over, is he? I won't have any shenanigans going on under this roof!'

'I've told you before, Grandma. We're not staying. We're going to visit Paulo's parents after this.'

Rose looked suddenly panicky. 'I can't let you go there hungry! Have more Yorkshires. Does anyone want more Yorkshires? Amber, pass the Yorkshires.' They could all feel another tedious objection coming on. 'On second thoughts, I'll do it.' Rose stretched awkwardly, her bosom (it's nearly always a bosom, post middle-age) cradling Paulo as she did so. Stoically, he carried on chewing his turkey.

'Tender, isn't it?' said Joe, impervious to Paulo's predicament.

Gemma swallowed a laugh.

'Aunty Ambie,' said one of the triplets, 'Uncle says you're a witch.'

'Which one?'

Tony hid his face behind a wine bottle.

'That one!' said the boy, pointing to the bottle and laughing so hard he spat out his potato, which landed on Paulo. He flicked it off good-naturedly.

'Kids!'

Gemma smiled at her boyfriend. He'd always been great around children — that was one of the things she'd loved about him before.

'Why did you call me a witch, Uncle? Is it because I'm not afraid to stand up for women's rights?'

'Oh please. You don't give a damn about women's rights. You just use that as an excuse to never help anyone out, ever.'

'That's so not true!'

'It is! You are a lazy little witch!'

'Ha! You see? You did call me a witch!'

'Just now, yes. But I categorically deny ever calling you a witch prior to that.'

'He actually called you a bitch,' said Joe, helpfully.

'Stop swearing everybody!' cried Ruth, trying to cover six ears at once.

'Witch, witch, witch!' chanted all the boys.

'Can somebody pass the gravy boat?' asked their father.

Amber rounded up her nephews. 'I am not lazy or unhelpful!' she said, between raspberry-blowing on little bellies. 'I work damn hard five days a week and want to rest on my days off. What's wrong with that? You try managing fifty employees!'

'Bet you're a delegator,' muttered Tony under his breath.

Luckily Amber didn't hear him, because she was too busy singing *Wheels on the bus* with her audience. 'The witches on the bus go cackle, cackle, cackle…'

'Does anybody want more Yorkshires?' hollered Rose, over the nursery rhyme hoo-ha.

Paulo laughed, winked and told Gemma, 'Can't wait till it's our turn.'

'Look at those two lovebirds, deep in private conversation,' said Georgia, clapping hallelujah hands together. 'Shall I go fetch the mistletoe?'

'Paulo's a good find. I wouldn't kick him out of bed,' said Grandma.

Therein followed a chorus of approval, enough to make Paulo blush.

'Don't embarrass the poor lad,' said Joe, returning to the table from wherever he'd been.

'Dad. Your fly.'

'Oh yes, sorry.'

'Did Gemma ever send you a thank you card for saving her life by the way, Paulo?' asked Rose, as she offered out mince pies.

'Give it a rest, Mum!' snapped Amber. 'We've barely finished mains yet.'

Paulo smiled politely. 'No. But she did say thank you.'

Rose clicked her tongue disapprovingly, and Gemma missed the woman who once spoon-fed her tea and told her tales of Turf Fen.

After checking his phone, Tony made an announcement: 'Norwich have signed Lionel Messi!' He looked around, clearly expecting a greater reaction to his important news which, judging by everyone else's reaction, wasn't actually that important. 'I'm nipping outside to check the finer details!'

'I must say,' said Grandma when he'd left, 'it's nice to see Gemma with someone who's not a loser for a change. Did she ever tell you about the fraudster, Paulo?'

That was the starting gun; the signal for her family to treat Paulo to a detailed account of Gemma's unlucky-in-love history till now; where she'd gone wrong, and what she should have done instead – which, according to her mother, was get run over by a bus sooner, so she could meet him. On and on they went – only ever pausing for breath when a triplet clambered over them. Gemma couldn't help drawing a parallel between the current setting and the room of writers. If she clouded her hearing enough, her family even sounded like a bunch of jabbering monkeys. Or maybe that was just the triplets. Either way, she needed a time-out.

'Excuse me. I've got to make a work call.'

She didn't mean to eavesdrop, she really didn't, but the door to the back was open, and the words channelled through.

'Love you too. I know it's hard, but… Look, I'll see you later, yeah? Okay. Love you. Love you.' Tony hung up, and blanched when he saw his niece. Ferrying her outside, he closed the door. 'How much of that did you hear?'

'Enough,' said Gemma, bobbing her head sympathetically. 'Uncle… do the rest of the family know you're gay?'

'What are you talking about? I came out years ago! Everyone knows I'm gay!'

'Right,' said Gemma, nodding her head as if to something she'd known all along. 'Right, yeah. Only, I wasn't sure after my bus crash if things were different and… Why are you keeping your lover all hushed up, then?'

It was clear by his manner that her uncle was wrestling with some great internal struggle. 'He's not a Norwich City fan.'

'That's nothing to be ashamed of.'

'You don't understand.'

'He's not… not Ipswich?'

'Don't be daft! I'd rather die!'

Tony was close to tears. Something bigger was going on than divided team loyalties.

Gemma placed an encouraging arm around her uncle. 'It's fine, you don't have to tell me. I won't let on to the family that you're seeing someone.'

'There's an age gap,' said Tony, awkwardly. 'I'm old enough to be his father.'

'That doesn't matter. As long as the relationship is… legal?'

'Of course it's bloody legal!'

'Right. Sorry.'

'It's… it's something else.'

'Yes?'

'I promised him I wouldn't breathe a word.'

'Then don't.' Gemma made for inside.

'He's a premiership footballer!'

Gemma stopped in her tracks.

Tony was covering his mouth and shaking. 'I shouldn't have said anything. I shouldn't! Oh, but it's been hard keeping it secret so long!' He started to sob.

Gemma hugged him, and even as she did, the burden of her own secret weighed heavier upon her than ever. 'I swear I won't tell anyone, Uncle. I swear.'

'If the press ever found out… Well, you can imagine the chants. The abuse he'd receive.'

Gemma's heart broke, both for her uncle and for the man she didn't know.

There was a rap on the door, and a squashed Rose face against the glass. 'Your pudding's getting cold!'

Linking her arm through his, Gemma escorted her uncle back to the warmth of the family, and the pudding. She whispered. 'Let's pray for a world where footballers can come out, and not be punished for it.'

*

'Round two!' said Paulo. Ringing the doorbell, he mumbled under his breath, 'All you need to remember is Mum's amazing, Dad's a prick. But it doesn't matter, because he's hardly ever here.'

'Got it.'

Between the ring and the answer, Gemma mentally drew axis. If her relationship with Paulo's family over the last three years were a graph, her days of knowing them x and her level of edginess in their company y, then the line would be depressingly straight and high. She longed for the point where they could all be at ease with each other, less try-hard. She told herself it was okay. This was not meeting number fourteen. This was meeting number one, and it was supposed to be awkward. Maybe it wouldn't be awkward. She wondered what Josh's parents were like. The door opened.

'Hello! Lovely to meet you both, Mr and Mrs Fernandez!' Gemma handed over her present.

Paulo's mother was a pretty Columbian wrapped in a bold print dress. 'Thank you!' she said, giving Gemma a Chanelscented kiss on each cheek. 'But please, call me Maria.'

No sooner had the woman named herself, than she was brushed away by a short man with fading hair. 'Juan's the name!'

'Won't you come on through,' said Maria, her restrained manner at odds with how she was clinging to her son's hand.

They trailed her into a perfectly styled house that belonged to a Real Housewives of Norfolk episode.

'You have a beautiful home.'

'Thank you.'

Out of nowhere, a deep sense of loyalty imbued Gemma. 'But if you ever want to sell, please let me know. I have an uncle who'd give his right arm to represent this property.'

'I shall be sure to do so.'

'Are you all right?' asked Juan, as they settled into cashmere-soft sofas.

'I'm fine, thank you.'

'Oh good. I wasn't sure – what with your accident – whether your face was supposed to do that.' Gemma looked confused, so he explained. 'I mean the whole nose-off-centre thing.'

Gemma cupped her hands over her face in dismay. 'Is my nose really off centre?' she whispered to Paulo.

'Not at all – it's perfect. Yo, Dad! The crash didn't do anything to her nose.'

'It didn't? Oh. Sorry.'

Maria smiled at her husband in a way that said she would murder him, after the guest had gone. His phone rang. Apologising, he left. Echoes of his son.

Maria shook herself, as if trying to shake herself back to the start. 'So, how was the family dinner, Gemma?'

'It was lovely. Thank you again, by the way. It's so kind of you to have us here.'

'Not at all. We appreciate you making time for us.'

'Likewise.'

Their inane chat carried on for some time. Dolls in a child's tea party, that's what they'd become. It was as if an invisible girl stood behind them, making them talk the way she thought women talked. Paulo watched the dolls like there was nothing unnatural about them at all. In fact, his smile said it was all going swimmingly.

Juan re-entered the room, and before long, he had launched into a monologue. Without meaning to, Gemma zoned out. It was an easy thing to do. She'd heard it all before, and besides, Uncle Tony was playing on her mind.

'They told me turning Norfolk into the centre of the world's banana trade couldn't be done – but I proved them wrong!'

Gemma suddenly heard. 'Bananas? Not… not second-hand cars?'

Juan laughed like she'd made a joke he didn't understand.

Maria calmly returned her cup to its saucer. 'Norfolk isn't the centre of the world's banana trade, Juan. That's why you spend half the year abroad.' Silence, tangible as a fifth person in the room. Maria cast the other aside. 'So, how long have you two been dating again?'

If you count my past life, three years, Gemma didn't say. 'Officially, two weeks.'

'And you're already living together and meeting families?'

Paulo slouched back in his place, completely at home with the speed of things. He gazed at Gemma. 'Yeah, but I saved your life, what, over a month ago now? We've been messaging regularly since then. And when you know, you know.'

Maria stared at Juan, who was back on his phone. 'I suppose I knew your father for twenty years before I moved in with him and… You saved her life, so… so it was probably written in the stars.'

'Exactly,' said Paulo and Gemma simultaneously, and that coincidence put a wide smile on Maria's face. For her, something had just been confirmed.

'Paulo tells us you're a teacher, Gemma.'

'That's right—' She would have gone on, but there was already a follow-up forming on Maria's lips.

'And how do you deal with bullying, these days?'

Paulo tensed up. 'Mum.'

'What? You haven't told her yet? It's nothing to be embarrassed about. They're the ones who nearly killed you.'

Gemma stared at her reddening boyfriend. He had never mentioned bullies – ever.

'His school did nothing. And it was fee-paying. Can you believe that? We—'

'Mum. This is hardly the appropriate time.'

'I mean, the gall of them! We had to pay for the privilege of getting our son beaten. I—'

'It doesn't matter, yeah? Look where those losers are now. And look where I am.' Paulo gazed in earnest at Gemma. 'Next to the most beautiful woman I've ever seen.'

'The experience was good for the boy,' said Juan, barely looking up from his phone. 'Knocked the cobarde out of him.'

Later, Gemma looked it up. "Cobarde" was Spanish for "coward".

<h1 style="text-align:center">CHAPTER TWELVE</h1>

She made some excuse to Paulo; something about Christmas drinks with work friends. He tried to dissuade her, to tempt her back to bed, but she had stood firm, and now here she was, shivering, waiting for Josh. He would appear, as he always did, not all floaty and ghost-like, but respectably, turning round the corner in a supposed stroll, with his hands in his pockets, and a hiya-smile on his face.

'Hi,' said Gemma, shy suddenly. Air left her when she spoke.

Nothing escaped his mouth – except a smile. 'Why are you acting weird?'

'I'm not acting weird! All I said was hi!'

'Yeah, but something about you isn't right, I can tell. If you'd rather forget this whole Francesca thing, it's fine. I totally understand. It probably won't help me anyway.'

'No, it's not that. I… I've moved in with Paulo.'

Eyes went wide. 'That's… soon.'

'And I've met his parents.'

'That's… soon.'

'Don't look at me like that. I don't have any choice. I need to speed up the love train.'

'Love train?'

'Develop my feelings for him. And the only way to do that is to live with the guy.'

'What do you mean *develop feelings*? I thought you were crazy for him already?'

'I was. I am, but…' Already, Gemma didn't want to talk

about it anymore. 'Actually, it's none of your business.'

Josh held up his hands in repulsed surrender.

'Let's just get in the car. Should be about a twenty-minute drive.'

'Oh, God. Twenty minutes of Christmas music.'

'Don't worry. I've set my stereo to stations that have banned it.'

They didn't say much to each other on the way there. It didn't help that most of the songs on the radio were love songs.

*

The house was caked in Christmas lights, and there was a wreath on the door. The gingerbread cheeriness of the scene filled Gemma with a hope the inhabitants would not mind her presence. Josh gave her an encouraging smile, a "here goes nothing", and she rang the doorbell.

'Can I help you?' asked a heavily made-up woman in a candy cane jumper.

'Hi, I'm Gemma. Sorry to bother you – and please tell me if this is a bad time – but I've come to ask about Francesca.'

The woman's fixed smile faltered, but then Josh held her hand with words, and she relaxed. 'You'd best come in.' Josh whispered something else. 'My name is Roberta, by the way.'

As the exterior suggested, the home was sickly sweet with tinsel and twinkle. *Just the way*, Gemma thought, *a home should be in the build up to the day*. Except, it did make the woman leading the way seem pale, in comparison. Even with all the foundation.

'Cup of tea?'

'I'd love one, thank you, Roberta. White, no sugar.'

Whilst her host was gone, she studied the pictures in the living room – one, in particular – the only one with Francesca in it. She stood before her parents, her arms round her double's neck. On closer inspection, her sister had a broader nose and tamer hair. Josh's eyes lingered just as Gemma's did.

'Mince pie?' offered Roberta, joining Gemma on the sofa.

'No, thank you. Look, I really am sorry for ambushing you like this. I'm happy to come back another time.'

'It's fine. But please – I don't know who you are, exactly. And what it is you want.'

Gemma checked with Josh. He nodded, so she took a deep breath, and let it out. 'My name is Gemma Higgins, I'm a secondary school maths teacher, and I was a friend of Josh's. Only, we lost touch a long time ago. I tried to get back in contact with him again, but then I found out what happened. I felt this need to meet you; to find out what Francesca was like; what they were like together.' Gemma's shame crushed her speech to dust, and she could lie no more. 'I'm sorry.'

'I see,' said Roberta. There was kindness in her smile. It just wasn't much of a smile. 'The way you are talking – forgive me for asking but… was Josh once your boyfriend?'

Josh's mouth stayed firmly shut.

'Um…'

'I understand. Handsome man, wasn't he?'

Gemma didn't look at him when she nodded.

'Kind and funny and a doctor. What more could anyone ask for, in a son-in-law?'

'I suppose they were perfect together?'

'Oh yes. Couldn't keep their hands off each other. It was a bit embarrassing at times. All their under-the-table play.'

Josh seemed pleased with himself, despite the sadness,

and Gemma longed to throw a mince pie in his face.

'My husband caught them at it in the garden once. Nearly had a heart attack. Could have been worse, I told him. One of our guests could have stumbled in on them.'

'Guests?'

'Yes. We were hosting my mum's eightieth, had lots of old dears pottering about. We could have had a *real* heart attack on our hands.'

Gemma laughed weakly.

'But of course, that was my Francesca all over. Loved a bit of the shock factor. Always a rebel and risk-taker. The trouble I had to put up with when she was a teenager, oh my gosh!' Roberta clasped her hands together, as if calling to the Lord. 'Drugs and drink, naturally. A string of unsuitable boys – one of them old enough to be her father. An abortion. An overdose. She ran away a couple of times. It was awful.' Roberta buried her face in her hands.

Gemma comforted her the best she could, given the strangeness of the situation.

When Roberta resurfaced, her face was wet. 'I'm sorry,' she said, 'for venting like this. Completely inappropriate.'

'Please don't apologise.'

'Something about you makes me trust you. I can feel you have a good heart.'

Gemma looked at Josh, but he shook his head – told her he hadn't put words in Roberta's mouth.

'Of course, the most shocking thing my daughter did, was get a steady nine-to-five, shortly followed by a nice, non-tattooed doctor boyfriend.' She laughed, bitterly. 'Sometimes, I think she did it to spite me; to say, *see, Mum? I can do it, when I want to – be respectable.*' Roberta clutched her now empty mug and stared at fairy lights. 'I'm sorry I argued so much with you, my love. I wish I could have been a better mother.' Her hands started shaking.

Gemma steadied them. 'You were the best. Don't ask me how I know it, but I do.'

'Thank you, Gemma. I'm sure this is hard for you too.' A droll smile, and a woman-to-woman look. 'You loved him, didn't you?'

Josh suddenly found the ceiling very interesting.

'Um…'

'Hate to break it to you, but he was smitten with my daughter.'

Josh did a double take. Following his line of sight, Gemma checked the doorway. Francesca's double was slouched against it – her expression a cross between disdain and pity. She was wearing a leather jacket.

'How long you been standing there, Jan?' asked her mother.

The answer was a shrug.

Roberta seesawed between the two twenty-somethings. 'Gemma, this is my daughter, Jan. Jan, Gemma's an old friend of Josh's.'

'Sorry for your loss,' said Jan, with more than a hint of defiance, like she was launching a pre-emptive strike, getting in there with her sympathy before Gemma had a chance.

'You too,' mumbled Gemma, feebly.

'Heading out with the girls now. See you later, Mum.' Jan gave a faux sailor salute. 'Gemma, nice ta meet ya!'

She left, leaving behind nothing but her impact. Gemma had a sense of how it might have felt, when Francesca was done with you.

'Sorry about her,' said Roberta. 'She's not been herself, since it happened.'

'Understandable.'

'They were very close, my girls. Fought like cats and dogs of course, but loved each other, fiercely. Jan was always so fond of Josh too. They were like brother and sister. He always looked out for her.'

'Josh was a very caring person.'

'Yes. I'm not surprised he died the way he did, trying to save my girl.' Her eyes filled up again. 'Still, at least they were engaged, when it happened. Although—' She paused.

'Yes?' prompted Gemma, gently.

'She called me. Hours before she died. A bit hysterical. Said she'd taken her engagement ring off to put on sun cream, and now she couldn't find it. It was lost in the sand, somewhere. Asked if I could drive over there and help her look for it.' Roberta laughed. 'Like a two-hour car drive was nothing!' The laughter turned to something sadder, as the thought passed her mind, for the thousandth time: *I should have gone.* 'I never knew if she found the ring, before she died. It was Josh's grandmother's. I hope she did. I'm sure she did.' Roberta shook her shoulders. 'Anyway, it doesn't matter. With or without that jewellery, they left this world together, as soulmates.'

Josh couldn't bear it. Began prowling the room with his silent anger, then left.

Now he was gone, Gemma wanted to ask more about the man: *What had his dress sense been like? Had he always worn the same shirt and corduroys? Did he wear aftershave? Where had he lived? Did she know his family? Where they were?* The Internet had told her nothing. The family had requested privacy at this very trying time.

Roberta wiped her eyes, muttering something about mascara, and Gemma knew she could ask none of those questions. She said, 'Is there anything I can do for you?'

'Not unless you can turn back time.'

For a second, Gemma was tempted to tell this grieving woman about the multiverse. To explain that somewhere, her daughter was alive and well and happy. Probably married to Josh with a couple of kids by now. But then, Roberta wouldn't believe her. She'd think her mad. Better to alleviate the burden of loss in the more traditional way.

'Do you believe in God?'

Roberta pointed to the decorations, to the Christmas cards, to the candles, to the miniature nativity scene. 'I'm trying. Can't you see? I'm trying.'

CHAPTER THIRTEEN

Huddled on the spot, Gemma fought off the cold. She had never known this place to be anything other than cold. What else could it be? Out of the blue she had come to this world; a world on the cusp of winter.

Before arriving at the gingerbread house, they had made their arrangement. When the interview was over, she was to give Josh a lift to the hospital. Minutes passed, and Gemma laughed to herself. As if a ghost wasn't perfectly capable of appearing wherever he damn well pleased, without such mortal things as cars.

The window opened, and Roberta asked if Gemma had locked herself out. There was nothing for it but to produce keys – 'Ah! There they are!' – and drive off, alone.

In the coming days, he didn't show up in the usual places. Having him around had been like having a buffer against all the worlds and their frightening possibilities. Without him, Gemma felt unprotected, and small. She wished she could shrink herself to the size of the woman in her head – just curl up alongside her, hold her hand, and sleep. After a while, she began to think Josh had been unreal all along. She never got much further than the beginning.

It would have been easier if Josh weren't preserved on the Web, but there he was, whenever she browsed, forever the hero who died for another. Why couldn't he have lived and died unremarkably, as millions of others do? *Why*, thought Gemma, wiping away angry tears, *why couldn't he have been like the rest of us?*

Diya tried, and failed, to draw out what was wrong, so she took her friend to church. It was that time of year, after all. There was a fresh Father. Gemma imagined storming the pulpit, teaching a new gospel. It was all she could do not to interrupt mid-sermon. *But you're wrong! You're wrong! You've missed out the bit about Pete and Marge and alternate realities and monkeys and everything! What do you know, preacher?*

Then again, wasn't she as lost as the rest of them? Hadn't Marge said God was beyond? Maybe everything Father said was true as well – only there was something wrong with her heart that she couldn't *feel* religion like others did – even after witnessing, with her own eyes, extraordinary, unexplainable things. Like ghosts. She stared at Diya and Tom, holding hands, enraptured and at peace, all because of Jesus's name. *At least*, she thought, *I have the same comfort as the believers. We all of us know, this life isn't it.*

When everyone else is happy, and you know that you should be too, Christmas is a very sad affair. She had expected Paulo to buy her sexy lingerie, but he didn't. He bought her tickets to the show she really wanted to see – and it must have cost him a bomb.

'Do you like it, babe?'

'I love it.'

There was no lingerie to put on, so she put on a smile. It was as if she had erected a wire fence around her emotions, beyond which was unencumbered happiness. Beyond the fence was wherever *he* was.

Paulo kissed her. 'I love you,' he said.

If only she could wipe Josh from her mind, she and Paulo could cut through the wire. 'I love you too.'

*

In the New Year, the door slammed open, and she was forced to shut his photo down. 'Aunty! Aunty! Play football with us!'

'It's pouring with rain, boys. Tell you what, when it stops, we'll go outside and jump in muddy puddles.'

'Yay!'

'A certain pig has a lot to answer for,' said Paulo, strolling into the room. 'Stop interrupting Aunty, she's trying to do some work.'

'It's okay,' said Gemma, switching off her laptop hurriedly. 'Lesson planning can wait till Roo picks them up.'

'What are we going to do with them in the meantime, then?' asked Paulo, as one by one, he dangled a triplet by their ankles.

'No, Uncle, no!' giggled Dwayne, meaning very much, yes.

Paulo beamed at Gemma, and she reflected him. It was the first time they had called him that, and he deserved it. He was wonderful with them. It had been the same in the old world. Despite paying his cleaner to iron his pants, he had always embraced the chaos and mess of children. It was part of what made him so perfect. It was why she had loved him so before, and why, she told herself, she would love him so again. Each day she lived with him, and was reminded of how things used to be, each time there was a nugget like now, when she saw things through an upside-down child's eyes, she could feel her affections grow. If only they would supplant certain other emotions…

'How about,' said Paulo, 'we jump on the bed, until the rain stops?'

'Yay!'

'Thank you,' said Gemma, kissing him on the lips like she meant it.

A couple of hours later, he asked, 'Ready to rock and roll?'

'Yep. *Think* I've got the last of the mud from my hair. Jesus, Paulo. Are you really wearing that suit to bowling? All you need is an oar and boater and you could be my old Cambridge boyfriend.'

'Gotta look slick for the boys afterwards.'

'I don't want you looking like you're trying too hard.'

'Relax, babe,' he said, slicking back hair and generally acting debonair. 'My natural charm will win Dee over.'

'It's not that she doesn't like you as such,' said Gemma, sliding herself into the Porsche. 'You just… got off on the wrong foot at the hospital, and I'd be much happier if you two could like each other. I think that might help me to—'

'Yes?'

'Nothing.'

Driving came naturally to him; he could do it with his eyes closed. They screwed up now, forming their own vision of the road ahead. 'I get it,' he said. 'I get how much easier it is to fit someone in your life, if those you love like your partner. Promise I'll be on my best behaviour tonight. How many fucks am I allowed?'

'Three. Don't use them all at once. And maybe cut down on the "babe-ing" too. That really annoys Dee. And try not to talk about money-related things.'

'Gotcha. Three fucks, no babes, no money.'

'Sounds like a tragic rap song.'

Paulo laughed. 'Mum loves you, by the way.'

Gemma blushed at the window.

*

Bowling got off to a bad start, mainly because Tom was wearing his favourite cardigan.

'Mate!' said Paulo, guffawing like he was eighteen, and pissed. 'You look like a fucking sheep!'

'Strike one,' hissed Gemma.

Diya did the glaring on her boyfriend's behalf.

Tom smiled and said, 'Nice to meet you, Paulo.'

'No offence, mate,' said Paulo, typing their names into the overhead screen. 'Does anyone need the barriers?'

'I do,' said Gemma, sheepishly. 'Otherwise my ball keeps falling in the cracks.'

'My boyfriend's name is not Sheep-Boy.'

'I'd prefer *ba-aaad* boy,' said Tom.

Diya shook her head at Paulo. 'You do realise what you've done, right? Given him a licence to make sheep jokes.'

'Wait, wait!' said Tom, excitedly. 'What do you call a singing ewe?' He paused dramatically. 'Lady Ba-Ba!'

Gemma laughed, but his girlfriend looked appalled.

'Like I was saying,' Diya grimaced, 'thanks a lot.'

'All right, give it a rest, mate,' Paulo said to Tom jovially, before getting the ball rolling and bulldozing every pin. 'Ha! Drinks on me!'

'I'll go with you to the *baaa.*'

Two rounds later, Tom had moved on. Unfortunately, his new subject was period poverty, and he was talking far more about sanitary towels than anyone wants to hear on a night out. Paulo took the lecture in his stride and pledged to make a large donation.

'See,' said Gemma to Diya, as their partners went for more beer. 'Told you he was nice.'

'You did,' said Diya. 'I thought he'd be all over-competitive and wanky. But he's been fine.'

'Yep.'

'I think it helps that the rest of us are crap at bowling.'

'Probably.'

Returning with their hands full, Paulo had a strained smile on his face. Guinness finally put a stop to Tom's monologue.

'Thanks for the invite,' said Paulo, 'but some mates are visiting this weekend, and we're meeting up in Flavorz after this. Maybe another time.'

'Well, why don't we move the Water Aid meeting to Flavorz?' said Tom, grinning at Diya like he'd just had the best idea in the world. 'I'm the chairman, what I say goes, right? Let's not cut this evening short, I know you girls have been looking forward to it for ages.'

'But it's short notice…'

'Let me WhatsApp the lads and see if they'd prefer the church hall or a nightclub.'

Gemma looked over at Tom's phone, saw him skim over the Volunteering for Veterans group, the Fundraising for Orphans group, and the Praying for Peace between Finland and New Zealand group, until he finally reached Water Aid.

'Sent them a message,' he said. 'Blue ticks… yep! Yep! They're up for it. Let's do this!' He downed his pint.

*

In a private room affordable to the likes of Paulo and his friends, sat two separate groups. In the one corner were several bearded men in sheep's clothes, stroking their beards pensively, pouring over well plans as they sipped on their ale. Tom was the only one among them with no facial hair. This may or may not have been why he was the only one plastered.

'Send them beer!' he kept shouting over the thump of music. 'Fuck the water! When you're down on your luck, what you need is beer!'

In the other corner were a bunch of rowdy men pouring shots into each other's mouths, whilst boasting about how much money they earned, and how many women they'd slept with.

'Hey, Tom! Tom!' slurred Paulo, beckoning his new friend over.

Tom stumbled towards him, then listened intently as some great secret was whispered in his ear. 'You're a genius!' he said, before stumbling back to his group. 'Lads! Lads!' he shouted. 'Alcohol is really hygienic! It could save a lot of lives!'

Everyone on his table ignored him.

'Right,' said Tom, swiping his phone with haphazard fingers. 'I'm setting up a new WhatsApp group. Who wants to join "Send beer to Africa"? Anyone? Anyone?'

Back over on Paulo's side, a glass smashed on the floor. One of Tom's bearded lot ran for a dustpan and brush.

'Wow,' said Diya, observing the carnage from a safe distance. 'It's like looking at a load of Paulos, and a load of hairier Toms. Our partners are quite different, aren't they?'

'Yes,' said Gemma, staring at her boyfriend, wondering where Josh would fit in all of this. Nowhere, was the answer. 'I'm sorry if you think Paulo has corrupted your lovely boyfriend.'

'Not at all,' said Diya, staring at Gemma like she was a ghost – someone she could see right through.

CHAPTER FOURTEEN

'You guys are in for a real treat.'

The class groaned in unison.

'What? Why are you all reacting like that?'

The student with the most un-tucked shirt took on the role of class rep. 'Because that's what you always say when a topic is extra hard. Or boring.'

'Or both,' said a girl who's lank, dyed black hair and mournful eyes suggested she'd given up on life, aged fifteen.

'Well this time I'm serious,' said Gemma, smiling enthusiastically to show how much she meant it. 'Today we are tackling…' she scribbled symbols on the board, 'algebra!'

'Algebra?'

More muttering and moaning – not all of it genuine, Gemma noted. Her two brightest were professing to be as glum as the rest of them, but she had clocked their clandestine smiles of satisfaction, quickly cloaked, before peers could accuse them of being geeks or freaks.

'Honestly,' said Gemma, 'There is nothing as intellectually beautiful as working out, through pure logic, exactly what X, Y and Z stand for.'

'Xylophone, yo-yo and zebra?' said some smart-arse.

'It is amazing how you can swap constructs over, from one side to another, rebalancing reality, in order to work out the true value of something. The Ancient Greeks…'

Out of the corner of her eye, she saw him come in.

'You all right, Miss? You look like you've seen a ghost!'

'What?' Gemma blinked at Josh.

He had the air of a student caught doing something he shouldn't. 'Sorry,' he whispered. 'I'll sit at the back.' He took the place of an absent student.

'Miss?'

Gemma clenched her pen tight, and her heart rode wild. 'Right. Sorry. Lost my train of thought there.'

'You were saying we've worked so hard recently, you think we should chill and watch a film.'

'*Fast and Furious*?'

'*Fifty Shades of Grey*?'

'Nice try, guys. Algebra!'

Gemma turned to the board, spoke what came naturally to her and, in time, a collective sort of calm and content came over the class as, against all odds, twenty-nine teenagers experienced the fulfilling gratification that comes with understanding an equation. Josh said nothing, the silent observer, invisible to all but one. Distracted by her responsibilities, Gemma managed to blank him out quite successfully. Until the bell rang, and the last of them had left. Then she could pretend no more.

Gemma leant back on her desk for support. 'What the hell are you doing here?'

'I was curious.'

'Curious?'

'You always spoke so passionately about your work, and your students. I thought it would be great to see you in action – and it was! You hold a class brilliantly... Miss.'

'Don't you "Miss" me!'

'But I did!' said Josh fast, like the words had just fallen out.

Gemma knew her own anger and hurt. She knew his too. For that reason, she kept her voice level. 'You're the one who chose to stay away.'

'I know. I'm sorry. I needed time with my own thoughts. Unfortunately, that took me a month.' He wound up his mouth. 'You know, because my thoughts are so grand and complex.'

She saw through the transparent smile. Something had changed since she'd seen him last. He was more ghost-like than before. Geometric shapes on the wall were visible through his chest. There was a transcendental curve where his heart should be. Perhaps he was ill – if ghosts could get ill – and she should feel sorry for him.

Fuck off, why should I feel sorry for him?

She slammed down her marking. Conflicting emotions were blowing her apart, and the debris rained indiscriminately from her mouth. 'Jesus, Josh! You can't just waltz back into my life! It's nice to see you again. I'm glad you're okay, even if you're looking a bit… under the weather. But for fuck's sake, in future, if you need some space, do me a favour and tell me, yeah?'

'Okay.'

'Don't just ghost me, like I mean nothing to you!'

A beat of anger in his face. He changed it to something more harmonious. 'I'm sorry I made you feel that way. Nothing could be further from the truth.'

'So what is the truth? Why are you fading away?'

He was trying to play it cool, but there was fire in his pale eyes. 'Just leave it, yeah?'

There was fire enough for the two of them. 'The least you can do is be honest with me! And if you can't manage that, fuck off!'

Shaking his head at the ground, he laughed at it, as if where he stood was the source of all that was wrong with the world, and deserved to know his contempt. 'I was depressed, all right? And I didn't want you to see me like this. Even less of a man than I was before.' He stared at her through his open palm.

She didn't know who his disgust was aimed at, and she didn't know what to say. In the dark silence, her thoughts swirled. *How could you have been so selfish? Of course he was depressed. He should be spending eternity in paradise with the love of his life. Instead, he's stuck here with you, in no-man's land. You turned your back on your friend. Bitch.*

'I'm sorry,' she said. 'I'm ashamed of how I just behaved.'

'It's okay. I get it. You weren't expecting me. And I was unfair to you.'

'Still, it doesn't mean that… Josh?'

'Yes?'

'I know I always freaked out in the past if you did anything traditionally ghostly.'

'What, like walking through solid objects?'

'Yes. But that doesn't mean I want you to hide yourself from me, now you're more… liminal. I'm sorry I made you feel ashamed of your form. Honestly, I don't care what you look like. I don't care if you vanish to the point you're just a voice in my head. I only want your happiness. And… Josh?'

'Yes?'

'Please don't vanish to the point you're just a voice in my head.' He started to laugh, but it wasn't enough. She needed to make things right. 'I have a theory about how to reunite you with Francesca.'

'Why are you talking to a desk?' asked Roz, looking at Gemma like she was crazy.

'Sorry. Didn't hear you come in.'

'That's because you were too busy talking to a desk.'

'Right. I was… planning what to say to Paulo later.'

'A bit strange, but okay. Who's Francesca?'

'Um, the secretary Paulo's shagging.'

'What? The bastard!'

'It's okay! We have… an *understanding*.'

Roz's eyes lit up. 'You do, eh? It's always the quiet ones. Does this mean you get a free pass too?'

Even though Gemma was decidedly not looking at Josh, she could see him doubling over. 'Sure.'

'Bet Diya doesn't approve!'

Roz had always been a little jealous of her best friend. Sometimes, she couldn't help a dig.

'We're kind of keeping it to ourselves, so if you wouldn't mind.'

'Consider it sealed!' said Roz, shutting a zip over her mouth. 'Anyways, what I came to tell you before I learned of your sexual deviance is there's a change of plans. Year Eleven are taking over Hades tonight, so we'll have to make do with Flavorz.'

'But they're all underage.'

'I know. Terrible, isn't it? You plan a night out for ages, and then a bunch of fucking teenagers blow up your hard work with excellent fake IDs.'

'Does it have to be Flavorz? I went there recently, and it's got a z on the end, and everything.'

'Tragic, I know, but hey-ho. It beats standing around talking to desks. Come on. I'll give you a lift home and you can dish some more dirt on your shit-hot sex life.'

As Gemma followed her colleague out the door, she mouthed to Josh that she'd meet him outside the apartment at eight; told him where it was.

'Swanky,' he said, with a smile she'd missed, and her heart

fluttered wildly. Then she saw a Year Seven crying through the window.

'You go ahead,' she said to Roz.

'But it's Friday! We should've been out of here *ages* ago. And I want to hear all about your shit-hot—'

'Another time. See you later.' Gemma made her way towards the child, and Josh watched her go.

*

Draping fake fur over her skin-tight dress, Gemma tottered out front. Totter is all you can do in skyscraper heels and fabric so clingy your legs might as well be bandaged together.

'What's with the penguin waddle?' asked Josh, laughing with his eyes.

She beamed back at him. Her insides hadn't stopped cartwheeling since Roz had dropped her off. 'I've had to dress sexy, that's what.'

'Why *had* to?'

'The place we're going. It's full of cool, RnB, bump and grind people. I'd like to fit in.' Also in some warped, revengeful way, she wanted to show Josh what he'd been missing. 'But even wrapped up in wolf skin, it's still bloody freezing.'

'We could go inside.'

Gemma shook her head and curled her arms around herself. 'That'd be too weird, having you in Paulo's apartment. I already feel guilty that he doesn't know about you.'

'Why guilty? You just don't want him to think you're a nutter who sees dead people – and that's fair enough.'

'It's kind of out of order, isn't it? Keeping your good-looking friend of the opposite sex a secret from your partner…' She mentally kicked herself.

'So, you think I'm good-looking?'

'No! Um, okay, you are. A bit. For a ghost. You're looking a bit less see-through than earlier on, anyway, so well done on that.' She gave Josh a thumbs-up and stared at him confidently. 'So, as I mentioned earlier, I've figured how you transition – find peace in the next world.'

'If you're going to say it's about the ring, I—'

'Francesca lost your grandmother's engagement ring right before you both died. And now you're hanging about on this Earth like a lost soul. Coincidence? Me thinks not!'

'Me thinks you're barking up the wrong tree.'

'All we have to do is find the ring!'

'All right, Frodo.'

'And, I dunno… place it on her grave, or something.'

'You're Tolkien the mick.'

'How can it be you've forgotten your fiancée and parents and countless other things about your life, but you remember *Lord of The Rings*?'

'And the *Doctor Who* theme tune.'

'You know what that tells us.'

They spoke in sync:

'I was massively cool when I was alive.'

'You were a massive geek when you were alive.'

They laughed.

'The brain's a funny thing,' said Josh. 'What it remembers. What it forgets. How's that kid from earlier, by the way?'

'I don't know,' said Gemma rubbing her head in worry. 'I think there's some safeguarding stuff I'm going to have to do. But I'd rather not go into it now.'

'Of course. Sorry.'

'Can we get back to you and Francesca?'

Josh shook his head. 'I can't believe I'm a ghost because of some piece of jewellery.'

'Maybe it's priceless? A grand, irreplaceable heirloom. Maybe you can only join her in the afterlife when you have a ring to bind you?'

He couldn't resist. 'One ring to rule them all.'

'Stop taking the piss! I'm trying to help.'

'How are we going to find the damn thing, anyway? It's been buried beneath sand for years. It's probably already been washed out to sea.'

'We have to try! And I have a plan.' Gemma paused for dramatic effect. 'We hire a metal detector.'

Josh raised a cynical eyebrow. 'A metal detector?'

'Yes! And maybe we try and interview your great-aunt whilst we're at the beach, too? I did some more research and found her address online.'

A cab beeped, and a very drunk science teacher yelled out of the passenger side, 'Dear, God! Now she's talking to bushes. Get in here, you crazy bitch, and let's get this party started! Woo Woo!' Roz waved a bottle and some liquid spilt onto the pavement.

'Hasn't she heard of Dry January?' asked Josh.

'See you later,' muttered Gemma under her breath.

'Sure.' Josh did his usual suppose-I'd-better-be-off slouch and suddenly, Gemma felt sorry for him. Did he ever get to do anything fun? Something that wasn't helping sick patients – or talking to her?

'Josh, why don't you come with?'

'Really?' It wasn't an excited "really".

'Yeah! Come on! Live a little!'

'That's all I can do,' said Josh, sardonically. 'Live a little.'

'Stop feeling sorry for yourself and get in the cab!'

Despite looking slightly scared of Roz, who was "singing" along to the radio, Josh got in.

*

They joined the others in the queue. There were ten of them in all; well, ten teachers and a ghost. Roz offered round her hip flask. The man in a wig and sunglasses was the only one brave enough to take a punt.

Josh asked Gemma, 'What's with that guy's get-up?'

'Still terrified of running into students, Terrance?'

'Indeed, Miss Higgins,' said Terrance between vodka-induced splutters. 'You'll never guess what happened to me yesterday. The one time I'm at the supermarket without my disguise – *the one time* – I bump into none other than… Francis Butcher!'

Everyone in the group recoiled, except for Gemma. 'He's not so bad, if you get to know him. He's going through a lot at home.'

'The boy's currently blackmailing me. Said unless I give him more help with his coursework, he's going to tell everyone I buy ready meals.'

The group made sympathetic noises, punctuated with terms such as "little shit".

'I don't understand,' said Josh. 'Why is buying ready meals so bad?'

'Because Terrance is a home economics teacher,' said Gemma, drifting from the group, feigning a phone call. 'And a lifelong member of HEAD. They're supposed to be boycotting ready meals at the moment, on account of the high salt content and inadequate labelling.'

'Oh look! The man wants to see my ID!' squealed Roz, embracing the bouncer.

'I'm obliged to ask it of everyone who passes these doors,' said the bouncer, staring at Roz. 'Even if I think the person looks forty.' He turned to Terrance. 'Take the wig off, mate. You look like a twat.'

In the dark were patches of strobe light and sticky floor, fumes of alcohol and drunken talk, but most of all, bodies that writhed to banging, RnB music.

'I love this tune!' said Josh, as Gemma said, 'I need to dance.'

They grinned at each other, and Josh followed her to the floor. At first, there was enough room for Gemma to move with no one, it seemed, about her. She was a woman dancing on her own, having the most marvellous time. Her colleagues whoop-whooped from the bar. After a while, the ground became crowded, and a man was right up behind Gemma, mirroring the grind of her body. Roz was ready to leap to her friend's defence, but then, as she got closer, she saw the look on Gemma's face – saw she was enjoying it. *Little minx*, she smiled to herself. *Probably lining herself up a threesome.* She staggered to the bar and messaged her husband.

It was Josh. It was Josh touching her body like that. Gemma had looked in his eyes, and she had seen the want in them. They echoed her own. In the dim, she deliberately made her gaze vague, until she had merged his face onto a stranger's. Now, his form was firm, his arms were wrapping themselves around her waist – his trousers were hardening against the small of her back.

'Gem,' said Josh, his voice desperate with restraint. 'Gem – you don't want this.'

'What?' she said, her voice dreamy, post-orgasmic-like, as

she felt Josh press hard against her.

'I don't like the way this guy is dancing with you. Tell him to leave you alone. Or walk away.'

And she saw, for the first time, people dancing through Josh; oblivious to his existence; intoxicated instead with their own joy, or sadness. There was a stranger – *a stranger* – pleasuring himself at her expense.

'Excuse me,' said Gemma, suddenly angry, and unable to look at Josh anymore.

'But we were having so much fun,' said the stranger, grabbing hold of her, and not letting go.

'Sorry,' said Gemma, staring at the man who, though handsomely built, did not have a face to match. Certainly at present, his face was gnarled into something ugly. He was squeezing her arm so tight, she could feel purple being made. She pulled again, to no avail. Like a fool, Josh tried to punch her captor. His punch went through several other revellers, and none of them felt a thing. He shouted obscenities that only made sense to Gemma.

'I'm not a bastard!' shouted the man to no one, and just before Roz and security reached them, Gemma kneed the bastard in the balls.

'Drink!' said Roz when the bastard had been kicked out.

Gemma necked what remained of Roz's hip flask. 'Thanks. Look, I hope you don't mind, but—'

'Of course! D'ya wammee to walka wit you! To a cab?'

'No thanks,' said Gemma, well-versed in drunk-Roz-talk. 'You might not get in again. Don't want to ruin your night.'

'Bar it's no safe to—'

'Honestly, I'll be fine! It's not that late, there's still plenty of people outside.'

'Okay!' said Roz, staggering towards a terrified Terrance.

'Love you!'

'You too,' said Gemma, making a beeline for the exit, before another friend could offer her company.

Josh followed her out. They said nothing. Gemma couldn't look at him. Before they got far, she thought she might faint, so she stopped in an alley by Hades. Away from the glare of streetlamps, she leant on brickwork. The music from inside the club pumped through her like a heartbeat. Her eyes were closed, but she could sense him, and when she opened her eyes, there he was. His body was arched over hers, and his hands were pressed against the wall – though of course, that was just an illusion. Letting her dress ride up, Gemma slipped her fingers beneath her thong, and let him watch her. His breathing was heavy.

'It kills me,' he said. 'It kills me that I can't touch you like I want to. Do things to you like I want to.'

'What is it you want to do to me?'

He whispered in her ear, and in her mind, her fingers became his, which in turn became his mouth and then, finally, his erection. She came and crumbled to the floor. Josh took a moment to compose himself, before planting his hand over hers, and Gemma cried because she couldn't feel the warmth of his hand.

'Most of all,' said Josh, quietly, 'it kills me that I can't protect you like I want to.'

Gemma threw her head back despairingly. 'This is all wrong. I've come to this world for Paulo. *Paulo*. You are only stuck here because you can't reach the love of your life: Francesca. Once I help you with that, everything will be as it should.' Josh looked as if he was dying to kiss her. She had to stop him trying. 'This,' Gemma flapped her hands between herself and Josh, 'this is just a… a wanton misinterpretation of feelings.'

'A wanton misinterpretation of feelings?' Josh screwed his eyes tight, as if enduring a painful flashback. 'This is like that time you described Paulo's eyes as kaleidoscopic ripples in an azure pond.'

'Shut up.'

'Gemma…' He said her name like he was about to say something after it, something scary like "I love you", so she intervened:

'You are a *ghost*, Josh. A ghost. Perhaps it's a good thing you've started disappearing. It helps me to see you as you are. I can't so easily pretend you're something else.'

'But you said so yourself. Since we reconnected today, my colour's started returning.'

'That's nothing to do with me. You're just feeling less depressed, now we've got a strategy to reunite you with Francesca.'

'But—'

'Josh, nothing can ever happen between us. It's pointless.' She blinked back tears. 'And I have it on good authority from those who govern the universe that Paulo is The One. I'm doing what I've always done historically, torturing myself with notions that the different choice is the better one. Queen of self-sabotage, that's me. But it has to end.'

'Right.' What life Josh had seemed to have left him. 'Shall we draw a line under tonight, then?'

'Great! Yes! Perfect!' She spoke in that overly bright way people drawing lines under things do. Her phone rang. 'It's Dee!' she told him. 'Hello?'

The reply was a squeal-cum-shout. 'I'm engaged!'

It was a two-hour drive to the patch of coast where the great-aunt lived. Two hours is a long time to talk when you're trying not to say too much, but they managed to do it the good old-fashioned English way.

'Nice weather we're having.'

'Yes, though it's set to change. The clouds they are a comin'.'

Josh laughed. 'Let me guess. One of your lyrics?'

'From *Songs to Shit Your Pants to*.'

The sat nav issued a fresh instruction, and the driver followed it. The map on the screen span itself into a tizzy, and a message flashed up: *Recalibrating*.

'Ah, bloody hell, not again!'

'I think it meant the other left, Gem. Would it be easier if I performed hand signals?' He said it kindly, without a trace of condescension.

'Yes please. I think it's a form of dyslexia – not knowing your lefts and rights.'

'It's very common. There's another roundabout coming up.'

'It doesn't have an exit to a motorway, does it?' asked Gemma, anxiously. She'd asked this at pretty much every roundabout they'd come across.

'Don't worry, no one's ever in a hurry to reach our part of the world. It's not even possible to merge onto a slip-road for miles.'

'Yeah but there've been roadworks, what if they built a

new route?' Gemma's head spun like her sat nav.

'What are you doing?'

'Checking for warnings of motorways. You know, the big blue sign with a giant, man-eating robot on it?'

'Look ahead. No new routes. Our only options are A and B roads.'

Gemma gave a huge sigh of relief, and took the exit to turn back on herself. They got stuck behind a tractor. 'Thank God. Now we can take our time.'

As they trundled along, Josh told her, 'There's no need to be so terrified of motorways. You're a good driver.'

'It's the thought of joining the rush that frightens me. Everyone else is moving fast; so sure of themselves. I'm afraid, if I join, I'll make the wrong call about their speed of travel, and mine. Maybe it's the mathematician in me, overthinking things.'

'Were you this nervous about it before your accident?'

'Yes. I've always been this way. Happy to scoot around the little lanes of Norfolk that I know – but not much more than that.'

She braced herself for the "typical female driver" line. He didn't go down that road.

'Knowing how you feel about driving long distances makes it even more amazing that you're doing this for me. I really appreciate it. Thank you.'

Gemma's grip on the steering wheel eased and she felt her anxiety lessen. 'You're welcome. I'd hoped to leave all fears back in the old world, but I guess some just stick.' She shrugged her shoulders. 'Anyway, thank you for being so nice about it. My ex – the one who stole my financial details – he yelled at me all the way to Liverpool once. Kept trying to push me onto the M6.'

'Twat.'

'Yeah. I'm glad you're not like him.'

She could feel Josh gazing at her, and she wished he wouldn't. If only he would study the fields or the grave-grey sky instead. It might make her stomach stop doing that funny, jittery thing it was doing.

'You're looking much more like your old self, by the way.'

'You said that earlier.'

'Did I?'

'Mmhm.' His smile retracted a bit. 'So… did you tell Paulo you were going to Clacton?'

'Yes. Told him I once went digging for bones there and was feeling nostalgic. It's a bit scary, how easy lying comes to me these days. I've lied to pretty much everyone since I came back.'

'Only to spare them the truth. That reality is downright crazy.'

Panic hit. 'Which lane? Which lane?'

'That one,' said Josh, calmly indicating.

She followed his direction. 'Why can't your great-aunt live in – I dunno – Winterton, or somewhere?'

He was going to say something.

'What?'

'No. Too cringe-y.'

'Oh, come on. What was it?'

'Nope.'

'Please?'

'Promise not to laugh? Or take it the wrong way?'

'Promise.'

'Fine. I was going to say, if I could, I would chauffeur you to the faraway places.'

She made a noise like she was watching a baby gurgle.

'You're taking it the wrong way.'

'Am I? Sorry.' She stymied her laugh. 'Well, thank you, anyway. That's very sweet.'

He winked at her affectionately, and Gemma realised the atmosphere was way too sentimental, considering they hadn't even reached Ipswich yet, and there was a whole load more suppression of feelings needed doing. Luckily, Gemma nearly ran over a cat.

Josh shouted, 'Cat!' just in time, and Gemma was able to pull off an emergency stop.

The end result was that the cat wasn't killed, but the mood was. They stopped at a petrol station for flowers and a cup of tea.

When they got back on the road, Josh stuck out his hand and said, 'Right,' and Gemma was reminded of The Conductor.

She allowed her mind to wander, and wonder how that man was doing. She hadn't seen him in a while, since she'd last gone to church.

'Have Diya and Tom set a date for the church yet?'

Gemma started. 'How did you do that?'

'Do what?'

'I was just thinking about… Never mind. The church is booked, yes. April 1st.'

'April Fool's day?'

'I know. It's the day Tom's parents were married. You remember I told you? His mum died of cancer last year?'

'Yes, I remember.'

'They wanted to honour her.'

'It's a touching gesture.'

'They're getting married at the same time too. Noon.'

'Nice.'

'Yes, it is. Josh, are you sure I didn't kill that cat?'

'Maybe in some other, Schrödinger universe, but not here.'

*

When all about them were bungalows, and the sea was a stripe in the bottomless sky, they'd reached their destination. Gemma parked up. Nervously clutching her petrol station bouquet, she climbed the hill to the right number, conversing quietly with her companion along the way.

'Wish your great-aunt knew we were coming. But she never picked up the phone.'

Josh was inhaling.

'Can you smell the salt?' asked Gemma excitedly.

'Almost. Or at least, I think I can remember what sea air is supposed to taste like.' He permitted himself a smile. 'I can envisage it.'

'What did I tell you? Now you're within touching distance of Francesca's lost soul, you can smell salt.'

Josh pulled a face. 'At no point did you ever say "follow me so you can smell salty sea air".'

'Okay, maybe I didn't use those exact words, but—' She stopped abruptly, because an elderly couple entered the house they were heading for. They were dressed in black. 'Josh, you don't think…?'

From around the corner came a bundle of middle-aged women, who also toddled through the door, who were also dressed in black. If there was any room left for doubt, each of the visitors was carrying a casserole dish.

'Yes. I do think.'

'Ah crap,' whispered Gemma. 'Trust me to accidentally gate-crash a wake.'

'Jewish people don't have wakes. They have shivahs.'

'Shivers? As in they feel cold, post-death?'

'No. Shivah with an "ah". Thank God we've got time to get out of here.'

A bouncy sort of woman snuck up behind Gemma. 'Hi! I like your coat. Perfect for a funeral. You brought flowers for Maureen too? Snap! Come on, let's go in together!'

Josh winced and made to snatch the lilies from Gemma. Of course, she was mortified to be walking into a stranger's shivah, but what could she do? This bouncy woman was practically frog-marching her forward.

'How did you know Maureen?' she was saying. 'I met her once at my cousin's neighbour's party. It was only that one time, but I felt like it was enough to really form a connection, and I'll miss her hugely.'

Josh looked as though, if he weren't already dead, he would have wanted to die. The door was open, but it was dark inside. All the curtains were shut, and the lighting was weak. Rumblings were coming from deeper in, but no one came to greet them.

'We'd better take our shoes off,' said Gemma's newfound sidekick. 'Everyone else seems to have – oo! I like this pair – smell that? Genuine leather, that is. My size too.'

'There's a jug of water and soap on the sideboard,' said Gemma, distracting the woman next to her so she wouldn't try on some unsuspecting person's loafers. 'Let's wash our hands before we do anything else.'

'Oo,' whispered bouncy lady, as she shook her hands dry. 'Like the décor. Retired spinster style is in at the moment.'

She ushered Gemma on. In the musty living room, a

candle was burning. Mourners milled around several people sitting on low stools, who wore the haunted expressions of those who have endured hardship. *Must be close family*, thought Gemma. Like Josh, she scanned them and the wider room, checking for anyone with a passing resemblance. Skullcaps, shawls and tissue paper skin were all she saw. The room was old. No one looked like him. Pictures on the mantelpiece had cloths draped over them. Blacking out images of the deceased was part of the shivah ritual, she supposed. Josh tried to mask his disappointment.

The bouncy woman coughed, and everyone turned to face her. 'So sorry for your loss,' she said, addressing the family on stools. She indicated to Gemma. 'We have brought you these!' She handed over her geraniums with gusto and Gemma, nudged on, followed suit.

Josh put his head in his hands.

'Thank you,' said the recipient, holding the flowers at arm's length. 'I'll just put them, um, on the table.'

'I can fetch you a vase!' The bouncy lady looked positively thrilled at the prospect. Gemma could only assume it was because she'd been gifted an excuse to nosy around. 'Where might I find a vase? No, no, don't tell me! I'll guess!' She opened a cupboard. 'Dang it! Towels! I'll try the kitchen.'

'There's no need, thank you.' An unshaven man had decided to intervene before the house was ransacked. 'I know you mean well,' he said, addressing both her and Gemma. 'But actually, in our faith, flowers are forbidden at this time.'

Gemma felt the earth sink from under her. Even bouncy lady looked a bit less bouncy. Josh was wearing a tried-to-tell-you face.

'Flowers represent life,' the man continued. 'And they are a distraction from the process of mourning. Gifts are usually food, so the family don't have to face the burden of cooking.'

If only she'd brought along some of her aunt's chicken soup. But who brings chicken soup to a meeting about a dead great-nephew? 'I'm so sorry,' said Gemma. 'I'm so sorry to everybody.'

'Not to worry.' said one of the hosts. 'We will be having prayers soon. You're more than welcome to stay.'

'Thanks, but I think I'd better… I hope I haven't offended…' How could she ask after a Mr and Mrs Cohen now? Or their deceased son?

Josh stepped in. 'Say, "May you be comforted from Heaven".'

'May you be comforted from Heaven,' repeated Gemma. Relieved to see everyone suitably touched, she left.

*

'That was the single most mortifying moment of my life,' said Gemma, removing a metal detector from the boot. 'And bear in mind, I have more than six million lives.'

Josh had been quiet, in the moments since. Now he spoke up. 'I don't suppose you saw her, did you?'

'Saw who? Oh. You mean your aunt? No. Sorry.' She felt guilty for her blindness. 'That's a good thing, right? It means she's… moved on. She's not restless like—' She stopped herself.

Josh finished the sentence. 'Like me.' His mouth curled up and closed.

'I'm sorry I couldn't ask after your family. You didn't recognise anybody?'

Josh shook his head.

Gemma, too, fell silent.

It was cold, as a new year tends to be, but not bitingly so. The salt-laced wind was being kind to them. They reached the point where grassy verge met sand. It was a dirty bathwater sea, and the sky was grey, but there was a gothic sort of beauty to the bleakness. Few people peppered the landscape. Those that were there were mainly dog-walkers. Now was not the time for tourists. Gemma peered further down the beach, to a pier that seemed to be crumbling before her eyes. No carousel music came from the decks. All that sounded was the song of the sea and the barking of dogs.

'Sad. How abandoned this place is.'

'And yet it's beautiful,' said Josh. 'Like someone old, who's kept her dignity.'

'Yes – that's it.'

'I swear I could feel her presence in the house. It was nice.'

'Maybe you were very close to her?'

'Maybe I was. The Jewish ritual around death – that came to me strongly back there.'

'I suppose it wasn't too long ago, when your loved ones were doing that for you.'

'Yes,' said Josh, making no dent in the sand. 'Why is it I recall fragments of ceremony, but not the people performing it?'

'I don't know. It's a big question.'

'I have a lot of those – big questions.' He stared at Gemma in a way she found hard to handle. 'How come I felt such a bond with you, from the start?'

She thought they'd agreed on an excuse. Perhaps he'd forgotten. 'I visited the fourteenth dimension, right? And you must have picked up on that.' Gemma began furiously punching buttons on her machine, the way she'd been instructed to. 'Maybe we can find out some answers today. I

205

think it's working.' She put on her headphones, took some coins from her pocket, and scattered them in the sand. Sure enough, when she hovered the metal detector over them, it issued a high-pitched screech.

The two of them spent hours combing the beach for treasure that couldn't be found. Gemma's frustration grew with each false alarm, but Josh, throughout the task, had an air of equanimity. As Gemma tossed her latest discovery into a rubbish bag, he examined some shells like a man who had all the time in the world; like it didn't matter that their hoard of bottle tops and broken toys was worth nothing.

'There's a mathematical name for this pattern, isn't there?' he said, admiring a fossilised spiral.

'The Fibonacci sequence,' said Gemma, distractedly, straining her ears for the sound of gold. 'Starting with zero and one, the next number is the sum of the two preceding it. Represented visually, the sequence forms a spiral like one found recurrently in nature. It crops up everywhere, from pinecones to galaxies.'

After a moment's thought, Josh said, 'Relationships spiral this way too. Grow and grow with each new shared experience.'

Ten minutes of searching passed, before Gemma replied, 'Not always. Feelings are messy, non-sequential things. They can start up high, end down low, and tread all paths in between.'

'I guess.' Josh smiled. 'It's only ever been one way with you.'

The machine had gone off. She hadn't heard him. Discarding the unearthed penny, she swore.

'What's wrong, Gem?'

'I stepped on your shell.'

'Oh. That's one way to stop the spiral.'

*

It was a late lunch. The cafe that sold fish and chips was shut, so Gemma made do with a corner shop sandwich. She didn't want to discuss how impossibly wide the beach was, or how there were millions of grains of sand. How, unless there was such a thing as fate, they were performing a fool's errand.

Instead, she said, 'I can't get over that woman at the shivah. I've never seen anyone so excited about someone's death. It wasn't even like she was a relative about to get an inheritance windfall.'

'I suppose she's a busybody sort of person who didn't want to be left out of all the grieving. You get a lot of visitors like that at the hospital.' Josh grinned. 'She was mourning whoring.'

'Oh, very clever.'

The grin grew even wider. 'No, wait: she was mourning whoring Maureen!'

The applause was sarcastic, but if she was being honest, she was impressed by his wordplay. A mother with a baby in a sling walked past. Their eyes met, and they shared a warm, mother-to-mother look. Gemma wasn't a mother yet, but she knew she was born to be one.

'You'll be great, when the time comes,' said Josh, quietly.

'Thanks!' Gemma picked up the metal detector and sighed. 'Right then. Back to work.'

*

A tin soldier was the last thing found, before she conceded defeat.

'Sorry,' she said, reining back tears.

She'd been so sure this would work. She'd had it all mapped out: Francesca's ghost appearing beside Josh the instant the ring was reclaimed. She'd witnessed them kiss, hold hands, and disappear over the horizon with pretty birds overhead. As she'd watched them go, acceptance had put his wise hand on her shoulder, and told her: "Enough". And just like that, Josh had become a memory to fondly look back on. Her heart was free. Her heart was Paulo's.

It had pained her, that picture, but she had wanted it for him. She wanted Josh to be happy. Now she had to face the fact she'd let him down and didn't know what to do next.

'I'm so sorry.'

'That's all right,' said Josh, looking out to sea, the picture of serenity. 'You know, I've been thinking: I belong here. Must be my aunt's presence.'

She heard the siren. In the corner of her eye, she caught the blue lights of an ambulance. Gemma felt suddenly choked, like she had sand in her throat.

'Don't worry. I'll see you home first, then—'

'No.' Waves were crashing loud against land, echoing the sound of her heart, breaking. 'Who will you speak to? They won't hear you as I do. You'll be lonely.'

'I'll be fine. I'll keep myself busy.'

'Doing what?'

'Same as back home. Volunteering at the nearest hospital.'

'No! I didn't take you to the edge of the world so you could leave me like this!'

'It's not the edge of the world.' Josh pointed to the horizon. 'Belgium's over there.'

'I don't care about bloody Belgium!' Her phone started ringing. Josh seemed perilously close to wandering off. 'Just wait there, please!' She answered the call. 'Paulo?'

'Where are you? Where exactly are you?'

'Um?' She plucked out a landmark and offered it.

'Stay right there! I'm coming!'

Gemma hung up, shell-shocked. 'He's coming.'

'Good,' said Josh, smiling like it was a hard thing to do. 'Now you won't be on your own, I can go. Take care. And thanks for all your help.'

'No! This can't be it!' She tried to grab hold of him, her fingers grasping at nothing.

Josh smiled, but his eyes didn't, and she started to cry.

'What's wrong?' said Paulo, making her jump.

In his embrace, she was torn. On the one hand, he was stopping her falling apart. On the other, she was being kept from *him*. She saw Josh mouth *goodbye*. His back turned. He was heading for the sea; the sea that had killed him before.

Suddenly, Paulo's physicality was suffocating. She wrenched herself free, and was ready to run. What did she care if she drowned in this moment?

She didn't notice a little black box fall from Paulo's pocket, or hear him ask, 'What's wrong?' once more.

The water's white fingertips were clawing at Josh, beckoning him home. And... could that be...? For the briefest second, Gemma thought she saw footprints; footprints where he had once stood. Almost as soon as she caught the marks in the sand, the tide washed them away.

The tide washed them away.

The landscape changed. Where sea-sky should be was Marge, drifting on a swivel chair, firing bullets in outer space. Gemma darted towards her, leaving Paulo far behind.

'Where is he?' asked Gemma breathlessly, as she glided from grains of gold to black matter. 'Is he here?'

'Nice to see you, too,' said Marge, resting her gun in her lap. 'I've no idea what you're talking about.' Something occurred to her, and she leapt off her chair. 'Get out!' she snapped, pushing Gemma back in the direction she'd come. 'Time is not constant! We've no idea how long this déjà vu bridge will last!'

'Déjà vu bridge?' asked Gemma, pushing back, trying to stand her ground.

'Yes, yes,' said Marge impatiently. 'Obviously. You've been repeating yourself, and now you've formed a bridge between your world and that,' she said, tossing her finger over her shoulder.

Gemma dodged her opponent and ran for the other side, stopping at the edge of the darkness. It was as if she was on a boat near the start of its voyage, and the shore was still in sight. She could make out two figures, frozen in time, but they were too far away to properly decipher. The other world was so close, she could dip a toe in its water…

'Don't fall in!' cried Marge, seizing Gemma's coat and dragging her back. 'That's the reality where you die of cancer at forty. You didn't want that, remember?'

'Right,' said Gemma, her head swimming. 'Marge, I don't suppose a ghost wandered in here, did he?'

'A ghost?' said Marge, looking nonplussed. 'Is your brain still messed up? How long has it been since your bus crash? Talking of time – quick! The gateway's closing!'

It was true. Space was swallowing up the beach, and Paulo. Soon they would be gone.

'It's cool. You can send me back later.'

Marge was pushing her again. 'There's no guarantee of

that. Last time, it was a cock-up on our part. We were obliged to make amends. But if you come here of your own accord…'

Gemma stopped fighting; the fourteenth dimension vanished; wind and waves resumed their motions. It was as if the Earth had paused for a minute just to rest, just to breathe, and now she had the energy to spin again.

Paulo asked, 'What's wrong?', whilst over his shoulder, Josh walked on water.

She heard *him* call, 'It's okay. I see Francesca.'

All too soon, sky bled into sea, and he was gone.

'You okay, babe? You look pale.'

'I'm fine, it's just… I'm not wearing make-up.'

'Ah.'

'Sorry. Didn't know you'd be coming.'

'It's okay. Figured you'd be shitting your pants on the drive home, especially now it's getting dark. So I hitched a cab.'

Gemma was genuinely touched, and overwhelmed by all that had passed. She cried for *him*.

'Babe!' said Paulo, hugging her. 'It was nothing, really. I've got a twenty-grand bonus coming my way!' He cleared his throat dramatically. 'When you told me Clacton held important memories for you, I knew I wanted to do it here.'

Cloudy as her tear-stained vision was, she could see what was coming.

Paulo began fishing in his pocket. His face fell, and his fishing became more desperate. 'Where is it? Where the fucking hell is it?'

'I could use my metal detector?' said Gemma, blowing her nose.

'Um, no! It's fine!' said Paulo, feverishly searching the beach. 'What you got a metal detector for, anyway?'

'Ah nothing. Just thought it would be fun. Thought I'd search for gold this time, instead of dinosaur bones. Sad indictment of the human condition, really, isn't it? That when we're children, we hunt for bones and adventure. And when we're grown, we hunt for wealth.' She wasn't sure why all this was coming out of her mouth. She simply felt this compulsion to talk and occupy her brain, so she wouldn't have to think. So she wouldn't have to face the inevitable.

'Here it is!' said Paulo, finding his black box which, after all, hadn't fallen so very far. 'Sorry it wasn't exactly smooth. Let's start again…' He asked her a question, and time stopped.

But the waves didn't stop. *It's like a tragic love affair*, she thought. Sea loved Land so completely, she wanted to pull him into her, till they became one. Land would tease his lover with meagre bits of himself. "Here, Sea, take these grains of dust off my back". But he would never give her any more than that. He couldn't, even if he wanted to. They were two different things, Sea and Land. But Sea would't accept this truth. Again and again she begged at his feet; a hopeless, never-ending tide of devotion. *What a fool.*

'Yes, Paulo. I will marry you.'

CHAPTER SIXTEEN

'Babe? I said do you want me to drive?'

'Sorry, I was in my own world.'

'Wedding planning already, eh?'

'Something like that.' Tossing the car keys, Gemma sagged into the passenger's seat. 'Thanks a lot.'

'You're welcome – wifey!'

He was monitoring her reaction closely, so she put on the show he'd come to see. Beaming, she twirled the ring round her finger.

'You sure it's okay?' he asked, with bright, eager eyes.

It was hot under his spotlight. Gemma removed her coat.

'Because if it isn't, we can always go back to the jewellers and—'

'I love it!' The belt was cutting into her neck, so she placed her hand on her chest to create more slack. As she did so, she felt her heart bang furiously against her, screaming, *let me out! Let me out!*

'Mind if I make some calls?'

'Not work ones?'

'No,' he said, setting up the hands-free. 'Spreading the news, of course! I'll put us on speaker, yeah? Mum first!' He punched the screen. 'Mum! Yo! Guess what? She said yes!'

Back came a grainy scream, and he carted Gemma away.

Several more conversations were had. The passenger drifted in and out of them, snatching pieces where she could:

'Yeah, man! She's so happy, she's speechless! ... It's gonna be a sick do, need to impress all the partners, know what I'm saying? … What the fu— This gear stick! Sorry, man, I'm driving Gem's car. It's a piece of shit. … Yeah, when we're married, I'm gonna buy her an automatic. … Yeah I know, it's gotta have five doors. We want at least three.'

'Children?' said Gemma, absent-mindedly.

'Yes,' said Paulo, relieved she was finally engaging. 'We said at least three, right, babe?'

Gemma nodded and slipped back in her own world, where she was setting things straight. Josh was with Francesca now. She would never see him again. That was a good thing. With him out of the way, she could dedicate herself wholly to her… She hesitated, before forcing herself to round up the thought: fiancé.

Watching her fiancé chat animatedly next to her, it was hard not to be touched by his enthusiasm. And hadn't he said he'd rather die than be caught in her little Suzuki? Yet here he was, willing to perish to save her negotiating the A140 once again. If she didn't feel a rush of love, certainly she felt a rush of affection. Perhaps this affection would spiral into something more, now her future had less… unwanted phantoms in it. She imagined her parallel self, and parallel Paulo, frolicking on that faraway beach, probably engaged too, by now. That woman was lucky, living her life without a handsome ghost-decoy. Well, lucky except for the oncoming cancer, of course.

Through the glass, buildings and fields, light and dark, blurred into one tangled mess. She would never see him again. Francesca was his destiny. Paulo was hers. It was written in the stars, and she just needed to swallow it. Her breathing became rapid and shallow. Paulo asked her what was wrong.

'Nothing,' she said.

'Everybody shut up!' yelled Georgia, tapping her spoon against a bowl of chicken soup. 'My daughter has something to announce!'

'Mum, it's too early.'

'Paulo will be here soon!'

'That's not what I meant.'

'Why should you wait for a man to announce your announcement?'

'Shut up, Amber!' said everybody but Gemma.

'Actually it's fine. I don't have anything to say.'

'She'd better not have gone and got herself knocked up,' muttered Grandma.

Gemma's smile took a nosedive because sometimes, she was crap at keeping secrets.

Grandma huffed and said something disapproving about relations before marriage. The others squealed and hugged and made congratulatory noises.

Behind backs, Gemma gave her mum a bollocking.

'Sorry, love,' she shrugged. 'Thought you'd given me the go-ahead.'

'Saying "I'll think about it" is not the same as—'

'You should have told me before I made lunch,' said Rose. 'I'd have cooked more food.'

'Aunty, my baby's still smaller than one of your peas. I don't need to eat more than normal.'

Her aunt looked at her like she'd said she was planning to starve some orphans, and then burn down their orphanage for good measure.

'Honestly, Aunty. I'm stuffed.'

'Here,' said Rose, dumping three fist-sized potatoes and two more lamb chops on Gemma's plate. 'We've got triplets in the family. Best eat for four to be on the safe side.'

'I don't want a bastard grandchild.'

'For Christ's sakes, Mum! They're engaged!'

'I don't want a bastard grandchild.'

'It's the meds. It's the meds,' said Georgia, talking through her teeth.

'When you getting married, then?' demanded Grandma.

Between gnawing on her lamb, Gemma explained, 'I'm not in any hurry. I don't know how pregnancy will affect me. I don't want to walk down the aisle feeling sick. Equally, I don't want to be a waddling blob of heartburn. We'll get married sometime after baby's born, I should think.'

'Baby? I don't want a nameless grandchild.'

'Don't worry, Grandma. They'll have a name. But it's too soon to think of that.'

For about the millionth time that week, Georgia patted her daughter's abdomen (and Gemma had only told her she was pregnant yesterday).

'Where are you going to live?' asked the dubious uncle/estate agent. 'Paulo's apartment isn't exactly baby-friendly.'

Gemma avoided her mum's eye when she said, 'We'll be staying at his parents for the first year, before we find somewhere of our own.' She pre-empted his next question. 'They live in Unthank Road.'

'Oo, golden triangle!' said the estate agent, sounding suitably impressed. 'If they ever want to sell up, give them my card!' He pulled out a bunch from his breast pocket.

'Thanks, but I've already got a stash.'

Georgia smiled like she'd been practicing it all her life. 'I didn't know that was the plan, love? You told me you felt awkward around them?'

'Yeah, but we'll be fine once we get to know each other. And I'm sure they'll be a great help.'

'You told me his dad spends half the year in Barbados.'

'Yeah. But his mum—'

'And Maria's diabetic.'

'What does her being diabetic have to do with anything?'

'Having a new-born's hard enough without nursing a sick person too.'

'She's not a sick person!' Gemma drew a deep breath. 'Mum. I love you. You won't miss out, promise. Maria says you can come visit anytime.'

'That's kind of her.' Georgia downed the gravy in her Yorkshire, neat.

Sensing an intervention was needed, Ruth delivered. 'When are you due?'

'My twelve-week scan's not till tomorrow, so I'm not sure, exactly. But I think August.'

'A summer baby. That's nice. I'm sorry. If I'd known, I never would have asked you to babysit the other day. You must be shattered.'

'No, as a matter of fact, I'm all right. Haven't been suffering from morning sickness either.'

One of the triplets stuck melted cheese up Ruth's nostril, laughed and said, 'Mummy's got a yellow booger.'

'What did I miss?' said Joe, ambling in as he did up his fly.

'Your daughter's pregnant!'

'Oh, that. Pudding ready yet, Rose?'

Ruth's face blanched.

'What?' said Marvin, clueless as usual.

She whispered back. 'Uncle Joe said the P word. But it's okay, I think we got away with it. They didn't hear him.' She raised her voice to a toddler-audible level. 'Now, children. Eat your lunch please.'

'No!'

'No!'

'No!'

'Honestly, Joe,' said Tony scathingly. 'I thought you'd be more excited about your first grandchild.'

'I am. Was chuffed to bits when I found out. But it's a bit early to—'

'Get in there, my son!' Tony looked up from his phone, 'Won't be a minute, guys!' and left the room.

Amber shouted after him. 'Fine one to talk! You care more about Norwich than the baby!'

Tony's head made a brief reappearance at the door. 'You are my nemesis, niece!' before disappearing again.

'You shouldn't goad him so much,' said Rose, gathering up gravy-soaked dishes.

'Whatever.'

'It drives me mad when he absconds mid-meal.'

'Stop organizing family-get-togethers when Norwich are playing, then,' suggested a cousin.

'No,' said Rose tartly. 'One is never too old to annoy one's brother.'

By the look on his face, it was clear Joe was getting mightily concerned about something. 'When's the pudding ready?'

This time, the triplets were listening. 'Pudding?'

'No!' shouted Ruth. 'No cake until you've had proper food first! Eat your pizza and chips!'

The triplets threw a collective tantrum, and chucked pizza

against the wall.

'You've got all this to look forward to,' said Ruth grimly, as she watched congealed cheese drip down woodchip, whilst three children cried and six hands tore at her limbs.

*

Paulo rang to say he was sorry, he wasn't going to make it back from London after all. Gemma said she didn't mind. Paulo apologised again. Really, she said, she didn't mind.

'How are you feeling?' he said.

She got asked that question a lot these days. 'Absolutely fine.' So fine, it was worrying, really. 'See you later.'

Catching her reflection in a shop window, she saw she was rubbing her belly again. Did she used to fondle the heart of herself so much? She couldn't remember ever being so attached to the middle before. But now, everything had changed. What was growing inside was the most precious and important thing in the world. The moment she had seen the blue line, had been a moment like no other. She had never known an explosion of love quite like it, not even when Josh… She stopped her thoughts there. In her brain, she had reached a terrible crack in the road, and couldn't cross to the other side. Where her baby should be curled up, safe, she felt a womb full of terror. Quick as she could, she dusted the feeling away. Her baby mustn't know her fear. What could she recall of the impact, anyway? Nothing. There had been the bus coming, and then a whole new reality. That was it. Drugs had numbed any after pains. What had she suffered, really?

There was The Conductor, doing as he always did, telling the traffic where to go, even as the drivers stared at lights.

Where had he been, the night she had crossed without guidance?

'Hullo,' said Gemma.

Too busy waving on cars. Nothing but a grunt.

A green man. Her turn to move. She thanked The Conductor for her safe passage, and he briefly looked proud.

*

Heavenly Coffee, as its name suggested, was close to the church. A dinky little cafe, there was barely enough room for its six tables. Diya had nabbed a spot in the corner, and was leafing through a bookbinder as she sipped on something chocolaty.

'Wasn't sure how much longer you'd be,' she said, watching Gemma squeeze into a chair. 'Otherwise I'd have ordered you something.'

She sounded on edge, but Gemma was too full to ask why. 'Can't put anything else in my mouth,' she said, massaging her belly. 'Now Aunt Rose knows I'm pregnant, I'm done for. Say goodbye to your nine-stone friend. You may never see her again.'

The laugh was nervous. Diya dropped her pen on the floor, then bumped her head on the table picking it up. 'Ow! How come Rose knows you're pregnant? Thought you were waiting for the scan to break the news?'

'I was. But then Mum took one look at me and asked if I was pregnant. My face gave it away. Thought I could trust her. Big mistake.'

'Aw, huuuuun. Never mind. Her heart's in the right place.' She knocked over her mug, rescuing it just in time.

'Is everything okay?' asked Gemma, tilting her head

quizzically. 'You seem on edge.'

'Who wouldn't be a bit stressed organising a Catholic, non-conformist, Anglo-Indian wedding in only a few months because you've got polycystic ovaries and want to start trying for a baby ASAP?'

Gemma raised her eyebrows.

'Oh, all right, you got me. That's not it.' Diya shifted in her chair. 'How are things with you and Paulo?'

'What do you mean?'

She was a reluctant agitator – fidgeting with her nails and looking deeply unhappy.

'Dee, what's up? Why are you acting weird?'

'I probably should have said something sooner, but it's still not too late…'

'Oh my God, is Paulo having an affair?'

'What?'

'Have you caught him with another woman or… man?'

'No! Why? Are you suspicious?'

'No! But he does work away a lot and—'

'Don't you trust him?'

'I do! He's clearly devoted to me, but…' *After all, I had an emotional affair for a long time. Maybe he picked up on that and wanted to even the score. Who could blame him?* '… but if you don't need to tell me about his cheating, what do you need to tell me about?'

Diya searched her empty mug for the right words, which turned out to be grotesquely cliché. 'I think you've settled.'

'Settled?'

'It's as if… the crash taught you life's too short. And all of a sudden, you wanted to fast-forward yours – love, engagement, babies – even if that meant settling for the first bloke you found when you woke up.'

'I'm sorry, most people wouldn't call being with a sweet, handsome, successful guy *settling*.'

Diya shook her head. 'You and Paulo, you don't have what Tom and I have. I'm sorry, you don't. When it's us, it's raw, it's real, it's effortless. But when I see you look at Paulo, all I see is someone trying.' She tried to take her friend's hand, but Gemma flinched, which brought tears to Diya's eyes. 'You can still have your baby, and be on good terms, but you don't have to marry him. Please, Gem. Don't trap yourself. I'll help you raise your child. You have an amazing family. Whatever happens, you won't be alone.'

'You had it in for him from the start! You never even gave him a chance!'

'That's not true! Okay, so he's not my cup of tea, but that wouldn't matter, if I genuinely felt like you loved him. Like you were happy.'

White-hot lava whirled inside Gemma. 'Who are you to question how I feel about him?'

Diya said nothing. Her friend burned in silence. The more she thought about it, the more the lava cooled, until eventually, it was no more than a pool of sadness.

'I'm sorry, Dee,' she said. 'You're right.'

Diya looked like she didn't want to be right.

'I haven't told you everything. The truth is… there was someone else.'

Whatever she'd been expecting, it hadn't been that. Diya's eyes nearly popped out. 'What?'

'Nothing happened,' said Gemma, hastily. 'But I wanted it to, and I couldn't stop thinking about him. The thing is, it was… complicated.'

'Oh. Was he married?'

Gemma still couldn't bring herself to describe him.

Diya interpreted the silence the way she thought best. 'It's because I'm so Catholic, isn't it? That's why you didn't tell me the truth.' This time, Gemma let her hold her hand. 'Look, just because I am the way I am, it doesn't mean you can't tell me anything you want, all right, hun? I'll never judge you. I only want to help.'

'I know.'

'You talk about this other man like he's in the past.'

'He is,' said Gemma, firmly. 'He's gone now. He's never coming back. And since he's been gone, things have been better with Paulo. I'm… I'm falling more in love with him.'

'Really?' Diya looked like a weight had been lifted.

'He's been so sweet – can't do enough for me. We're in a good place.' She said it in all sincerity, but she didn't want to dwell on the ins and outs of things any further. 'I'll tell you all about the other guy one day, but for now, can we pretend this conversation never happened?'

'Okay.' Diya's voice stilted. 'At least… at least my conscience is clear.'

'It is. It's how you live your life, and I love you for it.'

They squeezed each other's hand. Then they talked about other, non-heart-breaking things. When the time felt right, Gemma brought the conversation back to the baby.

'I'm still not suffering from sickness.'

'But that's great, isn't it? You're probably gonna be one of those women who sail through pregnancy. You hear of them, don't you? Those women who carry on bleeding, whose stomachs stay flat as pancakes, and one day they go to the toilet, and a baby plops out, and they say "oh, I didn't know I was pregnant".'

Gemma held her belly once more. Even after the bloat-fest that was Aunt Rose's lunch, there wasn't much there.

'But I *want* to feel pregnant. I want to feel that this is real; that it's not all in my head.'

'You're one hundred percent pregnant. You took, what, ten tests?'

'Fourteen.'

'Exactly!'

'But it's not right. Hormones are supposed to make me want to hurl my guts out, or at the very least become vegetarian. I just ate a whole lamb. And why isn't my brain foggy? And why aren't I tired? First trimester tiredness is supposed to be unlike anything you've ever experienced. Roo was a zombie her first three months. Uncle Tony took her to a Norwich match, and she managed to sleep through twenty thousand people singing *you don't know what you're doing*.'

'Yes, but she was pregnant with triplets. Her hormones would have been off the scale. Yours are chillaxing whilst they can.'

'Their chillaxing is stressing me out.'

'At least you're probably not pregnant with triplets.'

'I guess. I'll know for sure after my scan tomorrow.'

'Anyway, if you ask me,' said Diya, 'you *have* been an emotional wreck lately. You cried at a toilet paper ad, and you slammed my door so hard Tom's dad had to fix it back on its hinges.'

It was true she'd had her moments. But that had been less due to the hormones, more due to the fact the ghost she loved had run off to be with his true ghost-love, and the man she should love she did love, but not enough to be certain. Even though the universe had told her to be certain.

'Did I tell you what Paulo did yesterday?' said Gemma, perking up suddenly.

'No,' said Diya, warily.

'He brought me freshly baked banoffee pie – in bed!'

'That's impressive,' conceded Diya. 'I can see why you might be falling more in love with him.'

'I know, right?' Gemma pulled the bookbinder closer. 'This thing looks thicker than last time.'

'It is! I've added several more fabric samples.'

'Fabric samples?' Gemma flapped through different squares of cloth, each more Persian-rug-esque than the last.

'Yes. I was going to ask your opinion on chair covers.'

'Chair covers?' And then Gemma got very excited, because it had taken her a minute to remember such things existed. 'I think I've just experienced my first episode of baby brain!'

'Oh, well done! It'll be keys in the fridge by tomorrow!'

'In time for my scan!'

They high-fived, and things between them felt almost normal again.

CHAPTER SEVENTEEN

The doors parted, and her stomach flipped. It was no wonder. She associated the hospital with her accident, and the freak blip in her life, and him. Most of all, she was terrified the scan would confirm her biggest fear: that the lines had lied; that there was nothing inside her at all.

Slathering on alcohol gel, she sanitized her brain of such thoughts. In their place she installed a vivid image of Paulo's banoffee pie. *Much better*, she said to herself as she hastened her way through.

This was a wing she'd never visited before. Breastfeeding poster mothers smiled at her as she checked in at reception and made her way in. Nestling into a seat stuck to mint-green wall, she was reminded of the waiting room in the sky.

'Hey, do I know you?'

A bump poking out of a leather jacket loomed over Gemma like a prophecy. She looked up. A raven-haired woman, supporting her hips with her hands, was talking down to her.

'I'm sure I've seen you before.'

'Yes. We met at your mum's house.'

'That's it!' said Jan.

'How is Roberta?'

'Still depressed.'

'Oh. I'm sorry to hear that.'

'Yeah. You'd have thought a first grandchild would cheer her up.'

'Maybe counselling would help?'

'It's done fuck all so far.' Jan sat opposite Gemma. 'First scan?'

'That obvious?'

'You're in the Early Pregnancy Unit.'

'So are you.'

'Yeah, but I'm not really here. I was just walking around, trying to get this fucker to move, when I saw you. You're hardly showing.'

'Oh.'

'Mind you, I was the same till a couple of weeks ago. Nobody believed I was pregnant, then suddenly out of nowhere, whoosh!' At the "whoosh", she raced her hands from the top to the base of her bump, stressing the speed of change. 'I can't believe how much my skin has stretched in a short space of time, yet my body hasn't split, I'm still holding myself together. Women's bodies are amazing things, huh?'

Gemma nodded meekly. 'How did you find your first trimester?'

'I was hurling my guts out every day, and when I wasn't hurling my guts out, I was sleeping.'

'Oh.' Paranoia again, buzzing round her brain like an annoying fly. She swatted it away. *Come on.* She had survived near-death; survived discovering her body was divided a million times over. Carrying a baby was a comparative breeze. Besides, every pregnancy was different.

'Man, am I glad to be out of that phase now! I'm twenty weeks, but I don't wanna know the sex. I wanna be surprised.' She scanned the waiting area. 'Is your father a dick too?'

'I'm sorry?'

'I mean the baby's father. Has he fucked off?' She asked the question hopefully.

'No. He's stuck at work. But he'll be here soon.'

'Oh.' Jan rubbed her belly and stared at the wall. To blow up the silence that followed, she dropped a bomb. 'My sister was pregnant too.'

Gemma's heart stopped. *No wonder Josh chose Francesca.* She hoped, in the afterlife, babies could be born, families made…

'She aborted it.'

'I'm sorry, what?'

'She got rid of the baby. Didn't even bother telling Josh she was pregnant. Said it was her body, her choice. Which is true, but he still had a right to know, know what I'm saying? But that was typical her.' Tears pricked her eyes. 'Selfish bitch.'

'But your mum said…'

'Yeah, well, Mum's told herself all sorts of things since Fran died. She actually believes that crap she fed you.' The laugh at Gemma's reaction was cruel. 'Yeah, I heard it. How Fran had sorted herself out… how her and Josh were perfect together… how they were soulmates. Bullshit.'

'I don't understand.'

'He always wanted to help people, didn't he? Had some sort of doctor-Jesus complex. Kept taking her back, over and over, no matter how she hurt him. Always made excuses for her, put it down to the drink. He deserved better, and I told him so.' Jan stopped. She started crying. 'I'm making her out to be a bad person, aren't I? That's not what I meant.' Gemma put her arms round Jan, who gave more and more. 'Fran was the life and soul – she didn't need to be wasted to be fun. And she could be so kind. She did love him. Looking back, I think she was trying to push Josh away, because she wanted more for him. Only he was so fucking loyal, he gave her a ring.' Staring at the poster mother on the wall, Jan made a confession. 'Know what I think? I think she was so messed up, she wanted to kill herself. And he died trying to stop her.'

'Gemma Higgins?' A woman in white had opened the door and was calling her through.

Unnerved, Gemma replied, 'My partner's not here yet.' Jan wiped her eyes, and Gemma squeezed her hand. 'Maybe they can go before me?' She pointed to a couple three chairs down, who were already halfway off their seats.

'Erm, okay,' said the sonographer, eyeing the woman in a leather jacket. 'Are you all right?'

'Hormones,' mumbled Jan, clutching her maternity notes tight. 'I'd better go back,' she said to Gemma. 'They said to give it twenty minutes. Hopefully baby's in a better position now. Ooo!' She grabbed Gemma's hand and placed it on her stomach. 'Do you feel that?' Gemma felt what she longed to feel inside herself, and nodded. The kicks seemed to cheer Jan up. 'See you round,' she said, before disappearing down the corridor.

Jan left a quietness behind – the heavy kind that follows great disaster. The aftershocks of her revelations were making Gemma tremble.

Paulo arrived, breathless. 'Sorry I'm late! Have I missed anything?' He stared at his fiancé. 'What's wrong?'

'Thirsty. Could do with—'

'On it!' Eyes targeting the water dispenser, he headed for the kill.

After downing it in one, she rested her head on Paulo's shoulders. A shattered illusion is hard to bear. Jagged fragments of what used to be cut her mind. If Josh and Francesca were not soulmates, had he really seen her over the horizon that day? Or had he… had he lied to her?

With a knowing Mona Lisa smile, Poster Mother taunted Gemma. *Poor child,* she said. *You thought he cared for you? The truth is, he was bored of your company. Couldn't wait to get away. And as soon as he'd found a red-herring excuse to latch onto, he ran for the hills. Or, to be more accurate, the sea. You're a fool! A gullible fool!*

'You're wrong!'

'What?'

'Nothing. Sorry, Paulo.'

He held her whilst they waited, and it made her feel loved.

Jan came bursting round the corner. 'It's a girl!' she squealed.

'Thought you didn't want to know the sex?' said Gemma, her smile flimsy, but no less genuine.

'Changed my mind! Hey look, about before, I'm really sorry. I spoke out of line.'

'It's fine,' said Gemma, quickly.

'Okay. Well, good luck with everything, then!' With a wave and a covert, 'He's hot!' for Paulo, she left again.

'How do you know her?'

'I don't, really. Got chatting whilst we waited.'

The door opened, and the couple from before emerged, in their own happy bubble. Soon after came the sonographer, and she saw where Gemma was staring.

'Who put that there? Mad breastfeeding lobby. So insensitive.' Marching over to Poster Mother, the woman tore her off the wall, and chucked her in a bin. 'Sorry about that. Are you ready to come through now?'

Gemma wondered if her sudden sense of sickness was of the morning or nerves variety. Deep down, she knew. She began to cry, and the sonographer wore an oh-no-not-another-crying-pregnant-woman expression.

'Look at me!' said Paulo, planting hands on Gemma's arms, pushing her in like a malleable piece of clay. 'I know what you're worried about, but that's not gonna happen, hear me? Your body's coping so well because you're strong. You're fucking strong. That's one of the reasons why I love you.'

Laugh-crying, Gemma wiped her nose, and followed the sonographer through. Her fiancé squeezed her hand.

The lady checked medical details and made small talk. Paulo turned her to jelly with his charm, even as she squirted some over the mother of his child. Batting her lashes at him, she said, 'I don't normally let strange men call me "Angel".'

Paulo winked, 'Sorry, Angel.'

Gemma couldn't help giggling with exasperation and, yes, affection, at his bravado. It was almost enough to distract her from the fact miscarriages are most common in the first three months. But then, as beautiful black and white flashed on screen, her fear was momentarily put to bed. Even Paulo stopped talking of angels. The vibrant, thriving sound of her baby's heartbeat – rapid, full of life – filled the room. It was almost too full of life to be true. Surely no heart could maintain that pace, without, well, having a heart attack?

'The beat is so fast. Are you sure that's normal?' asked Gemma.

'Yes,' said the angel, smiling. 'Your baby is very strong.'

'What did I tell you?' said Paulo, kissing Gemma's forehead.

Suddenly, she was overwhelmed with love – not only for the baby, but for the man who made her baby possible. Her eyes glazed over as it hit her: she had more than one man to thank.

*

Now the scan was had, and everything was well and good, they agreed to move onto the next step. After much to-ing and fro-ing, both outcomes were settled on. The baby was Michael or Hannah.

'And the baby will take my surname, right, babe?'

'No. I don't want to be cut off from him, or her.'

'But it's only a matter of time before we're married. Why go through the hassle of changing the registration?'

'I guess…'

It didn't sit entirely comfortably with her, but she recognised the cold logic of Paulo's request. She bowed to the inevitable, and her fiancé toasted the imminent arrival of another Fernandez with an expensive steak dinner. For her part, to celebrate the semi-christening, Gemma bought a cute, neutral baby grow that read: *Mummy's little star.*

She addressed the little star as she ambled along the long grass. 'Michael/Hannah, could you start growing a bit faster please, so that I might have a bigger belly? I want to show you off to the world!' Wind whispered in her ear, like it was letting her in on a secret. 'Oh darling, I can't wait to meet you. I need you.'

The Broads had become her sanctuary, of late. Sanctuary from what, she couldn't put her finger on, but she had been avoiding the apartment if she could – even though, in this never-ending Narnia winter, the thought of central heating was appealing. Maybe it was her newly acquired maternal instinct, protesting at the bare bachelor nature of the pad called home. *Well, maternal instinct, it's pointless to swap designer, sharp-edges for child-friendly furniture when you're imminently moving in with in-laws.* Glimpsing the future, Gemma shuddered. She closed her eyes and gave herself the usual assurances. Once she lived there, her sense of dispossession would disappear.

Her relationship with Maria would flourish. They'd have a baby to bond over.

She reached their old spot and hesitated, before laying her blanket down. 'Did you know, bubba? Today is February 29th. It's a leap year. Today doesn't normally exist. It's a rare, rare day – and it's ours. Isn't it beautiful?'

She took in the view. There was mist in the air and frost on lavender-like reeds which shimmied in the wind. Violet sky gave itself to the water, before sailing gently downstream to somewhere else. The mist lifted a little, and Gemma could see beyond the river to Turf Fen stuck in time, and the far-off trees. Gemma found comfort in their buds; a promise of spring to come. Watching her breath do somersaults in the air, she marvelled at the fact she was breathing for two. Her hand reached into her pocket for the scan photo, and then she saw what couldn't be.

'Hello, Gem.'

The shock of him was breath-taking. It was as if a dam had been erected in her veins. Blood flow stopped. Life stood still. Somehow, Gemma knew she had to get it moving again. It was not just herself on the line anymore. Demolishing the dam, she replied coolly, 'Hello, Josh.'

'Sorry. I didn't mean for you to see me.' He took a place next to her.

Drinking each other in, they sat in silence. He was no less handsome than she remembered – though he was considerably more transparent; more so even than after his last long absence.

His gaze drifted to her left hand, and he tensed up. 'Congratulations. When did that happen?'

The moment you left me to walk on water, she wanted to say. Then again, she didn't want to add to his Jesus complex. Her smile was whimsical and false. 'It was a funny day, the day we went to the beach. As you left, and Paulo came, I had déjà vu.'

'Déjà vu?'

'Yes. And the fourteenth dimension opened up to me, and I strolled right in. Marge was there, and so was the world on the other side – the world where Paulo and I were doing exactly the same thing.' Gemma arranged her body so it was more erect, more proud, more convincing. 'He was preparing to propose to me on that side too.'

'That's… interesting. But hang on – I thought this was the only reality where you could meet The One?' Josh didn't bother to hide his contempt for the concept. 'Oh, I'm sorry, I mean, the man ranked number one.'

'Actually it isn't the only reality,' said Gemma, smiling because he was wrong, and that was all she had to smile about. 'There were two options. But I chose this one because it's more… perfect.'

Josh glared at Turf Fen. 'I see.'

'Witnessing our parallel selves strengthened my conviction that saying yes to him here was the right thing to do.'

'You sound like you're trying to convince yourself.'

'I've had to convince myself less and less, since you left.' *And more and more, now I see you again.*

Josh fell silent. 'I'm glad.'

If only for a while, she wanted to play his game of pretend. 'You're happy with Francesca?'

'Yes.'

Gemma pointed to the purple sky. 'How come you're not up there, then?'

Josh shrugged. 'I wasn't good enough.'

'Come off it! You were a doctor who sacrificed himself for another. If that doesn't qualify you for heavenly status, what hope is there for the rest of us?'

He shrugged. 'You know more about the beyond than I do.'

'I never got to see that far ahead.'

'Yeah, well, me neither.'

'So what *did* happen when you saw Francesca?'

Josh paused for a moment, staring at a sky bereft of birds. 'She took my hand, and it felt like home. We spent our days making love, talking of shared hopes, taking long walks on the beach.'

'Sounds idyllic.'

He nodded.

'But I know it's bullshit. I bumped into Francesca's sister. She told me you guys were on the rocks. That Francesca was a serial cheater.'

'Really?' He sounded almost amused. 'Probably a good thing I don't remember her then.' His flippancy was grating.

'I understand why you lied. You wanted me to forget about you, knowing we were hopeless. And that's great and all. I mean, I'm happier with Paulo now than I ever was with you in the picture, but still… I wish you'd been straight with me.'

'You're right. I did it with the best of intentions – but I went the wrong way about things. I'm sorry.' With crucifix arms, he stretched himself out. His firmly shut mouth said he didn't want to talk anymore; that now was the time for quiet contemplation.

But Gemma wouldn't give him the satisfaction of that. From the moment she had met him, he had stolen her peace. It was her turn to be a thief.

'What made you come back?' Silence. 'I said, what made you come back?'

'Nostalgia.'

'How did you know I'd be here?'

'I didn't.'

'Life in Clacton not all it's cracked up to be?'

'They don't listen to me so well over there. Sometimes, I think they don't hear me at all.'

Ha! Gemma wanted to say. *Serves you right!* She only wanted to say that for a second. Then she saw his face, and his sadness made her want to weep for him. It made her want to do anything for him.

When he next spoke, the words were so soft, they were barely formed. 'She was only five. I tried to tell them it was sepsis. They wouldn't listen.' His voice broke, and he collapsed his head.

He was right beside her. Instinct strong as gravity made her reach out – but she fell through him. Scientists will tell you, gravity is a weak force. 'I'm sorry,' she said, straightening herself up.

'Truth is, I've been working back in our hospital for a while. At least I'm of some use there.'

Gemma wondered if he had been within touching distance, beyond the walls, the day she had had her scan. 'Those junior doctors are lucky to have you.'

Josh smiled at her. 'Thanks.'

All this time, trying not to miss him. And hadn't she done well? Now, with one look, all her efforts were undone. Why did he have to have eyes like that? Eyes that held all the love in the world.

'You're looking well,' he said.

She couldn't bear to share her news with him. Her hand

met his.

Her hand met his.

They both froze, shocked by the bolt of a touch. Suddenly, Josh was more vivid than ever. She held on tighter, not daring to move, in case manoeuvring vanished the miracle. Finally, finally, her other senses had caught up with the ones that had known him all along.

Disbelief and joy were written all over his face. Shaking, Josh slowly lifted Gemma's hand, and slipped it beneath the open buttons of his shirt. Pressed down on his chest, the warmth, the life, shone through.

'Do you feel it beating?' he said.

She didn't want the fall and rise of him to ever stop. 'Yes.'

He reached out, but stopped midway. 'May I?'

'Yes.'

That was all he needed. He stroked her hair, and her face, and she found herself tilting her head, so that she might rest her cheek in his palm. It was beautiful relief to rest her head upon him. For the first time, she understood. She had been here before.

Too enraptured with him to have noticed, but now she looked. Where marshland had been were a thousand stars. If she ran to those stars, she'd be free to go somewhere else entirely. In that split second, she had a choice to make. She made it. She kissed him.

They were gentle at first – scared too much contact might shatter the miracle. Although there was beauty in the flicker of his mouth against hers, there was agony too. More, so much more, was being suppressed. After seconds of caution containing eternity, Gemma broke off. She didn't want half of Josh. She reached for his lap. Instantly, his kiss turned to fire.

Her blood had only ever gone through the motions before. Now it was raging, like the fiercest of storms, and she knew, years from birth, what it was to be alive. Josh carried her away. Fear of transformation had left him, and he had become bold. Pinning Gemma against a tree, he stripped off her coat, and all that lay beneath it. With desperate fingers, she unclothed him too. He lifted her up, so her naked body hung above the bowing reeds. Frantic, hungry kisses rained down on her like flecks of fire, protecting her against the cold, cold air. As the hairs on his chest rubbed against the smoothness of her breasts, she felt like she was drowning in the form of a man. What a glorious way to die. The physicality of Josh alone was enough to send her into ecstasy. Then he lifted her higher still, licking her, sucking her, consuming her inner flesh with wild, uncontrollable desire. On the brink of her orgasm, he stopped, and entered her another way. The force of him penetrating hard against bark made her skin tear. The pain only amplified the pleasure, and she screamed for more. Still the kisses came hard and fast and ravenous, and she felt herself come, but he wasn't stopping, even as the earth was shaking. And then, he was gone.

CHAPTER EIGHTEEN

Gashes up her spine; tides inside so strong, she could stand no longer. On the freezing ground, the swells of pleasure subsided into ripples, before floating away. Terrible coldness set in. Pulling her coat up over her like a blanket, she curled up in the foetal position, waiting for the moment to pass. Against the shadowy backdrop of her mind, a projector played *Sliding Doors*. History, re-written.

Tearing her mouth away from his, she told him they had to stop.

His lips refused to part from her skin. 'I can't.'

'Quick. Come with me. We don't have long. Do you see what I see? Beyond the marsh?'

'No.'

'Take my hand.'

With the grip of someone scared to let go, she led Josh to the world between worlds. Holding her hand, he was able to step inside. Both of them were on equal footing, real as each other, walking on dark matter among iridescent stars, and nothing else, save the wintery land behind them and the wintery land ahead. Gemma guided Josh to the brink of the mirror image.

'There, you can see us,' she said, blushing, as they watched their counterparts against the tree. There was voyeuristic pleasure in watching Josh fuck her. *Then again*, she thought, *the lovers were not him and her. They were two complete strangers. She was not the one screaming.* A rush of jealousy swept through Gemma, and she dug her nails into Josh.

Even though the pain made him wince, he did not relent his grip. The wonder of feeling her was still too great. He kissed her head. 'Let's go.'

And she knew he understood – understood that in the alternate reality, he was not a ghost. He was human flesh and bone, and they could have a life together. All jealousy forgotten, she smiled at the man she loved, and kissed him, and they laughed as they made to cross the horizon. What did she care if she died at forty? She would rather die young, having loved and known Josh as he really was, than live a hundred years without him. Her foot was inches from the precipice. Then a sickness came.

*

When she opened her eyes, the moon provided the only light. There he was, crouched beside her, fully clothed, looking for all the world like a broken man. She already knew, but she did it anyway. Sure enough, her hand slipped through him.

'So,' said Josh, with a smile that both was, and wasn't. 'Turns out I'm not a ghost after all.' Of course he was always going to figure it out. He was a doctor, a clever man. 'Did you see them? Pete and Marge?'

'No.' The betrayal on his face broke her heart. 'I did see the fourteenth dimension, though.'

'I knew it!' He stared at her accusingly. 'Surely you put two and two together? Surely you realised, when you had déjà vu, and I came alive, what it meant?'

'No,' she said, and that was true, of sorts. Everything was messed up, a blur, confusing.

'I felt alive once before, you know,' he said. 'That day on the beach. I felt the sand beneath my feet. I felt *weight* sink my body to the ground. But the sensation only lasted a split second, and when I looked back to see footprints in the sand, the sea had washed all trace of me away. It was over so quickly, I thought I must have dreamt it. But now…' His gaze melted the bones of her. 'Now, I am enlightened. I am not a ghost. I am a shadow – a shadow of a man in another world.'

'I don't understand,' said Gemma, her face bedewed with tears, though in her heart, she knew what was true.

'You do understand!' shouted Josh. All measure and propriety escaped him, and he began pacing the terrain like a wolf. 'Only you're refusing to acknowledge the truth because of some… some fucked-up idea that Paulo is for you! Look, you asked to go to a world where you'd meet The One, right? You were given two choices. This world was one of them.' Josh made a tah-dah sweep of his arms. 'Here I am!'

'No.'

'You weren't specific enough in your wording, were you? When you asked to meet "The One". You failed to specify that he had to be a real, living, breathing man – not just a man's shadow.'

'Josh…'

'I suppose in the other world, I'm one hundred per cent alive and well. Bet we're knocking babies out left right and centre.'

'Josh…'

'I don't know why you chose this world instead of that, but it's okay. We can fix it. All we need to do is wait for you to experience déjà vu again. That's the key to all of this. Whenever you have that experience, you form a bridge. One I'm sure we can cross!'

'Josh…'

'I suppose if I'm involved in your déjà vu, I become an

extension of the "me" in the other world, and take on my physical form. But that's just conjecture. We can quiz Marge on the technicalities of it all when we see her.'

'Josh…'

'It's a shame we can't exactly know when you'll have déjà vu again, but if I stick to you like glue from now on, hopefully we won't have to wait too long to cross that bridge.'

His words were hitting her like a train, and he was refusing to stop.

'Stop!'

At last, he fell silent.

Gemma took a deep breath. 'Okay, I admit, the instant you came real, I knew what it meant. But you must understand, our time was limited. Any second you could have turned back into… something intangible. I had to fit in a lot of thinking in a short space.'

'And you thought it better to satisfy your lust, rather than take us to the fourteenth dimension, where we could map out a whole life together.' Josh permitted himself a grin. 'And it's men who get accused of thinking with sexual organs.'

'That's not it.'

Josh snapped. 'Well what is it, then? Because believe you me, I'm struggling to comprehend your motivations. It's like you're denying me. Denying us! Why? I can only think it must be Paulo. That you are choosing him, over me.'

Her anger rose to meet his. 'You abandoned me so I could fall more in love with him, remember? This is your fault!'

'I want you to stop loving him now. You hear me?'

'I'm not one of your patients you can tell what to do!'

'But you must listen to me! I love—'

'Don't say it!' Clutching her stomach for all she was worth, she decorated the walls of her mind with lies: it was just sex, he meant nothing to her, and yes, she was deeply in love with Paulo. *Please, God.* such designs might make Josh despise her, so he'd never haunt her again.

Noting where her hand was, Josh knocked down the walls. He was a doctor, after all. A very clever man. 'I see. You're pregnant, aren't you?'

Tentatively, Gemma sat down. 'Yes.'

His manner wholly changed. He knelt beside her, like a man in penance.

'I'm sorry. If I'd have known—'

'It doesn't matter.'

'It does. I was a moron just now. Thinking only about myself. I'm sorry.'

'I cannot leave my baby. Even if that means I sacrifice a life of happiness with you, I cannot leave my baby.'

'Of course. I would never ask you to do that.'

She needed him to understand, completely. 'Any baby I have on the other side would not be the same as the one I have here, growing in me. Those other Gemmas out there – they aren't who I am. Not really. I don't care what Marge says. They are more strangers to me than a sister would be. At least you grow up with a sister – know their character, their hopes, their dreams. I know *nothing* of the other Gemmas. How can I abandon my baby, to be a woman I don't know? To be someone else's mother?'

'You can't.'

Shivering, Gemma got herself dressed. 'I had seconds to choose whether to stay here with my child, or leave this world and go to the one where you are, where they would not be. It was no choice at all. I do not regret it.' The tears were falling fast. 'But I also had another choice to make. Whether to…' she could not meet his eye '… whether to make love to you for as long as we could, or whether to walk away. I'm sorry I was so selfish.'

'Don't apologise. You showed me what it was to feel, and I will carry that to my grave.'

'But we don't know if you can die.'

His face had the strange quality of a man trying not to be sad. 'It's my ingenious way of saying I'll remember shagging you forever.'

Making light of the dark. She wanted to join in his game too, by shoving him playfully. But she couldn't. That was the point. She began the walk to the bus stop, him beside her.

'I'll come with you back to the apartment. Then I'll go.' *For good this time*, he didn't add. But they both heard it.

Silence on the bus. Then on the walk home, tension between them, thick as a fortress.

Josh was the one making futile efforts to break it, with that impeccable bedside manner of his. 'How are you feeling?'... 'Are you on folic acid?'

Succinct replies were all he got – brief, to the point, revealing nothing about the state of Gemma's mind. It was not until they reached the church, that she posed a question of her own.

'I suppose I'm an adulterer, then?'

'Yes. Though you shouldn't feel guilty about it. You've found yourself caught up in something beyond your control.'

'Thanks. But I still feel guilty as hell.'

They were outside the apartment block. The two of them stopped; faced each other.

'Now I think about it,' she said, 'the couple I saw on the parallel beach, they might not have been Paulo and I.' She stared at Josh. 'I think they might have been you and...' She broke off, before her heart could break anymore.

'It's good to know,' said Josh, with the bravest of smiles, 'that somewhere, you and I are planning our lives together.'

'I'm sorry I can't take us there.'

'Don't be. Now I know who I am, I can live easy with myself. I will leave you alone from now on, so you can revert to good-enough happiness with Paulo, and raise a family together. I hope, with the passage of time, that love becomes more than good enough.'

'You're condemning yourself to a lifetime of loneliness.'

'It's fine.'

'No it's not. I want you to be happy.'

'I will find happiness of sorts in my work. What right do I have to absolute fulfilment, anyway? How many of us get that in this world? Okay, so I won't know love from now on – but nor will I know hunger, or cold, or pain. My hardship is not a particularly great one – certainly compared to the lots of some. Please don't cry.'

She couldn't stop. 'What if your lifetime of loneliness is not very long? Look at you, Josh. You're almost invisible.'

'If I die, well, that is no more or less than the natural order of things.' He nodded to the place where her child lay, sleeping. 'Anyway, don't think on that. You have so much to look forward to.'

She felt life inside, and it gave her strength. 'I will miss you.'

'Me too. Goodbye, Gem.'

He was gone. Gone the way he'd never gone before; gone like a ghost.

There was nothing else to do but hold herself together, hold the bump that wasn't there yet, and say, 'I love you. I love you. I love you.'

CHAPTER NINETEEN

The next day, there was blood.

'Paulo!'

He ran into the bathroom. 'What's wrong?'

Stained paper in her hand. 'Why is it red?'

'I don't know,' he said, pale. 'Are you okay? Are you feeling okay?'

'Stomach hurts a bit.' She reached for a pad – something she thought she wouldn't need for months. 'I think it's spotting,' she said, through tears. 'Spotting is very common in early pregnancy. A bit of blood is perfectly normal. Nothing to worry about. Oh, God, I've soaked through this pad already.'

They looked each other in the eye and they both knew: this was too much blood to be normal.

Doubling over in pain, Gemma begged him, 'Take me to the hospital. Make them stop the bleeding. If they don't stop it soon, we're going to lose our baby.'

'I can get you to the hospital,' he said, shakily. 'But I don't think there's anything they can do.'

*

It was the same woman in white as before. No jolly small talk this time. Cold fluid on her centre, as the sonographer desperately probed for life.

'The doctor will have a word with you,' she said after a minute, refusing to be the one to say it.

'You said everything was fine,' said Gemma, struggling to censor the blame in her voice. 'Only days ago, you said everything was fine.'

The angel of death looked away.

*

In a quiet, private room full of support leaflets, the doctor delivered the news.

'Why did this happen to me?'

'We do not know,' said the doctor. 'Sometimes, for whatever reason, a pregnancy is not viable. I want you to understand, there isn't anything you could have done differently. This wasn't your fault.'

Except it was, wasn't it? She had done a bad thing, and this was her punishment. She wasn't really listening as the doctor told her what to do next, and how to take care of herself. As if she wanted to take care of herself anymore. Another cramp, as her body turned in on itself, and she fought off tears of pain.

'I'll leave you both alone now. Take as long as you need, but you are free to go when you are ready.'

Couldn't bring herself to move, or speak, so she stared at the wall. Somewhere beyond the wall, he might be. She wanted him, needed him. Yet at the same time, he was the last thing she wanted. First, and everything after first, she wanted her baby back. She cried out for her baby. Paulo hugged her, until the cries died down.

'Are you ready to go home yet?'

'Can't bring myself to move.'

'I can carry you?'

'Give me a few more minutes.'

'Okay.'

The few more minutes became stretched time. Paulo spent it unsure of himself – kept changing positions – pacing the room, or else standing still and gazing nowhere in particular, or sitting with his head lolled over his lap. After a while, his focus changed. It did not go with his designer jeans, but he put on his business hat anyway.

'It doesn't matter,' he said. 'We can try again.'

'Doesn't matter?'

'Sorry,' he said. 'Wrong choice of words. What I meant was, this one wasn't meant to be. It's sad, but there you go. You can do your grieving, and then we'll try again. What do you reckon? A month long enough to recover?'

'How can you? You can't put a schedule on this!'

'Having a set goal will be good for you, trust me. Focus your mind. And when we get pregnant again, you'll feel much better.'

'What if there's something wrong with me? What if I can never have children?'

'Then we'll deal with it. Tests, drugs, IVF, surrogates. Whatever. I can afford it all.'

'But—'

'Besides, high chances are there's fuck all wrong with you. It was just bad luck this time round.'

'We've lost our child, and you're telling me it's bad luck?'

Putting a hand on both her armrests, he penned her in. Square on, he goaded, 'Go on! Be angry. Punch me. Scream at me. Do whatever you like. Get it over with, so we can forget this ever happened.'

Too weak to lash out, but she did it anyway.

'That's it! Hit me again! I'm not going anywhere. I can take it. I will always take it – whatever you throw at me, and whatever life throws at me, I can take it, because I'm a winner. And you're with me — that makes you a winner too. Understand? You are down for now, but trust me, you are gonna get the fuck back up again.'

*

The pain was awful, but she didn't want it to stop, because when it did, it would leave nothing behind. Emptiness came all too soon. Gemma looked upon the mass of bloody tissue.

'I'm sorry,' she said to Paulo, 'I couldn't make it to the toilet on time.'

'No worries. I'll have the cleaner come clear it up.'

'You can't ask her to do that.'

'Well I'm sorry, babe,' he said, 'I'm not wiping that shit off the floor.'

'That *shit* is our child.'

'Yeah, sorry.'

'It doesn't matter. I'll deal with it.'

'You sure?'

Gemma nodded, and he left her to it.

'Be good for her,' she heard him say, 'help her face reality.'

What should she do? Collect the broken part of her, put it in a keepsake box, and stick it in the back of her wardrobe? She could… but the box would soon reek of death. Perhaps she should turn her baby into ashes, and fill a pretty urn. It would have to be a small urn, there wasn't much to burn. Or she could forget fire altogether, and bury the baby in her parents' garden. Trouble was, burials, ceremonies, they belonged, in her mind, to the religious. Even after all she had seen, she had no religion.

In the end, she told herself Paulo was right: it wasn't a

baby. And though she wouldn't go so far as to call it shit, she should quit being so sentimental. On the floor was a collection of dead, malformed cells – no more, and no less. Okay, so it had had a heartbeat, but a heart alone is not enough to make a thing alive. It was in that frame of mind that she tore off kitchen towel, wiped up the mess, shoved it in a bag, and threw it down the chute. She had been careful, as she did all that, not to look too closely, in case she could see a tiny hand, or tiny eye, impossible as that may be. Once that job was done, she got a mop and bleached the tiles, till she had wiped away all trace of her body. And her baby's. It was a baby again. But by now, it was too late to do things differently. Tears never changed anything.

*

Telling only her mum and Diya, she asked them to inform the relevant parties, so she didn't have to repeat her tragedy over and over.

'I know what it's like,' said her mum a few days later, holding her hand. 'Why do you think you're an only child?'

'You had a miscarriage?'

'Seven.' She bowed her head. 'I'm sorry if I got over-excited before the scan. I assumed it wouldn't happen again, because I'd carried enough pain on behalf of my child. Turns out, I didn't.' She pulled her daughter into her, and they both cried. 'I'm so sorry.'

'I can come back…' said Diya, who had just returned from the kitchen.

'No, no,' said Georgia, gathering herself together, heading for the hallway. 'I was about to leave. Lovely sari by the way.' She pointed to the crimson dress draped over the sofa.

'Thanks, Mrs Higgins. See you soon.'

When the door closed, Diya turned back to Gemma. 'You really sure you're okay being maid of honour? Because I totally understand if—'

'Of course I'm sure. The thought of you getting married – it's the only thing keeping me going.' She fanned out the base of the sari, and the sequins sparkled like tea lights. 'Thank goodness we didn't choose one with more fabric, eh? Mind you, I always knew I wouldn't be showing by the big day.'

Diya didn't know what to say to that.

*

The thought of negotiating an entire day with all the things that needed doing – dressing, working, leaving Paulo – was too much. Bearing in mind there were three hundred and sixty-five days in a year, fourteen dimensions, and a million parallel worlds, well. There was too much time about, full stop. To cope, Gemma had to stop thinking big. So she shrunk her mind-set to the micro; broke up her life. She found, by dividing her day into steps, skipping the more difficult ones, thinking only of the step she was on, things were much more manageable. Could she bear to get up and shower and eat and instigate a break-up? No. It was impossible. But could she get up? Yes.

Turning off her alarm, Gemma sensed the threat of mental breakdown. It was running its fingers over her lobes, trying to sneak its way in through the cracks. *Would this have happened even if you hadn't slept with Josh? Or did the betrayal kill your baby? Are you a murderer?*

'I don't know!' she said aloud.

Crying, she clasped hold of her stomach. A hole where her baby had been, and the whole of her was filled with ache. She ached for the loss of her baby. She ached for the loss of him. Imagining his arms around her, and all the comfort he could bring, she scraped the covers off her body. *Well done* — she was up. Now, a shower.

CHAPTER TWENTY

There came a day she felt strong enough to take the next step. Once she ended the charade, she would storm the hospital. Break down the doors till they let her in. Scream for him so all the wards – from cardiac to cancer – heard her cries, and he would hear her, and he would know, she was free. They would be reunited. Maybe one day, cross the déjà vu bridge together. If he hadn't disappeared already. Heart clenching at that terror, she entered Paulo's office. He was crying.

'Sorry, babe,' he said, angrily wiping tears and smacking his phone on the table. 'Stupid thing set me off.'

Gemma put her arms around him, like she'd never had to before.

'I'd set a reminder to stop grieving,' he said, laughing at himself. 'What kind of dickhead does that?'

'Don't. You're not.'

'I love you,' he said, nuzzling his head into her chest, circling her with his arms, and she knew, now was not the time to end them.

*

She went to the hospital. The speech was all planned out:

I have lost my child. I know talking to you, being with you, will heal me. But I cannot be healed – not quite yet, anyway. Paulo is still grieving, you see. It would be cruel to abandon him now. And I refuse to taint the purity of our love, or hurt Paulo further, by betraying him more than I have done already. For that reason, I must ask you to wait a little longer

She called his name all the way down the corridors. Her only answers were funny looks from porters.

'Hello?' said the intercom.

'I need to speak to Amanda – Matron – please.'

'Can I ask what it's regarding?'

'Josh Cohen. Tell her Gemma has come to talk to her about Josh Cohen.'

'One moment please.'

Not long after, Amanda opened the door. Before it could close again, Gemma blocked it with her arm, and barged her way towards the sick children.

'Josh?' she shouted, marching up the corridor, sticking her head in different rooms and shouting his name. 'Josh? Josh?'

A child ran to her mother, bug-eyed, scared.

'Shall I call security?' asked the ward clerk.

'No,' said Amanda, firmly. 'Gemma, you're clearly quite agitated. Josh is not here. He is dead, remember? Come through to my office. Let me help you.'

'No! He's here somewhere! He's just faded a bit, because he's been away from me too long. But I know he's still alive! He has to be! I need to tell him something! Josh? Josh?' She collapsed in the waiting area, and cried.

*

Nor could she find him in the Broads. Day after day, she followed the river, and the paths they had taken together.

In desperation, she had screamed at Turf Fen, 'Wake up! Rise up! Turn your sails! Help me find him!'

But these days, the windmill was not the ancient guardian of her childhood. It was a decrepit, tumbledown building that had stood, helpless, for over a century.

Diya's wedding was a week away – she had to do something to dispel the despair.

In the damp-pillow darkness, she whispered, 'Are you there, Tiny Tony?'

The quark-sized scribe was nowhere to be seen. She visualised a version of her uncle, perched on her shoulder, faithful as a parrot.

'Yes, I'm here.'

'Good. I'm sick to the back teeth of tears. I need you to fly inside me, peck at my brain, remove everything that reminds me of him, or my baby – basically everything that's breaking me, and dump it somewhere far away.'

'I'm not supposed to stick my beak in. I merely observe, and when your story comes to an end, I write all I have seen.'

'Please.'

'Besides, it would be unethical for me to jettison your feelings. You might require access to them later, as an important part of the grieving process.'

Her voice became as small as him. 'Please.'

He considered her, and there was sympathy in his eyes. 'I suppose, whilst I can't get rid of them, I *could* re-house your feelings.' Giant kisses came down on him. 'Temporarily, mind!'

'Of course! Thank you.' Gemma had forgotten what hope felt like. 'So… where are you planning to "re-house" them?'

'Our body has a great capacity for storage, when you think about it. There's all that lovely space between your ribs, for a start. And once it's no longer lodged between your ears, the volume of your despair will decrease significantly.'

'Perfect! Oh, I'll be happy for Dee's wedding, thank goodness!'

'Remember, this fix is only temporary. Once April Fools' Day has passed, I will have to put your feelings back where they came from, and you'll go back to being manically depressed.'

'Okay. Can you do the job now? I don't want to live like this anymore.'

'All right, keep your hair on.'

Taking a deep breath, she felt a calming influence rise up inside her. With the skill of a surgeon, the writer unscrewed the cap on her brain and scooped out all the unwanted things.

'There we go. That's the last of your pain out.'

'Thank you. I feel much better already. Can you see her, by the way? The other Gemma? Is she okay?'

'Ah yes. My actions haven't disturbed her one jot. Still sleeping like a baby.' He winced. 'Sorry.'

'It's fine!' And it was. For the first time since the miscarriage, Gemma's head was gloriously devoid of sadness.

'Oh good, glad I didn't put my foot in it.'

With that, the writer stuffed Gemma's baggage in her chest, until she felt suffocated, until she couldn't breathe.

'Too… much… filling… the… cracks,' she gasped.

'Yes, maybe it would be best to leave some space around your lungs. They need room to expand, after all.' He paused. 'I've got it – bones! On my scale, your bones are hollow! Let me fill you in.'

When he cried "done!", Gemma tried to sit up, but couldn't. Her heavier body would take some getting used to, but she would do it, in the end. And in stark contrast, how light she was up there! How wonderful it was to hear *I wonder what there is for breakfast*, rather than that tired old *I lost my*

The respite, the silence, was fleeting, because the other organ played its mournful song. 'Oh, but my heart,' she said.

'I suppose you want me to perform open-heart surgery as well?' grumbled Tiny Tony. He mined that pain too and made a home for it in some innocuous place, somewhere between a joint and a muscle.

'Thank you,' she said, flexing her knee under the duvet. 'But there is one more thing you could do for me.' She rested her hand on the last place still hurting.

'Your womb?'

'Yes.'

There was a short interlude whilst he travelled to where the baby used to be. 'It's just an empty bag,' he said, not unkindly.

'Tie me up,' said Gemma. 'Tie me up so tight, I don't feel the emptiness anymore.'

He did as she asked. When it was done, when it was all done, she felt numb and heavy, and not herself. But she felt better.

When the morning came, she told Paulo she'd had the craziest dream. He smiled and said it must have done her good because she hadn't look so bright in a long time. And she said, 'Yes. Let me cook you breakfast.'

In his bloodshot eyes, she saw he'd drunk too much the night before. 'It should be me, cooking for you.'

She shook her head. 'I don't need looking after anymore.'

CHAPTER TWENTY-ONE

Apocalyptic rains battered the land. For anyone unfortunate enough to be umbrella-less beneath the canopy of clouds, each drop of rain felt like a bullet. Yes, on that last day in March, with the thunder and the flooding and the Conservative gains in by-elections, there was a general end-of-days feel to the country. Then April came, with its blue-sky morning and singing birds and – miracle of miracles – yellow sun. April first, the day of Diya's wedding.

'Where are my bridesmaids?'

'What we must remember is, the weather's great now.'

'Where are my bridesmaids?'

Dressing the bad news with her best I-know-it-seems-hopeless-now-but-it'll-be-fine smile, Gemma said, 'Near Cambridge.'

'Cambridge! They were supposed to be here an hour ago! Let me speak to them!' shrieked Diya, snatching the phone off Gemma. Several dial-attempts later, she gave up. 'Ah, Gem, I've been hopeless since my manicure.'

She slumped in a chair and (clumsily, due to excessive amounts of acrylic) untied her tie-dye dressing gown. What with the bedhead hair, wild-eyed expression and mutterings about how she never wanted her cousins to be bridesmaids anyway – and why hadn't they come up the night before? Bitches! – the overall impression was of a woman, unravelling.

Imagining the Diya of normal circumstances, Gemma refracted the image. 'Aw, huuun. It's okay. At least they haven't been involved in a car crash.'

'A car crash? I didn't even think of that! What if they have a car crash?'

'They won't.'

'How do you know?'

'Law of averages. Chances of another member of your wedding party being involved in a catastrophic traffic accident is practically zero.'

'But not zero?'

'Theoretically, since we live in a multiverse where every outcome occurs—'

'Huh?'

'But never mind that!' Finding that road of optimism blocked, Gemma took an alternate route. 'At least the girls have their outfits. If need be, they can change in the car. And there's still hours to go! Plenty of time for them to get here.'

The bride's shoulders relaxed a little. 'You're right. Sorry I'm acting like this. I've missed him so much.'

'I know.'

'And I've been living with Mum.'

'I know.' Gemma poured a drink. 'Black, right?'

Diya nodded.

Tea was ever-present where they were. The cabinet behind them housed fancy teapots and the air smelt like a cross between Earl Grey and cumin.

Gemma opened a box. 'Croissant?'

'Can't. Too full of nerves.'

'Have some lamb biryani, then,' said Uma, entering the room with a giant cooking pot underarm. The smell of cumin intensified.

Uma, Diya's mother, was an Indian version of Aunt Rose. Like her counterpart, she was a matriarch who used food to lure in family. Whilst Aunt Rose's trap of choice was a roast dinner, Uma snared her prey with…

'Onion bhaji, Gem? I've made six hundred. They're in the kitchen.'

'She's not even joking,' said Diya, downing her drink as Gemma tucked in. 'I told her not to cook. Told her we had caterers. Knew if she was in charge, she'd overdo it. Would she listen?'

'I'm worried the caterers won't make enough food.'

'Mum, what are we going to do with six hundred bhajis?'

'I'll take them,' said Gemma, through her current mouthful.

'They won't be wasted, priya. Worst case scenario, we can always throw them at your father and his bit-on-the-side.'

'They've been married six years!'

'And Lakshmi needs taking down a peg or two as well…'

'Mum!'

'Only joking. As if I'd start a food fight on my big day.'

'My big day.'

'Of course, priya. It's all our big days.'

'Whatever. Mum, where is—'

'But that Lakshmi's a right cow. Did you know she told your father not to marry me? Thought we were, quote unquote, "ill-suited"?'

'She had a point,' said Diya, glaring at the biryani on her plate. 'I said I wasn't hungry, Mum.'

'You're lying.'

'I'm not lying!'

'You're getting stressed. You always get stressed when you lie. Have some naan.'

'I'm getting stressed because… argh!' Diya took out her frustration on the bread, breaking it into a hundred sorry-looking pieces.

Turning to Uma, Gemma said, 'Such a shame. Next to your cooking, no one's going to want my croissants.'

'That's true,' said Uma, eyeing the flaky goods like they deserved pity.

'Maybe you could drop them off at my aunt's house? She's just down the road. They'd go down a treat.'

'But my hairdresser's coming any minute.'

'*My* hairdresser,' said Diya, breathing into her mug like the tea dregs were oxygen.

'Here's the address,' said Gemma, scribbling it down.

'Oh yes,' said Uma. 'Only five minutes away. But surely it makes more sense for you to go?'

'Aunt Rose fancies herself a good cook, but I'm sure she's got nothing on you.'

It worked. 'Maybe I could take her a sample of my food, as well as your shop-bought rubbish? Oh, but wait – it's quite early for visitors.'

'My aunt's a crack-of-dawn woman.'

'Is she? Does she get up at five to pray, like me?'

'Oh no. She gets up to watch Piers Morgan.'

Uma looked suitably impressed, then faltered. 'Does the Piers Morgan show run on a Saturday?'

'Yes,' said Gemma firmly, before Uma had time to internet search it.

'I suppose it won't hurt to drop by quickly.'

'Not at all!' said the maid of honour, very much pleased with her own genius as she closed the door. She panicked, and opened the door again. 'Wait a minute, Uma! Leave a few of those bhajis here, would you?' She gathered several in her arms. 'Thanks! See you later!'

'What would I do without you?' said Diya, when her

mother was really gone.

'You'd probably have committed matricide by now.'

Diya threw a half-eaten bhaji at her. The doorbell rang. 'Hairdresser's here!'

In tandem, the best friends ran to greet her. The hairdresser's hair was, to put it politely, fashionably messy. As if to compensate for poor effort on the head-front, the woman was made up to high heaven, with too-blue eyes and too-pink lips.

'Eight a.m. on a Saturday,' was the first thing the hairdresser said, not sounding too pleased about it. 'You must be the bride,' she added to Diya, between gum chews. 'I'm Dianne, and I'm newly qualified.'

Diya's smile was decidedly fixed. 'Sorry, but you're not the lady I booked…?'

'That was my colleague. Food poisoning,' said Dianne, accusingly, like Diya and the colleague had conspired to get her up at eight a.m. on a Saturday. 'Had a heavy one last night. You're lucky I'm here. Why do you have onion in your hair?' She didn't wait for Gemma to answer. Knocking her heels against the tiles and the gum between her teeth, Dianne staggered inside, wheeling a metal suitcase behind her.

'Is this an April Fools' joke?' asked Diya, hopefully.

Gemma shook a head full of sorrow. And onion.

'At least someone is better than no one,' said Diya, trying to sound like her old self.

It turns out that, sometimes, this saying is not true. An hour later, Diya looked in the mirror, and cried.

'It's not my fault your hair is so thick!' said Dianne. 'I'm not used to working with your lot!'

'Thanks for your time,' said Gemma, rising to her feet, and showing Dianne the door.

'But what about *your* hair?' said Dianne, twisting her head as she was ushered out, suitcase in tow. 'It smells all oniony.'

'We can sort it. Thanks.'

'Wait! Am I being paid?'

Her reply was a slammed door. The doorbell rang a couple of times, there was some swearing through the letterbox, and then silence.

'What the hell am I going to do?' asked Diya, struggling to stem the tears.

'Uncle Tony,' said Gemma, dialling his number.

A sleepy voice wafted over. 'Hello?'

Gemma explained the situation.

'And just because I'm gay, you assume I can work wonders with hair?'

'You know sometimes, it's obvious you're related to Amber.'

'Shut up.'

'Of course that's not why I rang! I called because you used to be a hairdresser!'

A silence loaded with indignation then, 'Send me the details. I'm coming.'

The two women spent the next half-hour calming their souls – Diya through prayer, Gemma through eating onion bhajis – until Uncle Tony arrived with a bag full of straighteners, curlers and tongs.

'Jesus Christ,' he said, upon sight of Diya. 'You look like a nineteenth-century prostitute at the end of a shift.'

'Not exactly the look I was going for,' said the bride, miserably.

'Don't you worry, darling,' he said. 'I'll have you sorted out in no time. And Gemma?'

'Yes, Uncle?'

'Go wash your hair. It smells of onion.'

*

By the time he had finished with her, and the dress was on, Diya was a divine fusion of traditions. Rubies were dusted over her flowing white sari and, through the veil, a gold nose ring was visible.

'You scrub up pretty well too, niece,' said Tony, giving Gemma – beautiful herself in a crimson sari – the biggest hug. 'I'm sorry,' he whispered in her ear.

He was referring to the baby, but now was not the time. She shook her bejewelled, braided head, and was grateful for the commotion as Uma, Aunt Rose and Amber traipsed through the door. Diya looked as stumped as she did.

'I've invited them to the wedding!' declared Uma, by way of explanation.

'What do you mean?' asked Diya, trying to smile.

'Priya! You look so beautiful!' Uma showered her daughter with kisses, ignoring the pleas to remember the make-up. 'Not exactly what people will expect, but that's my girl! If only your father could be here to see you!'

'He's not dead, Mum. He'll be arriving in an hour.'

'The bastard.'

'You really do look fabulous!' said Rose, who was struggling not to drop an industrial-sized saucepan.

'Let me help you,' said Gemma, squeezing past Amber, who deliberately didn't budge. Once the poultry-based offering was safe on the table, Gemma asked, 'What are you guys doing here?'

'Uma said there were a couple of last-minute dropouts, and we've just got on like a house on fire, and we weren't doing anything today, were we, Amber?'

Amber looked sullen.

'I'm not going to lie, it was a shock to be woken up by a stranger bearing a hundred onion bhajis.'

'She told me Piers Morgan would have you awake,' said Uma, shaking her head.

'My niece can be mistaken, sometimes.'

'Excuse us.' Diya ferried her mum outside, but the words, 'You can't just invite people to my wedding without asking me!' were still audible.

'Is it my fault your father's family book new kitchens in for the same day as your wedding, forgetting they have done so till it's too late to rearrange, and then choose the new kitchen over you?'

Gemma did her best to drown out the argument. 'Rocking that dress, Aunt Rose. The cockatoo print is so pretty.'

'Thank you.'

'The feathery fascinator really tops it off.'

'I wasn't sure about it,' said Rose, adjusting the angle. 'You don't think it makes me look like a chicken?'

'No.'

Rose gave her daughter a told-you-so smirk.

'And Amber – loving the pinkness of your suit. It's very… Barbie.'

'Thanks. It's supposed to be ironic.'

'I feel quite left out,' said Tony, good-naturedly.

Right on cue, Diya re-entered, and said, 'I'm so grateful for what you've done, Tony. And there's still a space left at the wedding. I'd love it if you could join us.'

Tony looked down at his lucky Norwich shirt. 'City are playing today. Big match.'

'I understand.'

'And, well, I need to sort myself out.' It was true. Now things were more under control, Gemma noticed the unkempt stubble, and the uncharacteristic dark circles. 'But of course I'll come!'

There were hugs all round, during which time Gemma asked her aunt why she'd bought over so much chicken soup. 'We were trying to offload food. Now we've ended up with more than ever.'

Rose didn't get the right of reply, because the doorbell rang, followed by a lot of kerfuffle. Finally, the cousins had arrived. Diya was so excited to see the M11 survivors that she accidentally attacked their faces with nails.

'Don't worry!' declared Tony. 'Scratches are nothing we can't cover with make-up!'

'And nothing we can't heal with chicken soup,' added Aunt Rose, triumphantly.

*

During the hectic hour that followed, Tony made several hysterical statements: 'I'm not cut out for this! How the hell am I supposed to get the mother-of-the-bride and two bridesmaids done in so little time?'… 'Stop tripping over my straighteners!'… 'Our best player injured – we're doomed!'

'Have another champagne, Tony.'

'Cheers, I need it.'

'Sure you're okay, Uncle?'

'Yes,' he said, avoiding her eye.

Gemma screamed.

'Sorry,' said Amber. 'Didn't mean to spill that champagne on you.'

'It'll dry,' said Gemma, through gritted teeth.

A tiger-ish Uma stormed in. 'Priya! Did you invite Aunty Fatima?'

'Yes Mum. She R.S.V.P.'d no.'

'She says she wasn't invited. How could you do that?'

'I did invite her!'

'Are you calling Aunty Fatima a liar?'

'No. Maybe she forgot.'

'What are we going to do? I don't need this stress.'

'Why don't you just—' The solution was never finished, because Diya tripped over the straighteners. Everyone rushed to her aid.

'It's okay, Fatima can't come anyway,' said Uma, stepping over Diya as she checked her phone. 'She's in Belgium. Oh, and she says you did invite her. She just forgot.'

'Give me strength!' The bride exclaimed, praying silently. Instead of God, her cousin answered.

'Where's my necklace? I need my necklace! Has anyone seen my necklace?'

'Not your gold necklace?'

'Yes, my gold necklace! Has someone taken my gold necklace?'

'Michael Bublé,' said Gemma.

'Michael Bublé didn't take my gold necklace!'

'I know he didn't. I just think we should all listen to him and calm the fuck down.'

The talented Canadian did his best, but even his smooth tones couldn't quell the chaos, or locate the jewellery. Still, he provided a very nice soundtrack to people flapping about.

'Think I preferred it when it was just you and me, worrying about whether everyone would make it,' said Diya, with a nervous laugh.

Gemma held her hand. 'This is how it's supposed to be.

The storm before the calm. When you see him, you'll know. Everything will be all right.'

'I love you.'

'I love you too.'

'Your father's here!' screamed Uma, who (in-between checking whether this or that relative had been invited) had been curtain twitching. 'At least he's not brought his hussy with him.'

'Uma,' said Rohan curtly, when she let him in.

'Nice car, asshole,' she said, before making her solitary way to the church.

Leaving Diya to have a moment with her father, Gemma searched for her family. 'Amber? Aunt Rose? Time you guys got going! Aunty, what's wrong?'

Alone in the conservatory was Rose, wiping away tears. 'Sorry, Gem. Just replied to a friend's message. The one who lost her son a while ago.'

That had been all her aunt was going to say, but something inside told Gemma she couldn't let it drop. 'Which friend?'

Rose looked momentarily shocked, then not. 'I suppose because of the crash, you don't remember?'

Gemma shook her head.

'Leah from the institute. Her boy was only twenty-nine. Died trying to save his fiancée from drowning. I told you all about it because – don't you remember? – I wanted to set you up years ago, but you weren't interested, even though he was a doctor. Such a handsome lad. I can show you a photo.'

Gemma wanted to say "please don't", but her throat was too dry to make a word. Her aunt conjured up his face, and she felt as if her stomach had been torn out.

'Tragic, isn't it?' Dejectedly, Rose put her phone away. 'Died a couple of years ago now, but Leah hasn't been the same since it happened. Today is the first time she's reached out to me in ages. So sad that we're going to a wedding, when he didn't live long enough to...' Rose dabbed her eyes and readjusted her fascinator. 'Anyway, today is a happy day. Best foot forward! See you in a bit!' She left the room, calling for her brother and daughter, like nothing sad had just been said, and Gemma was left shattered.

'You okay?' said one of the bridesmaids, flustering in.

No. No, I am not okay. The greatest what-if of my life, the one I've been trying so hard to suppress, she has come for me now. She's like a mad horsewoman, riding round and round my head, repeating with savage glee, "What if you'd chosen the other life? What if you'd chosen the other life?". Crouching to the floor, I beg her to end her cruel campaign. But she won't.

'Gem, did you hear me? I asked if you're okay?'

'Yep! Just sorting out my shoe.'

'Cool. Well, we're leaving in ten.'

CHAPTER TWENTY-TWO

'What's the hold up?' asked Diya, sticking her head out the window.

'Traffic lights by the junction still buggered,' said the chauffeur, shaking his fist at an imaginary ombudsman. 'They wouldn't let us go so long with broken traffic lights if this was London! Oh, it's fine if Norfolk brides get delayed, but God forbid a London lass misses her wedding day!'

'Seems to have quietened down, they must've fixed the problem,' said Gemma, before Diya had a chance to hyperventilate.

'It's not far. We could walk?' suggested a cousin.

'In these heels?' said her more pessimistic sister. She started fanning herself. 'I'm having flashbacks of the M11.'

The car crawled forward.

'Thank God. We're moving.'

The pace picked up. When they got close enough, they saw that someone had taken matters into their own hands. Bold as brass in the heart of the junction, stood The Conductor. Lines of traffic stopped at his command, whilst he waved through straight-on and left-turning vehicles.

'Cheers, mate!' called out more than one driver through open windows.

The Conductor puffed out his chest.

'Fair play to the lad,' said the chauffeur, grumpily. He wasn't about to let the improvement of the situation get in the way of a good moan. 'Don't know what the authorities are playing at, though. Why do they think we pay road tax?'

Rohan leapt at the chance to discuss injustices in the tax system. 'Driver, did you know that when you take property values into account, we pay eighty per cent more in council tax than they do down south?'

The driver thought for a moment. 'So you're saying our hard-earned Norfolk tax subsidises London's fancy, LGBT traffic lights that get fixed as soon as they break?'

'Probably.'

'Wankers. Excuse my French.'

The women concerned themselves with other matters. 'Do you think he'll be okay?' asked Gemma, eyeing the on/off overcast sky. 'I mean, he's not usually out there on the road itself. Shouldn't he be wearing a high-vis jacket or something?'

Diya proceeded to hack at her cousin's bright gold sari.

'What the hell?'

'No one will notice. We can wrap round some fabric from the other side.'

'Where did you even *get* those scissors from?'

'She always carries scissors in her handbag,' said Gemma, nonchalantly. 'In case anyone attacks.'

'But cuz, you work for Amnesty. Don't you believe in disarmament?'

Diya didn't answer. She was too busy being annoyed by her father.

'Of course, the death tax has its roots in the 1800s, when it was introduced to help fund the war against Lecretin.'

'Dad, can you stop with the history of tax talk, please? It's my wedding day.'

'Yes, priya. Sorry, priya.'

'And driver, can you slow down, please?'

'Certainly, love.'

Swinging open the passenger door, Diya called out to The Conductor. 'I have something for you!'

The man looked up and, to his utter astonishment, an angel in a cruising BMW stuck a piece of cloth over his head.

'A makeshift safety vest. At least you'll be easier to see now,' sang the angel.

The man decided the golden threads were a gift from the gods. They saw him; what he did was important; they were grateful for him. His body swelled with a sense of validation, then he told the angel to move on.

*

After some last-minute adjustments to hair, make-up and saris outside the church, the organ played, and they were ready to roll. First in the procession, Gemma. The sun's warm hand on her back was soon replaced by the cool, floral air of the church. Flowers of every persuasion lined the pews; an eclectic mix with no scheme, only colour. It was as if the church had experienced a totally random explosion of joy.

Flanked by his bearded best man, Tom stood waiting by the altar, smiling the sweet, nervous smile of every groom who's ever waited. Gemma watched the light fill him when Diya approached. It wasn't from the stain glass that the light came. The look of shared love between Tom and her best friend was threatening to ruin her mascara. Blinking, Gemma drank in the perfect scenes that ensued, and the solemn vows, spoken in all earnestness. She spotted Paulo in the crowd, and his eyes met hers. He did a small wave. She nodded in acknowledgement, then turned away so she could witness the woman she loved, marry.

Waiting patiently with a champagne flute in hand, Paulo watched Gemma strike demure poses with the rest of the wedding party. *It all looks so fake*, he thought. Or maybe that was just his mood. When the photographer had his shots, the lady in red wandered over.

'You look beautiful,' said Paulo, handing over a drink.

'Thanks, you're looking rather dapper yourself.'

A breeze passed them by, and it sounded like one long *shush*. The flattery stopped. On the outskirts of all the saris and suits and Sunday hats, they listened to others talking, laughing. Now and then, a familiar (or not-so-familiar) face cornered them into small talk, before making an excuse to leave, so the pair could stand alone in silence again.

'Dee's side are much more interesting,' said Paulo after a while.

'Why?'

'Because they're not do-gooding beardos obsessed with clean water supplies.'

'Thought you liked Tom's friends?'

'And they don't try to talk to me about fucking taxes.'

'You haven't met Dee's dad. Anyway, maybe if you didn't tell everyone you're an investment banker, they wouldn't talk to you about taxes.'

'What have taxes got to do with what I do?'

'You're right. Sorry.'

Another silence. Paulo searched his glass for an icebreaker, and found one in a joke. Gemma didn't laugh. The photographer had drained her of smiles.

When the joke fell flat, Paulo snapped, 'I'm getting a top-up. Want one?'

'No thanks.' Adrenaline had held her together, but she could feel it slipping away, washing its hands of her, insisting *job done*. Only, the job wasn't done. There was the reception, and hours more celebration to endure.

Her fiancé returned, and she felt like she was splitting apart, like she was having an outer-body experience. By the graves, she became her soul, which floated on high. She bore witness to herself and Paulo, as they drifted around, examining long-dead names, because they could think of nothing better to do. She had to say, they made a handsome couple.

'Have you thought about what you want to happen to your body, when your time comes?'

'Nope.' He said it very certainly, and then just as certainly, made his mind up. 'I'll pay for a tomb and a great big fuck-off monument. You?'

'I want to become ash, and be scattered by Turf Fen. You know, the windmill by—'

'Yeah, I know the place. Meant to take you there because it's romantic and that. Never got round to it.'

'Maybe because you find the Broads boring?'

'Maybe.'

Their stroll was cut short. Already, they had reached the final grave. 'There's very few buried, aren't there?' said Gemma. 'They ran out of room for the dead a century ago. Do you ever worry that our planet can't contain us all? That one day corpses might overflow, and soil the earth?'

'What a fucked-up thought to have – especially on a wedding day.' Paulo drowned his sorrows a bit more. 'And no, babe, I don't worry about it. For one thing, humans decompose quickly. For another, plenty of people get cremated.'

'And some drown.' For a moment, Paulo looked at her like he was repulsed. Putting aside the way it made her feel, she laughed. 'You're right. Sorry. Don't know why I'm being so macabre.'

'Watched any zombie movies lately?'

'Oh no. After my experience, I never want to deviate from rom-coms again.'

'What experience?

'Nothing.' Again, he looked repulsed. She turned to the last of the stones: *Violet Morgan. 1901. Aged 40. Cancer. Much loved wife and mother.* Absent-mindedly, Gemma ran her hands over the word mother, and some of the M crumbled away. Horrified, she whispered her sorry to the grave.

Paulo made a hash of smiling. 'Not all things last.'

They both knew what he meant. Gemma wanted to speak.

'No, babe. Let me go first.' He took a deep breath. 'I know you've hung on longer than you wanted to because of… what happened.' He gave her a chance to respond, but she couldn't, so he carried on. 'I think one of the main reasons I love you is because of how we met. I mean – what an amazing story, right? I helped save your life and that – that's quite a boost to my ego.' Gemma laughed a bit. He looked relieved to have done that to her. 'Yeah. I like telling guys I'm your hero. Your number one.' His voice moved from solid ground to a far more tenuous place. 'And then, because you might have died without me, I believed we were meant to be. I reckon a part of you thought that too, right?'

The memory of how she used to think was crushing. It made her head bow low.

'But at the same time, I always had this niggling sense I was more into us than you were. It felt like I was manhandling you along our relationship.'

Another nod.

'Thought so. But I kept pushing that theory aside, because it couldn't be right. My whole adult life, girls have thrown themselves at me. Especially when I wanted them to. And I wanted you, so that's how it had to be.'

'But why did you want me? It can't just be that I boosted your ego?'

'Because you're better than I am!' The confession erupted from him, taking them both by surprise. Paulo regained his composure. 'I mean, I know I'm great and all, with the making money, and the being successful and being handsome, yada, yada, but where I fail is… is probably where it counts.' For the first time in the two lives she had known him, Gemma witnessed a look of self-loathing pass over his face. He shook his head, shaking that imposter away. 'And that's where you come in. My lovely, kind, work-overtime-to-help-some-poor-kid other half. You have enough goodness for the both of us.'

'Rubbish! You are a good person! You look after your mum. And you always give generously at fundraisers.'

'Only because I want to give more than my rivals. Deep down, I don't give a shit. I want to, because I know I should. But I don't.'

'You did that heptathlon.'

'Only because I wanted to beat the competition.' He laughed. 'You see? I'm not motivated by the right reasons. But you…'

His "you" was loaded with so much adoration, it could have been directed to a goddess. 'Paulo, I cannot exist to be the better half of you. We are two complete people and I think, after all, we are too different.'

Her fiancé toasted his glass in bitter agreement.

'If you recognise the flaws in yourself, Paulo, and you want to change, you should do it. You can't act like a parasite, living off someone else's good bits, just because you can't be bothered to make the effort yourself.'

Paulo nodded sadly, and his gaze fell on her engagement ring. 'I thought if I gave you that, it would make you love me, as I love you. Stupid, huh?'

Gemma put her hand on his. 'I am sorry. I'm sorry I couldn't love you more. I tried, I really did.'

'What is it that made you try, by the way? Bazza said he thought you were a gold digger, but after I punched him in the face, I told him that wasn't true.' His eyes begged her for confirmation.

'Of course that's not why!' She hesitated, wishing she could pluck perfect words from thin air; as if perfect words existed. 'I wanted the perfect father for my child.' She smiled a bitter, sorrowful smile. 'I'm sorry for using you like I did. I think, until recently, I didn't appreciate how disingenuous I was being. You didn't deserve to be treated the way I treated you. You were so good to me.'

'Not good enough.' Clenching his knuckles so they covered his mouth, Paulo asked, 'Do you think we'd have been happy, if our baby had lived?'

It was the first time she'd heard him use that word since the day the baby was lost. 'Yes.'

He paused, then said, 'I don't. I tell you how things would have gone down. I carry on loving you like hell, you carry on being distant, and in the end, I'm so pissed off, I shag my secretary.'

She froze. 'Is that an admission?'

'It is.'

'Before or after the miscarriage?'

'Last week.' Exchanging his empty glass for a full one, Paulo downed it. 'I was fed up of all the sadness. And, as I've tried to explain, I'm a bit of a dick.'

There was a lot mixed up in her pot of emotions, but anger wasn't a part of it. How could she be angry at him for being unfaithful? She had strayed too. When it boiled down to it, they just weren't compatible. 'To be honest,' said Gemma, quietly, 'I've wanted to end things for a while. But then I didn't want to hurt you so soon after our loss. And I've been confused. And I guess, a big part of me hoped everything would just fall into place. I should be wise enough to know by now, life doesn't work like that.' Her mouth curled up, like paper in a burning flame. She took off her ring, and handed it back. 'Thank you for being brave enough to end us.'

'You're welcome.' Shoving the worn symbol of love in his pocket, he forced out a laugh. 'Sorry it was in a graveyard after your best friend's wedding.'

'Admittedly, your timing could have been better.'

'It was the way you looked at me from the altar. Like I was a stranger; like you didn't love me.'

'Did I? I'm sorry.'

'Enough of the sorrys.' His voice was not strong enough to mask the shaking. 'We've both of us made enough apologies to last a lifetime.'

'Okay. You're sure you'll be all right?'

'Course I will. But what are we going to do now?' Someone was ushering the congregation on to the reception. 'I can whack on a smile, carry on being your plus-one for the day? I owe you that much.'

'No, you should go. Pack my things if you want. Or else I'll do it tonight. I'll be gone by morning.'

'Fine.' He balanced his glass on a grave. 'All the best, babe.

I'm off to stuff some money in a stripper's thong.'

A kiss on the cheek, one last breath of his aftershave, and the illusion was over.

CHAPTER TWENTY-THREE

Canapés were being served on "The Norfolk Lawn of the Year", on the grounds of a fine country house. Someone who reminded Gemma of Marge (not because she was Chinese, but because she had a clipboard) was slaloming between the guests, anxiously eyeing up the damage a hundred stilettos were doing to the prizewinning grass.

'Is this your first wedding reception?' asked Gemma politely, as she chewed on an onion bhaji.

'Mmm,' said the woman, with a smile that suggested she regretted dabbling in the wedding venue market.

'Well, it all looks great! The maze especially is—'

'Oh my God! Is that man hammering stumps into the grass? Who brings cricket to a wedding? Sir! Sir!' Removing her heels, she bolted for the man forming unauthorised holes.

Past the game of cricket, big hats bobbed this way then that over paths of green, among peals of laughter. Gemma observed the fun from her spot, at the peak of a gentle incline, not knowing what to make of it.

'Fancy a go?' asked Tony, sidling up beside her.

'Why not?' said Gemma, stepping over the memory of The Waiting Room. This was not the fourteenth dimension – this was Norfolk, where charming hedgerow mazes were just that.

'I'm sorry about you and Paulo,' said her uncle, as they made their entrance.

Not wishing to overshadow or ruin Diya's day, she had said nothing. When people had asked where he was, she'd said he'd been feeling unwell, gone home early, sent his sincere apologies. 'How did you know?'

'Eavesdropped back at the church. Now then, which way should we turn?'

They walked in silence for a bit, going back on themselves more than once. Gemma brushed the shrubs on either side as she went. If ever a feeling of claustrophobia came for her, she looked to the sky, and the world felt reassuringly grand again.

'If it's any consolation,' said Tony, 'I don't think he was right for you. He had nice aftershave, but your values were too… different.'

Prosecco-quaffing guests tottered into their path. Between giggles, they managed to say, 'You're going the wrong way!' before tottering off again.

'Can we stop a minute?' said Gemma, resting her body against the wall of green. She stared at her finger. The light was making it look like she had gangrene.

Tony examined her sharply. 'You have the age-old air of someone who's loved and lost. But I know it's not Paulo you're grieving.'

She said nothing. Then a quiet, ashamed, 'Yes.'

'Tell me about him.'

'I can't. It's—'

'Don't say it's complicated. That's too cliché for a girl as bright as yourself.'

'Okay, it's… problematic.'

'Can I help you solve the problem in any way?'

'I don't know. I don't know what to do. I've no way of contacting him. I don't have his number. He doesn't really live anywhere.'

'Dear God! Are you in love with a homeless man?'

'No, no, he works. He's a doctor.'

'Thank goodness! Not that there's anything wrong with being homeless, but most folk would say, doctor trumps homeless man.' He coughed. 'Can't you go to his place of work?'

'I've tried, but I can't. Security won't let me into the children's ward, not without…' She wanted to say "not without a shadow doctor bending people's minds", but of course, she couldn't say that, so she improvised. '… Not without a sick child.'

'Maybe you could borrow one?' said Tony, pensively.

'How can I *borrow* a sick child?'

'Take one of Roo's.'

'But they're perfectly healthy! And I want them to stay that way!'

'Me too, me too. Nothing serious. Perhaps a broken ankle?'

'Uncle!'

'I'm not suggesting you *deliberately* maim one of the angels. Only that you make yourself *available* for the inevitable moment they injure themselves, because they're such nutters. If you could be the one to take them to A&E, problem solved!'

'Brilliant plan, thanks. There's just one flaw, apart from the million others. Even if I *am* their guardian during an accident, there's no guarantee he'll be at the hospital when we are.' Gemma dropped her head in her hands.

'Okay. Hmm, how else to pinpoint your mystery man's whereabouts?' Tony made a camp show of thinking. 'I know! Why don't you hire a private detective?'

'Trust me, that wouldn't help.'

'Why not?'

'Um, patient-doctor confidentiality.'

'Right.' He didn't sound convinced, but a passing conga line distracted him. When the final man had passed on, he said, 'Favourite haunts? Why don't you go to places that *mean* something to you both?'

'I have, but I still haven't found him. He swore never to bother me again, and worse…'

'Worse?'

She could scarcely bring herself to speak the fear. 'He's… he's sort of sick. For all I know, he might already have…' Her voice died.

'Oh, you poor thing!' Tony grabbed her hand to steady it. 'Can't believe they're still making him work! Damn NHS, so short-staffed they drag people from their death beds. You must do all you can to find him, whilst there's still even the slightest chance. Think, think very carefully. Is there any anniversary he might commemorate? Somewhere you might expect him to turn up, if he's still with us?' Someone shot him. 'What the—' he spluttered, wiping away water.

'Ha-ha,' said a little boy with a pistol. 'Happy April Fools' Day!' He scarpered off before Uncle Tony could scold him.

'What did he say?' asked Gemma, quietly.

'The little shit said it's April Fools' Day. Why? Is that significant?'

It was a long shot but… 'I told him Dee was getting married today at noon. Maybe, because of the date, he remembered?' Gemma checked her watch, and lost hope. 'But it's way past noon. Even if he had turned up, he'd be gone by now.'

'Fortune favours the brave, and blow-dried. I blow-dried your hair today.'

'Right.' For the first time in ages, Gemma had a sense of direction. 'How the hell do we get out of here?'

'I'll lead the way!'

'Sorry, Uncle. We never did get to the centre of the maze.'

'It doesn't matter. Love is more important.'

'How are things with you and… your mystery man.'

'We broke up. I found it too stressful to lead a double life, and he found it too hard to come out as a gay footballer. I believe he's currently dating Miss Manchester.'

'I'm so sorry.'

'Bloody football and its macho culture, eh?' His stab at light-heartedness sounded leaden.

The way out seemed less convoluted than the way in. At the border, she said goodbye. The last she heard of him was the Norwich score.

'The Canaries are one nil up, and it's only the first minute!' he shouted, to wedding guests who really didn't care.

'Have you seen the bride?' asked Gemma, breathlessly.

'Nope!' replied the venue manager, briskly. Her clipboard lay discarded on some gravel. In its place was a red cricket ball, which she proceeded to hurl at Rohan. It smashed him on the knee. He collapsed to the ground, wincing theatrically.

'Howzat!' screamed the bowler, arms raised, questioning Uma the umpire, who slowly raised her finger in the air.

The venue manager began celebrating wildly.

'It's not fair!' moaned Rohan.

'Nor is your husband leaving you for his mistress,' retorted Uma, with a look of such unadulterated satisfaction it seemed that, in her eyes, ejecting her husband from the present game had settled a higher score.

'Guys! The wedding breakfast is ready!' called Diya, holding up the train of her sari as she approached them, revealing bare feet. 'Oh, Mum. What have you done to Dad? Why is he rolling about on the floor?'

'Because the asshole slept with his tax advisor.'

The venue manager suddenly seemed to remember who she was and what she was meant to do. 'Right! In, ladies and gentlemen! Everyone in!'

'Except my husband, right?' said Uma. 'He's still out?'

'Ex-husband, you mad woman,' muttered the ex-husband, hobbling off.

Diya hooked her arm around Gemma's and rolled her eyes. 'Parents! I— What's the matter, hun?'

Gemma faced her best friend. 'I'm sorry. I'm so sorry. I've been lying to you for a long time. I want to tell you the truth – all of it – when it's not your wedding day. The man I mentioned before, the one who is not Paulo – this could be my last chance to find him. If I leave, it'll only be for a short while. I'll miss some of the speeches but—'

If she was shocked or hurt, she didn't show it. 'Go,' said Diya, 'and stay as long as you need.'

'But I—'

'We've got a videographer. You can watch it later. Go.'

Gemma said *I love you* without moving her lips, and Diya heard.

*

Lovelorn and pennant, Josh kneels at the altar. Upon seeing her, he protests, but then, once she explains, his mind is changed. Yet still, they can't hold hands.

'Soon,' she says. 'Soon. All we must do is wait for something to happen twice. When the bridge is made, I will walk – nay – run to the other side, where you are flesh and blood, as I am.'

'But what if it is not soon?' he says. 'What if you are old by then?'

'Where I am going, time does not flow in one direction. I will be able

to travel backwards. Journey from old to young.'

'How do you know?'

'I know.'

'What if I have died already, and this conversation is imaginary?'

'It isn't.'

And so, in God's place, they exchange vows of happy-ever-after. Life has become a waiting game, but at least they can play it together.

That was her romantic vision, anyway. In actual fact what happened was that Gemma arrived sweaty to church, burst through the doors, and realised she was gate-crashing a wedding. The bride, groom, congregation and priest all stared at her, before the onslaught of scandalous gasps and gossipy whispers commenced. The bride turned to her groom, giving him a look best described as murderous.

The priest cleared his throat for quiet, and spoke to Gemma. 'So, young lady, you wish to speak now, or forever hold your peace?'

'Um…' Mortification had made her momentarily dumb.

'I knew it!' screamed the bride. 'I knew you were having an affair!' The scandalous gasps and gossipy whispers reached fever pitch. The wronged woman began attacking her beloved with flowers.

'All right, all right! I admit it!' said the man, shielding his face from the relentless bouquet jabs. 'But I swear I don't know who this woman is! I swear it!'

'I'm not having an affair with him!' said Gemma, hurriedly, relieved to have regained the skill of speech. 'I didn't mean to interrupt; I was, er, looking for my handbag. Thought I might have left it here.' She glanced from side to side. 'Nope! Not here. Sorry!' Everyone was looking at her like she was a lunatic. Keen to prove them mistaken, she blurted out, 'Seriously, guys. I'm so sorry. I'm a bit all over the place because I suffered a miscarriage and broke up with my boyfriend. I mean, fiancé. But anyway, enough about me. Enjoy the rest of the day!' She legged it.

Scarlet with embarrassment, Gemma sought solace in a shady spot, under a great oak. Of course he wasn't here. It was long past noon. What if she never saw him again? What if he was dead? Before she could weep tears of unimaginable sadness, she was interrupted.

'What is it with you and hijacking religious ceremonies?'

'Josh!' Where was he? All she could see were stones of the dead. 'Josh? Josh?' Part of the tree seemed to shimmer, and a faint outline of a man appeared beside her. She repeated his name like an incantation. As she did so, his outline grew stronger, and his frame slowly filled.

'I'm here,' said Josh, smiling.

Stupid hope made her reach for him. She caught a splinter on the bark. It was nothing to her. All that mattered was his presence. Hot tears, hot emotion, poured out. 'I thought I'd never see you again!' She let her tears run their course, as she listened to him say her name, softly, softly, like gentle rain falling on a river, until she could speak again. 'I've missed you! Oh but, Josh, you look so different. More faded than ever, like a real ghost. Are you okay?'

In his clear eyes, she saw the graves beyond, and his deep, deep longing for life; for her. 'I'm fine, now I'm with you.' There was a pause, whilst each took in the wonder of the other. 'I lost weeks to lost consciousness, but actually, that was preferable to being awake.'

'I'm so sorry I did that to you, Josh. To us.'

'It's not your fault.'

She closed her eyes because, just for a moment, she didn't want to see the pain she'd caused. 'What happened exactly, after we said goodbye?'

'I carried on as normal at the hospital for a couple of days. Well, that's not quite true. Anyway, I blacked out sometime in February, woke up in April. I was on my way to work, when this joker played a trick on a passer-by, and I clicked what day it was. Half of me didn't want to come. I knew that if I stayed away from you, maybe in a day or two, I'd stop existing completely. Then I wouldn't have to endure this half-life anymore.'

'Don't. The thought of you dying. I can't bear it.'

Josh stared at her intensely, like an artist studying his muse. 'But there was this other part of me – the one that had to lay eyes on you, one last time. It meant breaking my word, but I figured what you couldn't see, couldn't hurt you. I never set out to gain your attention.'

'I know. So were you there? At Diya's wedding?'

'No. I slept too long. Luckily, you arrived as I realised I was too late.' His smile mirrored all the joy she felt to be with him again. Then his hand moved closer to hers, and what couldn't be was there in front of them, and suddenly, the smile was gone.

'So you heard my outburst?' she asked, quietly.

'Yes.'

What followed was a speech forged from love. No one else could have comforted her so. But even as his words cradled her soul, his hand was making her cry. That hand so near, yet so—

'Far away, in that other world, I am kissing you,' said Josh. 'I can feel it.'

That picture made the crying worse.

'Or, you know, I could be getting mixed up. Maybe we're just taking the bins out?'

A snort of laughter.

'That's better. Don't cry.'

'What if we can't ever get to the place where we take the bins out together? What if I never replicate another piece of that world? What if we remain stuck here, a woman and a shadow forever?'

'Then we will share a lifetime of friendship, companionship, love. And that's something.'

'True.'

'But something is not everything; everything you deserve.' Though he had no need for air, he took a deep breath. 'You need to be... touched. I want you to know, if you ever feel the need for... intimacy – the kind of intimacy I cannot provide – you have my full blessing.'

'I never want another man to touch me. I only want you.'

'But I cannot. As I am, I cannot.' Frustration made his voice tremble. 'No matter how much I want to. I cannot expect you to live a life of celibacy, whilst you wait for some indefinable point in the future – a point that might not ever come.'

She gazed at the mouth that couldn't kiss hers. 'I have never been more certain of anything in my life.'

'I am holding you to nothing. There is plenty of time for you to change your mind.'

Scandalized gasping and gossipy conversation drifted their way, as the congregation began to spill outside.

'I wonder if they married?' asked Gemma. 'Oh God, let's not hang around to find out.'

Josh followed her to the road. 'They did. Look! There's the happy couple.'

The couple who looked anything but happy shuffled out of the church, clasping each other's hands like they were being forced to at gunpoint.

'At least they made an informed decision,' said Josh, shrugging his shoulders.

Gemma mumbled in agreement, as jealousy struck. How was it fair that folks such as them got to have, and to hold? But then she remembered she had Josh, in a way she didn't before, and she could have flown to where she needed to be. 'Josh Cohen, do you promise to be my plus-one at Dee's reception, and spend the rest of your life with me?'

Josh grinned. 'I do.'

CHAPTER TWENTY-FOUR

Within a few days of their reunion, Josh looked as real as the next man. With him alongside her, the return of the manic depression – as promised by Tiny Tony – never materialised. Two football seasons passed. Norwich City were twice crowned Premiership and European champions, and Uncle Tony was insufferable. Metaphorically, Josh held Gemma's hand through every monologue on the superiority of The Canaries.

'I can't take it anymore,' she said, banging her head against the banister. 'If I have to hear one more time how Norwich won The World Cup, I swear to God...'

'You can do this!' said Josh, employing his best sports coach impression; squatting and gesticulating like he had a whiteboard behind him, and that whiteboard was covered with the most ingenious tactics ever thought up in the history of man. 'I believe in you!'

'Don't make me go back in there.'

'You have to. She's made a Delia Smith pie.'

'You're right. I've got to do this. For the pie.'

Josh fist-pumped the air. 'For the pie! They should make that into a t-shirt.'

Re-joining the party, Gemma left an amused observer by the door. She indulged in a thought experiment. What if all the others shuffled along one seat, freeing a spot next to her? Not that there was any room left around the table, but her imaginary scenario played out rather like something she'd learnt at university. Hilbert's Grand Hotel was a famous mathematical paradox explaining the curious nature of infinity. In that paradox, although the hotel is already full, because it has an infinite number of rooms, it is always possible to accommodate one more guest. And in her thought experiment, the one more was him. And they could all see him. And he could participate. And wouldn't that be nice?

'… no less than *seven* World Cup winners in our team! Guess you could say Norwich won The World Cup for Wales.'

'I don't like football.'

There was silence, followed by a blue and rasping reaction so convincing, Ruth felt compelled to perform the Heimlich manoeuvre on her uncle.

'Gerroff me!' he spluttered, between having his rib cage hoisted unnaturally high.

'Sorry, Uncle. Thought you were choking to death.'

'That was funny,' said a triplet.

'Marvin! What do you mean you don't like football?'

Marvin shrugged.

'How could you bring someone who doesn't like *football* into the family?' asked Tony, who couldn't have glared more scathingly at Ruth if she'd brought a convicted killer into the family.

'He said he liked it.'

'Did I?'

Tony's voice was dowsed in hurt. 'How long have you known?'

'Dunno.'

'Paulo liked football,' said Georgia, in that forlorn tone she reserved for Paulo-related topics.

Josh grinned with a here-we-go. Gemma said, amiably

enough, 'Man City, so… nuff said.'

Georgia sniffed on purpose. 'Met any other nice investment bankers lately?'

'No. Oh, Mum. Don't cry.'

'It's the onion.'

Rose took offence. 'The onion's cooked.'

'Beautifully, may I add,' said Joe, worried as ever that any slight on her cooking might result in less cooking.

'Getting any action between the sheets, Gem?'

'Who wants to guess how many clean sheets we kept last season? Anyone? Anyone?'

'I'd rather not discuss my sex life, Grandma.'

Ruth made a belated attempt to cover six ears. 'Less S. E. X. talk around the children, please!'

The children were less concerned about S. E. X. and more concerned about a shortage of chicken nuggets. 'More, please! More!'

'Here you go, sweeties,' said Rose, dishing out "more please, more".

'You know lots of sex keeps a woman looking young. That's why I look so old, ha!'

'You're eighty-five, Grandma. You're supposed to look old.'

'Forty-seven! And we played over sixty games! It's an all-time record!'

'Why do you keep looking over there, Gem, grinning like a Cheshire cat?'

'I'm admiring the triplets' door mural.'

'You were supposed to scrub that off,' hissed Ruth to her husband.

'Was I? Sorry, I was doing the washing up.'

'Men!' said the feminist, with her trademark eyeroll.

No one had asked for it, but Rose gave everyone an extra scoop of mash, anyway.

'Oh gosh, we won't have room for the Delia Smith pie.'

'That's not the attitude,' said Joe, picking up his fork with gusto. 'Come on carbs, let's be having you.'

'Your family are awesome,' said the man only Gemma could hear.

Through a mouthful of buttery goodness, the estate agent asked, 'How's the new flat working out, Gem? Don't you ever get lonely, living by yourself?'

*

Their situation was the source of a million in-jokes. Home was a snug, rented flat, and the routine was comfortable. They would go to work, return, and discuss their day, their hopes, and all the quirks of existence. Free time was spent on the Broads. Roz bought a boat, which, because it had an engine and did not rely on rowing, Gemma took to borrowing. Down the river she would glide with him. Tourist sailors took the same narrow routes as them but, somehow, it always felt like they had their own slice of Heaven. The willow trees, the outbursts of woodland, the wildness of the grass, the storks with their long beaks and the swans with their long necks, all that nature belonged to them. At least, that's how it felt. Gemma and Josh would bob along the water, pointing at all the houses they'd like to buy.

'Look at that one there! The one with wisteria for walls! No car in a drive, just a boat in a harbour. That's the life for me. Can't you see us there, lazing on the hammock, waving to passers-by?'

'I don't think he's waving to you. I think he's shaking his

fist and saying "damn tourists, ogling my property all day long".'

'What do you expect if you buy a house in a national park? You numpty!' hollered the driver of the boat behind them.

For two years they lived in their own world – a world no one else could possibly penetrate, or understand. It was "us" and "them". A single outsider was offered a way in at the start – but she dismissed it. A pat on the knee, a tepid smile, and a "have you heard of yoga retreats? They're great for curing post-traumatic stress" was Diya's answer to fourteen dimensions and the shadow man.

Later, Gemma complained to him. 'Bit rich of her. She believes in some Almighty, water-to-wine making man in the sky, but my story? Oh, that's too wacky to be real.'

'Go easy on her,' Josh replied. 'What she believes is based on centuries of scripture, works of art, and generations of shared experience. What you've told her has no precedence. And, to be fair, the bus did hit you pretty hard.'

'So what should I do? Keep pushing the truth on her? Or tell her I went to her stupid hippy hotel and am no longer loopy?'

'The latter,' said Josh. 'Except *really* go to the stupid hippy hotel. Sounds like a place of pliable minds. Somewhere I can whisper in ears and have some fun.'

A verbal spar was on the cards – something they both relished.

'You're not going to make vulnerable people stand on one leg for hours on end, are you?'

'Oh no. I'm sure I can come up with something far more stimulating than that.'

'Didn't you swear a Hippocratic oath to do no harm?'

'Not in this lifetime.'

Fake outrage.

'You're so uptight! Maybe you should take up yoga?'

They both burst out laughing, and almost kissed.

*

In those two and a half years, Josh and Gemma built a life together. It was exactly the life he had promised – one filled with companionship, friendship, and love. They were almost perfectly content – almost.

For Gemma, hope was the thing. To a greater or lesser extent it was always there, drifting over her like a cloud. Sometimes that was okay – if the cloud was up high. On those fair-weather days, Gemma didn't expect a moment to become any more than what it was. Doing the laundry was just doing the laundry. She had *not* been here before, nor was she likely to be. She was not about to be taken to a higher place. Hope was distant from her mind, almost not there at all, so long as she didn't look up.

But on days when clouds of hope hung so low, they were in her face, obscuring her vision, it was a different story. Quotidian tasks had the potential to be life-changing, and she became acutely aware of this fact. So something as simple as reading a book had her pumped with adrenaline.

When she finished *Great Expectations* and the world remained unchanged, the comedown was terrible. To stop herself going crazy, and because she was out of wine and apples, she went to the supermarket. Before long, she was sure she had performed this shop before… Yes! This was it! She was positive this time! Life was on a loop, the bridge must be near! Her eyes hunted the aisle for the connection to his world – a connection that never materialised. Same old apples and oranges in crates. She must have imagined the sense of familiarity. Disappointment, again. As she picked up the fruit, she tried to pick herself up. *Never mind,* she told herself. There was always a chance the next chore would be repetitive, in the way she needed it to be.

For his part, Josh didn't complain about the downside of their circumstance – but there were occasions when a darkness crossed his face. Like when his partner's dinner with Diya and Tom turned into a double date. The other man – Jayden – kissed Gemma on the cheek. It was a nothing kiss – no more than a polite, how-do-you-do peck. But it was more than Josh could manage. In times such as this, the jealousy was more than he could stand. Making his excuses to Gemma, he sat elsewhere. Not long after, in a reversal of gender roles, the men left the table to visit the gents.

'Sorry to spring his mate on you, hun,' said Diya. 'But you'd only have said "no" if I'd asked. His beard is impressive, isn't it? Newly single, or I'd have tried to set you up months ago. I know you have a thing for doctors.'

Gemma switched her gaze to Josh, alone at the end of the bar, looking very much like he needed a drink. No one was serving him.

Catching the apology in her eyes, he banished the darkness from his face and said, so only she could hear him, 'It's okay. You carry on. Have fun. And, by the way, my offer still stands.'

He meant his offer for her to sleep with other men. Just the thought of it made her stomach lurch. Especially when, over their calamari starter, Jayden told the "amusing" anecdote of the patient with diarrhoea.

Quickly sensing the room didn't share his bowel-based humour, the medic coughed. 'And, erm, how about you,

Gemma? As a teacher, you must have some funny stories?'

'Well, one of my students called me the shittest teacher ever today, and when I told my Head about it, she said there were days she was inclined to agree, and this was one of them.'

Diya gave her evils. *Try harder*, she was saying.

Fuck you, Dee. Fuck you for not believing me.

Jayden and Tom's phones buzzed in sync. 'It's the Send Beer to Africa group!' They both chuckled over the message.

'You're not *seriously* planning to send beer to Africa, are you?'

'Course not, Gem,' said Tom. 'It's just become a group for funny memes.'

*

When they got home, she said, 'I'm dying for a cuppa.'

'Sorry,' replied Josh through a forced smile. 'You're going to have to make it yourself.'

Returning from the kitchen, Gemma slumped on the sofa. 'World's shittest maths teacher. They don't print that on mugs, do they?'

'You're not! That kid's confused right now – but he won't always be. One day, he'll look back and realise you were the best. The only one who gave him a chance.'

'Thanks.'

Josh stared at her shoulders. At the end of the day, he could only pretend to put his arm around her.

'I need you tonight.'

On the nights she needed him, Josh would instruct her what to take to bed – butter or ice, or a silk tie. Then, like a lover in a film, projected onto her by some unseen director,

he would slide over her body, performing the actions of a
man upon a woman. Her hands followed his every command;
the objects she held became his touch – replicas of his kiss
and friction. She would close her eyes and remember three
years ago; the one time paradise had been real.

CHAPTER TWENTY-FIVE

The September sun had a sad tinge to it, like a lover, bidding a final farewell before a long separation. Clouds kept passing over it, getting in the way of goodbyes.

'It's a bit nippy,' said Gemma, zipping up her coat.

She wasn't complaining, merely stating. In fact, the susurrus of breeze, the marsh-earth aroma, and steady purling of water, had her infused with a deep, meditator's peace. Exhaling into the horizon, she spread her peace all the way to Turf Fen, lording over its surroundings like a shrine on the other side of the river. Josh, as usual, had nothing to say on temperature variations.

'You look beautiful.'

'Thanks.' A smile that contained a thousand love-yous, before Gemma switched her focus. 'See that butterfly?' she said, bowing to the pretty, fluttering thing. 'It seems so small, compared to the grass, doesn't it?'

'It seems so small compared to the grass, doesn't it?'

The riverbank, the windmill, the sky and its goodbye sun became a black canvas full of stars.

'Josh!' screamed Gemma.

'Run!' He grabbed her hand, sending a shock through her skin and bones. Together, they ran.

'What the—' spluttered Marge, as two running people ground to a halt before her.

'Hello again!' said Gemma, breathlessly. 'This is Josh!'

'Hi, Marge! Heard a lot about you!' Barely glancing Marge's way, he squeezed and kissed Gemma for all she was worth.

She could have basked forever in the glow of his heat, the strength of his touch, and the sound of his beating, beating heart! Laughing, she returned each of his passionate affections.

Marge coughed.

'Sorry.' Gemma dragged herself from the moment, suddenly remembering time was against them. 'I made a mistake, back when I had to select a world to go to, and I'd like to go to that one there, please!' She pointed to the Broads on the other side, where two lovers were sat, admiring a butterfly. 'And I'm taking this man here with me!'

'You can't just flip-flop between realities!' said Marge, flapping her clipboard flamboyantly. 'You made your bed, I'm afraid you have to lie in it!'

'No! I swear to God, if you don't help us, we'll do it anyway! We'll jump!' Gemma led Josh firmly by the hand, right to the edge. One more step, and they'd be where they wanted to be.

'Don't!' screamed Marge. 'Unless this is dealt with properly, the whole universe will implode!'

'Come on, Marge. We're not one of your poor, impressionable writers.'

'Oh, all right, it won't implode. I only said that to deter you because I don't want more paperwork. The red tape's getting worse by the millennium.'

'We don't have time for chit-chat!' shouted Gemma. 'The portal could close any second! And a leap of faith might be our only way in!'

'Calm down, Gemma,' said Marge, consulting her admittedly large pile of paperwork. 'Where we are, time is moving light years faster than it is in these wormholes, either side of us. You've got plenty of time to enter one or the other. And whilst you might not destroy the universe if you jump, I must warn you that if you do so without the writer's consent, there's a high risk you'll live in that world as a quantum shadow, like this guy, here. I'm sorry – who are you again?'

Gemma spoke before Josh could reiterate who he was. 'The worst-case scenario isn't so bad,' she said, feeling the tug of the brand new Broads like a magnet, pulling her in. 'We can be quantum shadow buddies till the end eh, Josh?' Looking more hesitant than a moment ago, he held her back, even as she persevered with wishful thinking. 'Surely shadows can touch each other?'

Marge consulted her clipboard. 'No, they can't. And oh, sorry, it seems I was mistaken. Becoming a shadow is not your worst-case scenario.'

'What is, then?'

'You could cease to exist the instant you break the barrier. Just break up – *poof* – into individual particles!'

'Oh.'

'So we need to do this right,' said Josh, firmly. 'Gain the writer's blessing.'

Gemma felt a sudden rush of blood to the head. 'How fast did you say we were moving again, Marge?'

Marge fired her gun and, contrary to past shots, the bullet was invisible to the naked eye. 'Time is currently moving at a rate of two light years a minute,' said the shooter, matter-of-factly. 'Like I said, Gemma, you have plenty of time to make a measured decision as to which world you grace with your presence. So please – let us go through the proper channels. Let us get Pete and the writers on board.'

'Do as she says,' whispered Josh. 'We can wait.'

'Okay.' Dizzy; she felt dizzy. How many beats a minute

did a racing heart make? Over a hundred? But if time really was moving as rapidly as Marge intimated, it would have to make more than that – much more. No wonder her body was struggling to keep pace with such an insane clock. She had to sit down. As she lowered herself, Josh never let her go. Joining her on a blanket of spacetime, he wrapped himself around her, and she gazed at him, ignoring the stars encircling them. Light-headedness turned to light. There was only him, wonderful him, and oh, how he made her heart beat.

'God, I love touching you,' he said, stroking Gemma's face. Marge looked visibly ill. 'No wrinkles,' he said softly, like it just occurred to him too. 'If time's moving so fast, how come we're not aging, Marge?' Again, he barely looked at the HR manager.

'Atomic bonds.'

'Atomic bombs?' Gemma's mind exploded with the sudden, petrifying fear her love had triggered a Hiroshima.

'Not bombs, you dodo, *bonds*! Atomic bonds with the wormhole worlds are regulating your cells!' She said it with the patience of a fallen saint. 'Can we get back to the matter in hand, please? Although… I'm not sure I can tolerate two lovebirds in my vicinity much longer. Would you mind very much if I summoned Pete on my own?'

'You mean, you'll negotiate the Problem and Solution Room on our behalf?'

'Yes, anything beats… For God's sake, is he trying to get you pregnant with his hands?'

Gemma couldn't answer.

'I can't take much more of this.' Marge turned her back to them, and shouted over her shoulder, 'Can you hear me over all your saliva-exchanging?'

'Yes!'

'I need to verify the facts.' Another consultation with the clipboard, before she tossed her hand like she was throwing something in a bin behind her. She was pointing at Josh. 'You're Jeremy… Cohen?'

He winced. 'Yes.'

She read up on him. 'Ah, that's nice. That's nice.' Tore her eyes from the papers. 'Congratulations on being so romantic. Can't say there's many who'd do what you did.'

'Er, thanks. And what did I do, exactly?'

She pointed to the bubble where the lovers were most content. 'See there, where Gemma wants to take you?'

'Yes?'

'That is one of the two worlds where you are not already dead. The only other world where you live on, is the one where Gemma was accidentally killed. In that messed-up world, a part of you knew there was something missing from your life; something not right. So you split yourself. You became a quantum shadow, and you travelled through multiple realities until you found the answer you were looking for. That answer being this lady before us.' Marge gestured towards Gemma in a manner that suggested the answer was a bit of a let-down.

'Aw, Josh! You became a quantum shadow and travelled through multiple realities for me?'

'What can I say, Gem? I bloody love you.'

'Oh please, stop snogging so audibly!' said Marge, who was either pretending to gag, or actually gagging. 'Seriously, knock it off. You haven't long left.'

They were knocked. 'What do you mean? You said we had plenty of time?'

Propelling herself to face them, Marge pointed her clipboard at Gemma. 'I said *you* have plenty of time. You,' she said, turning to Josh, 'not so much.'

'Why?'

'Well, there are two things that can dissolve a quantum shadow. One: if you are too long separated from the being you have a connection with, in your case, Gemma.'

'We figured that. It's why, whenever I was apart from her too long, I started to fade.'

'Yes, yes. But that can be remedied, if you reconnect before the final atom gives up the ghost. However what we cannot remedy, is death.'

'Death?'

'Well, death and time. See, in the place where you originate, Jeremy, time is moving inordinately fast. Everything went a bit tits-up when Gemma died, falsely. The world's orbit was knocked off kilter, as it were. It hasn't been in sync with its parallel brothers and sisters since the day of the bus crash.'

'What are you saying?'

'I'm saying you're eighty-nine over there, Jeremy. Your time is almost up. And when your original body dies, I'm afraid you, its quantum shadow, will cease to exist.'

Perhaps it was the doctor in him that meant he was used to the idea of death. It didn't faze him. Or at least, once the flash of fear had passed from his eyes, it appeared as if death didn't faze him. 'That's the second time I've heard you use the phrase cease to exist, and we only just met. I kind of think you like it.'

'I do, Jeremy. It's got a nice, apocalyptic ring to it. Appeals to the pessimist in me.'

'How much longer does he have?' asked Gemma, digging her nails into Josh's skin, like if she only held onto him tight enough, he wouldn't die.

'Not long,' said Marge, casually buffing her gun on the hem of her skirt. 'Cancer.'

Josh kissed Gemma on the forehead, told her it was okay.

'How can it be okay?' she shouted. 'Marge, I don't understand.'

'Well, why don't you have a good think about all I've told you, whilst I go fetch Pete. See you in a bit. Unless you've already ceased to exist by the time I get back, Jeremy, in which case, it was nice meeting you.'

Josh gave a respectful salute, which pleased Marge. With a smile, she treated her clipboard like a baton, stepped through the manmade whirlpool, and disappeared.

'Not much of a people person for an HR manager, is she?'

'How can you joke?' asked Gemma, tears in her eyes as she pinched at his shirt – short, repetitive pinches; a nervous tic.

He put his hand on her wrist to calm her. 'I can feel your pulse,' he said, as if such a thing was the most wonderful thing in the world.

The nervous tic slowed. Gently, she traced his stubble instead. Each insignificant bristle felt like a miracle. She wanted to fuse the fibres of him into her fingertips as his kisses butterflied over her.

'It doesn't matter,' he said. 'If I die now, it doesn't matter. I have been touched by you. I have felt your skin on mine. I will die a happy man, one who knew all that was worth knowing.'

If an astronomer could have set his telescope to the right coordinates, he would have caught the only two lovers in the whole night sky, floating on an unseen sea, surrounded by stars. There, in the Corvus constellation, the observer would have witnessed a man, comforting a woman, brushing her hair and body with the most tender of strokes. Through the lens, he would have charted the caresses, the shaking, uncontrollable emotion, the undoing of a dress. But mortals – they had no place in the heavens. This man and this woman, the astronomer would have thought, they must be gods.

A double take at the spyglass. Surely this was a mistake? There had been two lovers a second ago.

*

First came the disbelief. She called his name repeatedly, fully expecting him to emerge from somewhere, anywhere, with just the words to put her mind at ease. But there were no other sounds, only her voice, calling for him, with all its desolate echoes. After a while, she gave up, and wept. How long she wept, she didn't know. There was no sun in her sky, telling her stories of day and night. There was only darkness and the eyes, the countless eyes, twinkling with indifference, watching her weep, doing nothing about it. Doing nothing to bring him back. At some stage, she realised, there was a place where Josh, or a version of Josh, lived on. She ran to the cusp of the perfect butterfly world. There he was, frozen in time, his head leaning into the Gemma he knew, as her gaze followed the flight of a natural wonder.

'I'll do it!' said Gemma, spreading her arms like angel's wings, ready to leap to the blissful abyss. So what if she disintegrated upon impact with that place? It would mean her pain was disintegrated too, and wouldn't that be heaven; to have her pain blasted till it was no more than atoms scattered across the universe. And if she became a shadow of herself, well, at least she would be able to follow him. At least she would be able to see, if never touch. That would be better than nothing. How she craved her old life now! She should have been grateful for what she had! She wished the déjà vu had never happened! She would do anything to have Josh back as he was, except… She supposed he still would have died. Only he would have done so on Earth, somewhere unworthy of him. 'If you had to die,' she said, after a while, 'I'm glad you died among the stars.' She was about to do it. She was about to jump. But then, *what if?*

Hello, old friend.

Her old friend was changed, somehow. As if she had taken a gap year to find herself and returned, enlightened.

What if you wait for Marge and Pete and the writer? What if they give you permission to possess the body of the woman you want? If you wait for them to return, you might just get everything.

You're right.

That was the last of her internal conversation. Crossing her legs Diya's backward yoga way, she balanced on the edge of the world, and stared at him, only him, as the wind from that place drifted in, calling to her, *Come, come.* And oh, how she longed to.

It might have been seconds, or hours, or days later, when someone put their hand on her shoulder. 'I am sorry for your loss.'

'That's okay, Marge,' said Gemma. Her voice seemed far away from her own throat. Now he was gone, she felt disconnected from life, even her own body.

'Do you know where we are?'

'No.'

'We are currently floating in Apollo's constellation. Are you familiar with the legend of his son?'

'I was, once.' She wanted to tell Marge she didn't care. What should she care of the world and its tales? Josh was dead. But she hadn't the strength to say that.

Marge spoke on. 'It is a famous story from Ancient Greece. Orpheus, son of Apollo, and Eurydice were deeply in love. When she died on their wedding day, he followed her to the underworld, where he begged Hades, King of the Dead, let him return his bride to the land of the living. Hades granted him his wish, on the condition that Orpheus did not look at her during the journey. Orpheus agreed, and guided his wife back to life, always one step ahead, never looking behind. The passage was long and arduous, but finally, Orpheus reached the Earth's surface. Elated, he turned around so he could finally rest eyes on his beloved. But Eurydice had not yet completed the journey – she was still inches away from him. The instant her husband's gaze touched her skin, she died again. And this time, Orpheus could not go back for her.'

'What am I to make of that?' asked Gemma, eyes brimming with tears.

'It means,' said Marge, smiling kindly, 'that you should count yourself lucky. Unlike Orpheus, we can give you a second chance.'

'Really?' She cried into Marge's embrace. The skeleton of her comforter was surprisingly soft, and when Gemma untangled herself, she saw that hope had arrived.

Pete, Amber, Uncle Tony and Aunt Rose – or people who looked extraordinarily like them – were standing before her. They were all performing the sympathetic, cock-headed pose of those wishing to express their sincerest condolences.

'Pray, accept our sincerest condolences,' said Pete. 'He must have loved thee very much, to have turned himself into a quantum shadow for thee.'

'Yes, he did.'

'Normally I expect people to complete their own cryptic crossword puzzles, but since thou ist grieving, just this once, I allowed Marge to carry out the task on thy behalf.'

'Thank you.'

'Selfless was two down,' said Marge.

'Indeed,' said Pete. 'Anyway, I've brought the writers with me to try and sort things out, here and now. Rose is the author of the woman whose body thou wishes to inhabit.'

'Hi there!' Rose was holding a laptop under her arm. It looked out of place. Perhaps because, in another life, the laptop would be a roast chicken. 'I take no issue with you overriding my Gemma. In a way, it will make things easier. I've become rather attached to her you see and, well, knowing what I know…'

'I don't care if I die of cancer at forty,' said Gemma. 'I would rather die young, than live a single second more without him.'

'Ah, that's very sweet,' said Rose, typing into her laptop. 'It seems you know what you're letting yourself in for, and I can spare my girl suffering, so it's win-win all round!' She beamed at Gemma. 'I'll put my girl to sleep, and you can jump right in. Won't take a tick.'

For the first time since he left her, Gemma felt at peace. 'Thank you.'

'Guess I've got to wake my girl back up,' said Tony, tutting as he punched in his keyboard too.

'Sorry I caused you extra work.'

'Don't worry, it's not *your* fault,' said Tony, glaring at Amber as he emphasised the "your".

'What?' snapped Amber defensively. 'I gave Gemma the only two choices where she'd get to meet Josh. Is it my fault she picked the wrong life?'

'You could have been a bit straighter with me. You know, told me that in one of them he'd be like a ghost.'

'Excuse me for not wanting to give away any spoilers,' said Amber. 'I'm not here to be the fall-guy. Um, why did you drag me here again, Pete?'

'We need thy permission to put thee,' Pete put his saucepan-sized hand on Gemma's shoulder, 'into thee.' He pointed his staff yonder.

'I already gave it.'

'Thy did?'

'Yes!'

'Oh. All right then, thy can go.'

'Thanks, Amber.' Gemma suddenly thought to ask: 'Um, what have you been doing since I accidentally died? You've had nothing to write about.'

'I do what every writer does when the story comes to an end,' said Amber. 'I move onto the next one.'

'What is the next one?'

But Amber had already made a hole for herself to vanish into. Pete nodded, like everything was panning out as some prophecy had predicted. 'When the writers give the go-ahead, go forth, unto thy new world,' he said. 'In the blink of an eye, thee will be thy mirror image. Time will seem to have never stood still at all. The butterfly will soar, as before.'

Marge shook her head. 'I don't think you know what you're talking about sometimes,' she said. 'You use your thys, thees and thous so interchangeably.'

'Will I remember everything, like last time?' asked Gemma, indifferent towards Pete's bizarre use of language.

'No,' said Marge, firmly. 'It causes too much trouble, you having intel on the fourteenth dimension, bed hopping between worlds whenever déjà vu so much as winks. I've had

Pete re-program the database. As soon as you leave here, you will completely fuse into that other woman. Her memories and experiences, will be your memories and experiences.'

'What about *my* memories of Josh? Of his shadow?'

'They'll be gone. Forever.'

Silence whilst sadness bubbled inside Gemma, then settled. It was with tranquillity and acceptance that she said, 'I'll be kissing my whole history goodbye, not just him.'

'Oh, for goodness sake, woman! You're not changing your mind again, are you?'

'No, Marge. I love him. But I don't suppose—'

'Yes?'

'I don't suppose you guys can put me back to the start, can you? Back to when the bus first hits me, and I first meet him.'

There was a distinctly don't-push-it glint in her eye when Marge said, 'Sorry, no can do. But don't fret. As far as you'll be concerned, you will have lived through it. You will *remember* it.'

'Done!' said the copycat aunt and uncle in unison, folding away their laptops.

'Farewell then, child,' said Pete. 'Until the end of thy days.'

*

The setting sun was getting in her eyes, so she blinked, and turned away from the butterfly. Lying on her side, her body made a sheet and pillow of the grass. Suddenly, there was extra weight.

'Gerroff!' she said, laughing, more at his Tardis t-shirt than anything else. 'You're squashing us!'

Josh laughed too, and flipped her over so she could see

him, and the sky. Somehow, he seemed brighter than up there. His soap and ground coffee scent merged with the breeze. Words that seemed to have a life of their own, danced in her ear.

'I love you.' She could feel the warmth of the words on his breath. 'Ah, isn't it great about Dee and Tom?'

'I know. With her ovaries, she thought she'd really struggle, but they got pregnant immediately.'

'It was meant to be,' he said, patting her swollen stomach. 'You're going to have a best friend, little Layla.'

Layla kicked, and her parents cooed in delight.

'I was thinking,' said Gemma, 'I'd love to have Tony and George as her godfathers.'

'Brilliant!' said Josh. 'You know I love those guys. Show me the cover again.'

Gemma took out her phone, making Josh supremely happy.

'Love it.'

What he loved was a photo of the newest *Time Magazine* cover. Under the heading *World's most influential couple* was a picture of Tony and his husband, each on their own resplendent thrones, completely naked, save for crowns. Tony's modesty was covered by a canary blown up to the size of an eagle; his husband's by a Premiership winner's medal. Both halves of the world's most influential couple were pouting like underwear models.

'Apparently it's art,' said Gemma, struggling not to laugh.

'But in all seriousness,' said Josh, joining her struggle, 'I am so proud of them.'

'And this world,' said Gemma, her heart full of generous spirit. 'Who would have thought millions of football fans would unite in their support for gay players?'

'I know – everything's just perfect,' said Josh, soaking up the last of the sun on his face. 'Hey, Gem, do you remember the first time we came here, to the Broads?'

'Course I do,' she said, with a playfully coquettish smile.

'Fancy a re-enactment?'

'They do say history has a way of repeating itself.'

Chest on hers, heart beating on hers, he kissed and held her tight. Cocooned between them, surrounded by so much love, was their baby. Gemma saw her whole life stretched out in front of her, with Josh, with her family, and the future was beautiful.

www.ingramcontent.com/pod-product-compliance
Lightning Source LLC
Chambersburg PA
CBHW061639190726
48289CB00006B/1663